Dear Readers,

Have you ever heard the song "Fore She Was Mama" by Clay Walker? Well, that's what kept playing through my mind while I was writing this prequel to the Sisters in Paradise series. The lyrics in the song talk about two little boys who find a box of pictures of their mama taken back before she was their mother. So, I applied that idea to Aunt Bernie, who has been a matchmaker in the Sisters in Paradise books.

Bernie's story dates to a year or so before the first Sisters book, back when she still owned the Chicken Coop bar on the Oklahoma side of the Red River, and lets you peek into her life before she was the sassy, nosy, and bossy Aunt Bernie who lives out behind the Paradise in her little travel trailer.

As a thank-you bonus to all y'all, you get three for one in this book. You get Aunt Bernie's story and then two novellas about more sassy women who could so easily share DNA with her: "Chasing Dreams" and "The Matchmakers," original stories offered for the first time in paperback and e-book formats. After all, who wouldn't want to sail away with three old gals who've retired on cruise ships with one goal in mind—to play matchmaker on every trip they take? Or maybe to go along on a road trip with three octogenarians, each choosing one destination on their bucket list, and wind up two-stepping at a dude ranch, busking in Nashville, and basking on a Florida beach? There's a little matchmaking going on in all of these stories, so sit back and see who gets the job done the best.

As usual, there's a whole basketful of folks who helped me take the journey from starting with an idea to going forward to create the book you are holding in your hands today. I would like to thank a few of them. First, my readers for asking for more books centered around the Paradise in Spanish Fort, Texas. Then Deb Werksman and all the folks at Sourcebooks for giving me the opportunity to write this prequel. My gratitude to Folio Management for representing me and to my agent, Erin Niumata, who has been on this journey with me for more than twenty-five years. Thanks to my family, who have stood beside me through all the ups and downs of living with an author, and who have supported me this past year when we lost the love of my life, Mr. B. Every one of y'all have made me the author I am today, and I deeply appreciate you.

Happy reading!

Carolyn Brown

# Also by Carolyn Brown

*What Happens in Texas*
*A Heap of Texas Trouble*
*Christmas at Home*
*Holidays on the Ranch*
*The Honeymoon Inn*
*The Shop on Main Street*
*The Sisters Café*
*Secrets in the Sand*
*Red River Deep*
*Bride for a Day*
*A Chance Inheritance*
*The Wedding Gift*
*On the Way to Us*

## Sisters in Paradise
*Paradise for Christmas*
*Sisters in Paradise*
*Coming Home to Paradise*

## The Paradise
*Meet Me in the Orchard*
*A Little Christmas Matchmaking*

## Lucky Cowboys
*Lucky in Love*
*One Lucky Cowboy*
*Getting Lucky*
*Talk Cowboy to Me*

## Honky Tonk
*I Love This Bar*
*Hell, Yeah*
*My Give a Damn's Busted*
*Honky Tonk Christmas*

## Spikes & Spurs
*Love Drunk Cowboy*
*Red's Hot Cowboy*
*Darn Good Cowboy Christmas*
*One Hot Cowboy Wedding*
*Mistletoe Cowboy*
*Just a Cowboy and His Baby*
*Cowboy Seeks Bride*

## Cowboys & Brides
*Billion Dollar Cowboy*
*The Cowboy's Christmas Baby*
*The Cowboy's Mail Order Bride*
*How to Marry a Cowboy*

## Burnt Boot, Texas
*Cowboy Boots for Christmas*
*The Trouble with Texas Cowboys*
*One Texas Cowboy Too Many*
*A Cowboy Christmas Miracle*

# Chasing Dreams

## CAROLYN BROWN

sourcebooks
casablanca

Published by Sourcebooks Casablanca, an imprint of Sourcebooks
1935 Brookdale RD, Naperville, IL 60563-2773
(630) 961-3900
sourcebooks.com

*The Matchmakers* originally published in 2022 as an audiobook by Audible Originals.
*Chasing Dreams* originally published in 2023 as an audiobook by Audible Originals.

Cataloging-in-Publication Data is on file with the Library of Congress.

Printed and bound in the United States of America.
KP 10 9 8 7 6 5 4 3 2 1

*There have been several elderly women who have been a huge influence in my life. Some are still living, and some have gone on to claim their halos and wings, but all of them pop up in my mind on occasion when I need advice or a giggle. I won't call you out by name, but please know that I love every one of you.*

# Table of Contents

# A
# SUMMER
# TO
# REMEMBER

# Chapter 1

BERNIE THOUGHT SHE HAD heard every bar joke and had definitely seen a lot of situations that made her think of one she had heard in the forty-plus years she had owned the Chicken Coop, a bar in Ratliff City, Oklahoma. But she changed her mind when the rubber rooster above the door crowed loudly and she looked up to see her first customer for the day. This group beat all she had ever seen.

The faded sign, which had hung a little crooked since the last tornado swept through and kissed it, declared that the place was officially called the Chicken Coop, but it was commonly known as Bernie's Place. The sign to the right of the door said LEAVE YOUR COCKY ATTITUDE OUTSIDE. Bernie had had it made special after she'd had to take care of a brawl a couple of decades ago, and there was still a hole in the ceiling to remind her customers that she kept a sawed-off shotgun under the counter.

Expecting to see a Friday night customer, she couldn't believe the parade of three that marched into her bar. She blinked several times, but the sexy fellow leading the way didn't disappear. If she'd been forty years younger, she would have stripped him out of his jeans that hugged a perfectly fine body and snatched the shirt that showed his ripped abdomen up over his head. Then she would have thrown him back on her bed in the apartment behind the bar and climbed his frame.

That silly notion came to an abrupt halt when she looked beyond Mr. Sexy with his dark green eyes with gold flecks and long, silver hair and beard and saw her red-haired niece, Clara, following him. Clara had to be looking thirty in the eye now, and Bernie hadn't seen her in almost a decade, so what was she doing in Ratliff City?

Bernie's first thought was that her twin sister, Vernie Sue, had sent Clara to pass out pamphlets to a revival meeting that was about to happen at the little church there in town. From the expression on Clara's face, Bernie wouldn't have been surprised if the girl broke down in tears. But she'd have to deal later with whatever bad news Clara was bringing, because right behind her was Hershal Bennington. He was an old flame of Bernie's from the nineties, or maybe it was even the eighties, and he carried a bowl with a dead goldfish in one hand and a handsome little Chihuahua in the other.

"That looks like the beginning of a brand-new bar joke," she muttered.

Mr. Sexy claimed a barstool and flashed a brilliant smile. "Love the rooster and the sign. By the way, my name is Nash Murphey."

"Any kin to Hoot Murphey?" Bernie asked.

"He's my grandpa," Nash answered.

Clara put her hands over her eyes and began to sob. Bernie didn't need that kind of aura in her bar, especially on a Friday night when things would be hopping in a few minutes. And why would she be crying because Hoot Murphey was Nash's grandpa? To Bernie's knowledge, Clara had never been to Ratliff City. If she even mentioned coming to the Chicken Coop to see Bernie, her mama and grandma would have tied rocks around her and thrown her in the river. So how would she know any of the people who lived there?

Then Hershal broke down and started weeping like a little girl. The Chihuahua commenced to howling. The rooster above the door crowed again to signal that two bikers wearing black leather jackets had arrived. Hershal hugged the goldfish bowl to his chest, set the dog on the bar, raised one hand toward the ceiling, and commenced to praying—out loud—and asking God to raise his poor Goldie from the dead.

"Is this still a bar?" the one with Mad Dog embroidered on his leather vest asked.

The one with Snake Eyes on his vest raised an eyebrow. "Did someone die?"

"Evidently Goldie did, but I'm not sure who she is, or if the girl is crying because the woman died, or if she's upset because the guy at the end of the bar is related to Hoot Murphey," Bernie answered. "But I'll sort it all after I get y'all whatever you want. What can I get you guys?"

"Two pitchers of beer, and we'll sit over there by the jukebox," Mad Dog said.

"I've seen weepy drunks at a bar. Even been one a couple of times, but I ain't never seen a goldfish and a little bitty dog cause such a ruckus," Snake Eyes added.

Bernie nodded in agreement and started drawing up a pitcher of beer. In her rattled state, she hadn't even asked what brand they wanted. "Coors?" she asked.

"Budweiser," Mad Dog said. "And you better make that four pitchers."

She set the half-full pitcher to the side and shoved a clean one under the right spigot. "Y'all headed down to the rally at Turner Falls? You sure it's safe to ride after drinking all this beer? I might warn you that there's very few bathrooms between here and there."

"Our friends will be coming in for a cold one in a few minutes. They're about a mile behind us," Snake Eyes answered and then chuckled. "And, honey, we don't need a men's room. We can make do with a bush or a tree."

"How many more are on the way?" Bernie pulled a tray out from under the bar and began to load it with mugs.

"Ten more," Mad Dog threw over his shoulder and led the way to the far corner.

Clara raised up, took a look at the bikers, flopped her head down on the bar, and began to cry even harder.

"This is a bar!" Bernie growled and pointed toward Hershal. "If you want to pray, you can pick out whatever church in town that you like best and go there. I don't give a tiny rat's ass who Goldie is; you can mourn her somewhere other than here. This whole scene takes the cake, the frosting, and even the scoop of ice cream on the side. So, stop your caterwaulin' or get out." She whipped around and shot her finger toward her great-niece.

Hershal stroked the fishbowl, stared up at the tobacco-colored ceiling, and asked God to forgive his sins and not strike him dead on the spot. "I loved you, Goldie, and you've been the best friend a trucker has ever had."

"Hey, now!" Bernie snapped. "Enough of this crying in my bar. Either dry it up or leave, and that goes for the both of you. Are you saying that dead fish is, or was, a better friend than I have been? Did you forget about all those nights you spent with me?"

"I cheated on my girlfriend with you, and I cheated on you with a couple of cute little waitresses out in the Panhandle..." Hershal took a red bandanna from his hip pocket and blew his nose loudly. "I thought God had forgiven me, but He must have remembered all my past sins when I stole that dog, and He..." His voice got higher and higher until it was nothing more than a squeak when he said, "He killed Goldie."

Earlier that day, Bernie had made a breakfast run to the convenience store for a burrito and a six-pack of root beer. There hadn't been a storm cloud in sight, so she didn't think Hershal, or the bar, was in danger of lightning striking. But on second thought, Bernie had no doubt that her twin sister could conjure up a hurricane all the way from the Gulf of Mexico to the dry land in southern Oklahoma because her granddaughter was sitting on a barstool. Vernie Sue had always been Bernie's absolute opposite. She still had a perfectly straight halo and perfect white, fluffy wings. If any relative didn't believe that, Vernie Sue would lay hands on them and pray for their doubting souls.

According to Vernie Sue, Bernie had horns hiding under her red hair, which might be the gospel truth. But if the twin sisters could each put a number on the amount of fun they had had in life, Bernie would have gotten the trophy.

The rooster crowed again, and more bikers pushed into the bar.

"Hey, Bernie!" one of them yelled and raised a hand. "Good to see you are still open and that the pandemic didn't close you down."

"Almost did," she shouted above "Cry to Me" playing on the jukebox. The lyrics to the Solomon Burke song might not be totally appropriate to the situation, but the title dang sure was. Hershal was still sniffling, and Clara looked like she might break into sobs any minute.

Nash whipped a hair tie out from his pocket and pulled his silver locks back into a ponytail. Then he picked up the tray loaded with empty mugs. "I'll take these and come back for the pitchers. You probably need to straighten out whatever is going on with these other two."

"Thank you," Bernie said.

"Gonna be a hot Fourth of July," one of the skinny bikers with a Gator embroidered on the back of his leather vest said as he made his way back to the table. "A good cold beer is just what we need to get on down to the rally."

"Y'all supporting cancer for kids this year?" Bernie asked.

"Yep," he answered. "Some stupid weatherman said we were going to get rained out, but he's wrong. We never get rain in July, not in these parts. We can barely scare up a little breeze."

"Ain't it the truth," Bernie agreed and turned back to Hershal and Clara. "Okay, what is going on here? I swear this looks like…" She didn't get the last words out before they both started talking at once. Finally, she stuck her fingers in her mouth and whistled so loudly that the dog hunkered down and covered his eyes with his paws.

Nash had returned to his stool, so she nodded his way. "You were here first, and you were willing to help, so you get to talk first—and make it fast before Hershal falls off his stool and goes to meet his maker."

"Grandpa said you were talking about selling your bar. I'm interested in buying it," he said. "That and I would like a beer, but I'm glad to come back there and draw it up myself."

"Okay then, get to it, and we'll discuss selling this place after I hear from these two." Her finger shot up toward Hershal. "Now you."

Hershal crammed the bandanna back into his pocket. Years ago, when he and Bernie were both young and had their fling in her apartment at the back of the bar, he had been almost as sexy as Nash. She glanced over her shoulder and shook her head. *Nope,* she thought, *there ain't ever been a man that good-lookin' in this bar. I wonder how old he is. His face, body, and eyes say one thing, but his hair tells me another.*

She took a step down the bar. Her nose wrinkled at the smell of a dead fish and a sweaty older man with thinning hair and enough wrinkles to bury an army tank in. "What's the matter with you, Hershal? Make it quick because that nasty smell is going to run my customers off."

Hershal's lower lip trembled, and he nodded at the Chihuahua sitting on the bar. "That is for you, and it's cost me my precious Goldie. She was dead, floating belly-up…"—he said between hiccups—"when I got home off my truck route about an hour ago. I tried to revive her, but it was too late."

A vision of Hershal giving a goldfish mouth-to-mouth resuscitation flashed through Bernie's mind. She stifled a giggle, but it wasn't an easy feat.

"Poor thing has had to suffer for *my* sins, just like David's son did in the Bible."

"When did you get so religious?" Bernie snapped. "And why did you bring me a dog of all things?"

"I'm past seventy years old now, so I figured it was time to get right with the Lord and get a seat in heaven reserved for me. I started going to church when I could, and I got myself baptized, but I saw this dog and fell off the wagon. I'm afraid God has done gone and gave my place away," he moaned.

"What in the hell are you talking about?" Bernie asked.

"Remember when you rode with me on a weekend trip to New Mexico all them years ago?"

"A lot of water has run under the bridge and whiskey been poured since those days," she snapped.

"Yes, it has, but I cheated on you back then, and I'm making amends by bringing you Pepper," he answered.

"We were never dating, Hershal. We were just having fun, and for the record, you were not the only one I was having a good time with, either. Now, take your dog and dead goldfish and go home," Bernie said.

"I thought we were in love," he groaned between sobs.

Bernie sucked in a lungful of air and let it out in an aggravated whoosh. "What does a dog have to do with anything?"

"You saw one in a yard just like this, and you said that you thought it was adorable. You even said if you had one, you would name it Pepper because what we had was as hot as a habanero pepper," he answered. "I've been looking for a critter just like that little guy ever since, and I found this one yesterday in the Texas Panhandle. I stole it, and…" He pulled out the bandanna and blew his nose just as the rooster crowed again.

"Hey, Bernie." Hoot waved. "I see you've already put Nash to work. Did he tell you that he wants to buy this place?"

"Yes, but we'll have to talk about that later," Bernie said and then shifted her gaze back to Hershal.

"Beer or whiskey sour, Grandpa?" Nash asked.

"Whiskey sour and make it a double," Hoot answered and headed back to a table to join the bikers.

The Chihuahua's little feet seemed to be tapping out the beat to the song "Storms Never Last," by Jessi Colter and Waylon Jennings, playing on the jukebox when he crossed the bar, wagged his tail, and licked Bernie's hand. He was a cute little thing, but Bernie was thinking of retiring, not adopting a dog. And she didn't care if the title of the song reminded her that the three-sided squall in her bar would soon be gone and done with.

"He likes you," Hershal said, sniffling.

Bernie picked up the dog and handed him off to Clara. "Hold this thing while I get this sorted out with Hershal."

"Nothing more to talk about. I sinned by cheating on you, then sinned more times than I can count after that, and now God is sick of forgiving, and he's punishing me for stealing the dog. It's like the straw that broke the camel's back. He punished me—God, I mean, not a camel—for all of it by killing Goldie," Hershal declared.

"It's a goldfish!" Bernie was at her wit's end. "It's not even something you can pet or that will play with you."

Hershal shot a dirty look across the bar. "Don't you talk about my Goldie like that! She was always there for me and listened to all my troubles when I came home off a route. I read a chapter out of the Bible to her every night. I believe that she was saved before she died."

"Did she bring you a cold beer?" Bernie asked in an icy tone, tired of Hershal's tirade about a blasted goldfish and sinning. Forget about warning people not to get cocky in her bar. Next week she was making a new sign to hang on the other side of the door: WHINERS WILL BE SHOT ON THE SPOT.

"That's enough! I'm taking my Goldie home and giving her a proper burial, and I'm never coming back in this bar again." He growled as he slid off the barstool with his goldfish bowl sloshing water out onto his shirt all the way across the floor.

"Take your dog with you," Bernie called out.

"That's your dog, and his name is Pepper." Hershal slammed the door behind him, and the movement caused the rooster to crow again.

Bernie turned to Clara and said, "Now, your turn. Does your mama know you are here?"

"Mama don't care where I am. She and Grandma

both are so mad that they said I would have to live in a box under a bridge if I didn't do what they wanted. I was begging Mama to let me stay with her until I could get on my feet and telling her what had happened when Grandma walked in the door. Mama blurted it all out to her, so I got a double dose of lectures. After five hours of driving, my ears are still scorched. It's a wonder that Fritch, Texas, didn't burn to the ground because someone as horrible as I am set foot in Mama's house. According to them, I'm a bigger sinner than the goldfish man is."

"Go on back to my apartment and take that animal with you." Bernie nodded toward a closed door. "Go through the storage room, and the living quarters are on past that. We'll sort this out after I close tonight."

"You mean I can stay?" Clara asked.

"I don't kick kinfolks out," Bernie barked. "There's food in the fridge if you are hungry."

"Can I take a beer with me?"

Bernie almost smiled. "Of course, but you might want to take that bottle of whiskey that's half-full instead. Looks to me like you might need it."

Clara picked up the whiskey with her free hand and headed toward the door at the end of the bar leading through the storage room and on back to Bernie's little apartment.

"Maybe I was wrong about her," Bernie whispered, and then turned around to face Nash. "Now let's hear what you've got to say."

"Short story is that I'm a burned-out lawyer, tired of working eighty-hour weeks, and am interested in a change. I came to Ratliff City to visit my grandpa, and he said that rumor has it you are looking to retire," he said as he drew up four more pitchers of beer.

"How old are you?" Bernie asked.

"Thirty-five. I often get asked that question. It's the premature gray hair. It turned when I was just finishing up my law degree." He picked up two pitchers, one in each hand, and headed toward the bikers' table.

He stayed a few minutes and talked to his grandfather and the guys in leather, then returned to the bar. But he didn't sit down. "I did a lot of bartending to make spending money while I was in college and law school. I got to where I dreaded going to work at the law firm every day, so six months ago I quit and wandered around the whole lower forty-eight states for a while, trying to figure out what I wanted to do. A week ago, I landed here and told Grandpa, and Grandpa said that life is too short to do something you don't like. Then he asked me when was the last time I was truly happy."

"Tending bar, right?" Bernie asked.

"Yes, ma'am," Nash said. "If you need to go talk to that crying woman, I'll be glad to take over until you get back."

Bernie poured herself a double shot of Jameson and took a sip. "She needs time to think and have a drink or two before we talk. I *am* interested in selling my bar, but it's been my home for a large chunk of my life, so I'm not passing it on to someone who doesn't love it."

"I understand," Nash said. "How about I work for you free of charge for six weeks? If you like the way I take care of this place, you sell it to me. If not, I leave with no hard feelings."

"Any help I've ever had just got in my way and made me cuss," Bernie told him.

"I'm not just any help." Nash flashed a brilliant smile. "I'm interested in buying this place, so I need to know the ropes. Maybe at the end of six weeks I'll decide to go back to being a lawyer. Who knows? It'll mean tying up future sales for a while on your part, but no salary for me while you are thinking about whether you'll sell it to me. What do you say?"

"I'll give it a go, but it's on a day-by-day basis," Bernie agreed. After all, she would be getting free help, and that could give her more time to try to help Clara out of whatever fix she had gotten herself into.

"Fair enough," Nash said. "Since I'm here and already working, can you tell me what all goes with this place? Do you have it listed with a Realtor?"

"The place has three acres. The parking lot and bar take up one of those, and there's two back behind the place. There's a two-bedroom apartment beyond the storage room." She pointed toward the door where Clara and the dog had disappeared. "Lots of trees, squirrels, and a few deer live back there. I do not have it listed, and don't intend to. If the Universe means for me to retire, it will give me a sign, not a fancy-dressed Realtor out to make a buck off my property. Besides, what if someone bought it and then tore it down to build a convenience store? If I sell, it has to be to a person who will promise to give me the first rights if they don't want to keep it." She looked up when the rooster crowed and waved at two women wearing scrubs.

"Hey, Bernie!" they both said at the same time.

"Two margaritas?" she asked.

"You know us too well," the taller one said and hiked a leg on a barstool.

"Ladies, this is Nash, who's going to help me out for a few weeks to see if he likes living here in Ratliff City and bartending. Nash, these are two of my weekend regulars, Dolly and Loretta."

Dolly raised a dark eyebrow and grinned. "Well, we might just stop in after our shifts every weekday if you keep this little hunk of eye candy."

Loretta sat down on the barstool next to Dolly. "I feel like I'm a part of the old video that Dolly Parton and Billy Ray Cyrus was in. What was the name of the song?"

"That would be 'Romeo,'" Bernie answered. "It's still on the jukebox. Why would you…" She frowned, but soon it turned into a grin. "Now I get it. The older woman gets the young stud."

"Oh, yeah," Loretta said. "But how is he a young stud with all that gorgeous hair?"

Bernie snuck a sideways peek at Nash and found that their comments hadn't affected him at all. He just might be the one who could run the bar if smart-ass and flirty comments didn't faze him. "He's only thirty-five," she whispered.

Dolly's brown eyes lit up. "That's even better."

"Are y'all still liking the weekend shift at the hospital?" Bernie asked.

Dolly covered a yawn with her hand. "Love it from Monday through Thursday. Not so much Friday, Saturday, and Sunday. On those days both of us wonder why we ever went into nursing or agreed to work twelve-hour shifts."

"We're gettin' too old for the long hours three days in a row. We are grandmothers for goodness' sake and shouldn't even be teasing you about your new help," Loretta said and took the first sip of the drink Nash set in front of her.

"But," Dolly followed her cousin's lead, "the younger generation doesn't want to do weekend work. They want to party from Friday night to Sunday evening,"

"Are y'all named after *the* Dolly and *the* Loretta?" Nash asked.

"Yep, we are," Dolly answered. "Our mamas are sisters, and they love country music. They vacation in Nashville every single summer."

"Do you live here in Ratliff City?" he asked.

"A few miles east of here, but not all the way to

Tatums," Loretta said. "Where do you come from? I haven't seen you around these parts."

"Dallas, Texas. I used to be a lawyer," he replied and looked up to see half a dozen people coming through the door.

"Hey, Larry, how's life treatin' you?" Bernie said and waved.

"Horrible." Larry laughed. "I'm so dry, I'm spittin' dust. Don't that damned old rooster ever get tired of crowing?"

Bernie grinned at the same thing Larry said every time he came into the bar, which was several times a week. "What are you having this evening?"

"Make it a pitcher of Miller," Larry answered. "The high-end stuff, not that light junk."

"You got it," Bernie said and left Nash to take care of the rest of the people who came in right after Larry.

The bar was never fully packed to capacity, but business was steady all evening. A few minutes before two, Bernie flashed the lights and the last of the customers slowly made their way to the door. Nash grabbed a rag and began to wipe down the bar.

Bernie poured up a shot of Jameson and took a sip. "Rule number one. You can clean up right before opening, not after closing. At night, I get a shot of whiskey or a beer, prop up my feet for ten or fifteen minutes, and then go home. I am always too tired to put things in order after working eight hours."

"Sounds like a plan to me," Nash said as he twisted the top off a bottle of beer and sat down at a nearby table.

Bernie plopped down across from him, stuck her tired feet up on a chair, and then pushed another one toward him. "That's a bartender's footstool."

He nodded and followed her lead. "So, how did I do?"

"Just fine, but after six weeks you might be ready to throw in the bar rag and go back to wearin' three-piece suits," she said. "One night does not a bar owner make."

"Well, Miz Bernie, I loved the evening. If all nights are like this, I will never go back to the courtroom," Nash declared.

"What makes you think you can afford to buy my place?" she asked. "We haven't even talked about my price."

He combed his silver hair with his fingers. "Grandpa says you are a fair woman, so I'm not worried about that. Tell me about your apartment in the back."

"Two bedrooms, a little living room, and a small kitchen, plus a nice backyard that looks out over those two acres I was telling you about. I have my morning coffee out there every morning and feel like I'm at a fancy resort," she answered.

"This just gets better and better," he said. "A job I know I'm going to love. A place to live so I don't have to pay rent. Working from six in the evening until closing. Sounds like a chunk of heaven to me."

"That's what it has always been to me," Bernie said with a nod.

"What is rule number two?"

"Never put your pickle in the customer's jar," she answered without hesitation.

"Does that mean what I think it does?" he asked.

"Yep, it does," she answered. "I learned that lesson early on. If you sleep with one of the customers and things go south, they'll whine to their friends, and you will lose business. So, keep your jeans zipped up when it comes to the bar bunnies."

"Yes, ma'am," Nash said with a smile and a nod. "And rule number three?"

"Two is enough for the first evening," she told him.

# Chapter 2

BERNIE HAD NEVER TIPTOED back into her apartment, not in all the years that she had owned the place, but she did that morning after she locked up the bar. She hoped that Clara had cried herself to sleep, and that the story of whatever had brought her to Ratliff City could be put off until the next morning. Like always, she had had enough talking by closing time and wanted to take a shower and crawl into bed. She was on her on the way to her own bedroom when she heard a dog bark. She peeked out the kitchen window and saw Clara sitting in one of the two lawn chairs. The Chihuahua was in her lap, and the bottle of whiskey she had taken from the bar lay empty on the ground.

Bernie poured herself a sweet tea, added ice, and carried it outside. She had hoped to get a good night's sleep before she had to hear Clara's sad story—or, worse yet, deal with the fallout when the phone calls started coming from her estranged sister, Vernie Sue, and Clara's mama, Marsha. Evidently, the stars were not aligned in her favor that night. She sat down in the second chair. "I figured you would be asleep."

Clara handed Pepper to Bernie. "He seems friendly, but I don't like dogs." She slurred her words. "I'm a cap…I mean, cat…person. C.A.T." She spelled the word out slowly. "I can't sleep, Aunt Bernie. I'm looking thirty in the eye in the fall, and my life is in shambles. I have no job or even a place to sleep. Everything I own is in the back of a car that made it from Fritch to here on nothing more than fumes and a couple of earnest prayers that, according to Mama, God don't even hear from the likes of me."

"Your mama and grandmother don't know what God hears or don't hear," Bernie fumed.

"I should be on my way up a ladder to success, and here I am…drunk, homeless, and trying to make sense out of why my family…" She used the back of her hand to wipe her wet cheeks.

"Stop feeling sorry for yourself," Bernie scolded. "When life gives you lemons, you add a touch of maple syrup or honey, and Jack Daniel's or Jim Beam, and make a whiskey sour. You don't whine about how bad you've had it. You pull up your big-girl panties and show everyone that you are strong enough to take on anything that gets thrown at you. Tomorrow you are going to have one hellacious hangover," Bernie scolded. "But it's a case of choices and consequences. You drank too much, and now you have to pay the price."

"Story of my life." Clara hiccupped. "According to Mama and Grandma, I make bad choices, and they're right. But they say they have to pay the consequences because I embarrass them."

"Been there. Done that." Bernie chuckled. "That's their choice. They could learn to love both of us unconditionally and tell their friends to go to hell, but since they don't, then embarrassment is their consequence to pay."

"I am very drunk," Clara said. "I was going to ask you if I could work for you, but that good-looking guy beat me to the punch."

Bernie patted her arm. "If you are going to stick around southern Oklahoma, you *will* work, starting tomorrow morning. And you *are* drunk. For tonight, you have a bed and tomorrow, when you are sober, we'll talk about the rest. So, go to bed and sleep off your feel-sorry-for-me attitude."

"You sound like Mama and Grandma, only without all the rules." She raised her voice a couple of octaves to perfectly mimic Vernie Sue's high-pitched tone. "'If you don't change your life, we won't even come visit you in the box or makeshift tent where you live in a nasty back alley or under a bridge. God has already turned his back on you for your poor decisions, so don't expect us to take you in with open arms if you don't agree to change and get right with the Lord.'" Clara buried her head in her hands and began to sob again. "It was their way or the highway. I chose the latter, and here I am in bed with the devil, according to them."

Bernie had seen her fair share of drunks through the years. Mean ones that she had to grab by the ear and toss out the door. Happy ones that she took their keys from and made sure they had a ride home. She would take either of those two over a melancholy one. Next time Clara was throwing a bawling fit in the bar, Bernie was definitely *not* giving her a half-full bottle of whiskey.

"I can leave in the morning and take my feel-sorry-for-me attitude with me," Clara declared and stumbled back inside.

"I wouldn't be so lucky," Bernie told Pepper. "I guess it's just me and you, and I'm tired, so let's go to bed. I'll get you a collar and leash ordered tomorrow, but for now, I'm going to trust you not to get out on the road when I let you out the back door to go potty. If you mess on my floors, I will feed you to the hungry coyotes that come around."

Pepper whined, flopped down on her lap, and covered his eyes with his paws.

"I'm glad you understand," Bernie said as she carried him into the house, forgetting all about her unopened bottle of tea sitting on the ground beside her chair.

She peeled off her work clothes, shoved them into a hamper, and headed to the shower. But she couldn't even get that done in peace and quiet that evening. When she went into the bathroom, she found Clara was sitting on the floor with her arms wrapped around the toilet, giving back all the whiskey she had drunk that evening. Bernie sat down beside her and held her long red hair back. Years ago, Bernie's hair had been the same color, but now it took a regular visit to the beauty shop and a bottle of light-red copper hair dye.

"I'm sorry." Clara gagged again. "I'm a lightweight when it comes to drinking."

"I'm not surprised," Bernie said. "My sister and your mama would probably be in your shape if they even ate a bite of my butter rum cake."

"Don't mention food of any kind." Clara moaned and stood up. "I think it's all out of my system. Is my room the one with the pink bedspread?"

"Yep, it is," Bernie answered. "Mine is the one that looks like it came right out of a bordello."

"I like yours better than mine." Clara staggered out of the bathroom and headed across the hall.

Bernie watched her hold on to the walls until she reached the room where she would sleep that night. "No wonder Vernie Sue and Marsha are fearful of you not being right with the Lord," she fussed as she turned on the water and adjusted the temperature. Then she shed her clothing and stepped over the edge of the tub to take a shower.

When she finally got to bed, the ceiling became a movie screen to replay the events of the night. She had figured the Universe would send her a sign when it was time to sell the bar. Now that she had more than one, she wasn't so sure she was ready to step back and retire.

*You are seventy years old,* the voice in her head said. *You should have sold this place twenty years ago. I've sent you three good solid signs. There's a young, sexy guy who wants to buy your place. You know that he comes from good people. Hoot and Darlene Murphey are the salt of the earth. Then there's the death of the goldfish and a new dog to tell you that it's time to put this place in the hands of someone else before you drop dead like that silly goldfish. And a niece who needs a job, so you can make it part of the contract to keep her around to work when you sell the place. What more do you want?*

It seemed as if she had just gotten to sleep when Pepper yipped right at her ear. She awoke to find him standing on his hind legs and pawing at the bed with his front paws.

"What do you want?" she asked.

He barked again and ran out of the room, down the hallway, and into the kitchen. He growled several times before she reached the door. She cracked it a few inches, sent up a few swear words when the bright sunlight hit her eyes, and even more when she looked at the clock and realized she had only been sleeping four hours. Pepper was a blur when he ran over to her full bottle of tea, hiked his leg on it, and then kicked at the dirt and dried leaves with his back legs.

"That might look like a miniature fire hydrant to you, but from now on, you better get your sorry little self on out into the woods and pick out a tree to take a leak on," Bernie growled.

She couldn't remember the last time she was awake so early, and according to the heat flowing in from outside, the day was going to be another scorching one. "Damn dog," she muttered. "What was Hershal thinking? I don't like to be up at this time of morning."

The dog started back toward the porch, but then he saw a squirrel and took off into the wooded area after it.

"You are on your own, Pepper. I'm going back to sleep," she said and turned around to see Clara standing so close that it startled her.

"Holy hell, girl!" Bernie gasped.

"I didn't mean to scare you, but do you have some aspirin? My head is splitting," Clara moaned.

"You need my hangover cure," Bernie said. "Sit down at the table and I'll fix it for you."

She peeled a banana and handed it to Clara. "Eat this first."

"I can't," Clara said. "I'm gagging just looking at it."

"Yes, you *can*, and yes, you *will*," Bernie said in a no-nonsense tone while she rustled around in the cabinet for an individual container of applesauce. "Then you will eat this, and after that a piece of toast with two aspirin and a cup of coffee."

"Why not just coffee?" Clara shaded her eyes against the sliver of light bouncing off the sugar bowl in the middle of the table and hitting her in the face.

"Because I said so," Bernie snapped.

Clara took a tiny bite of the banana. "You sound like Grandma."

"Rule number one…" Bernie shook her forefinger at Clara. "You are never to compare me to my sister. That will get you thrown out, and I won't even send a cardboard box with you to use as a home under the bridge."

Clara nodded and took a bigger bite. "How many rules are there?"

"Too many for you to remember with a hangover, but you will learn them as time goes by," Bernie told her. "For today, just remember the first one."

Clara finished the banana. "Why are you and Grandma so different? And that isn't doing jack squat for my headache."

"Vernie Sue was always the little angel with her blond hair and pretty blue eyes. I was the spitfire, ornery twin, with my red hair. We should be in that book of world records as the most different twins ever to be born."

"Do you believe in God?" Clara asked.

"Of course I do, and I have the T-shirt with *I love Jesus, but I drink a little* on the front to prove it." Bernie chuckled.

Clara would be a terrible poker player. What she was thinking was written all over her face. "Are you serious? Do you wear that in front of Grandma?"

"I did at the last reunion," Bernie answered. "I was only there for about five minutes. She told me that I wasn't welcome in a blasphemous shirt like that, so I left. That was a long time ago, and I haven't been back."

Clara put her hands over her eyes. "When she found out I had been working as a bartender, she told me I was acting like you and that I was going straight to hell."

"I've heard that sermon before," Bernie said.

"Mama didn't take up for me," Clara moaned.

"Pity party was over when you went to bed last night," Bernie reminded her. "Grow an attitude and don't worry about what other people—not even your kinfolks—think of you."

"That's easier said than done." Clara's tone said she was about to start crying, but she sucked it up and went on. "When Mama retired from her job with the FBI and got all involved with Grandma's church work, she got the same outlook as Nana Vernie Sue."

"When was that?" Bernie asked.

"When I was about five years old. I could never do a blessed thing right, but things got even worse after that."

"What about your dad? Is he all up in the church, too?" Bernie asked.

"No, but he does go sometimes, just not every Sunday. Basically, he talked to Luke and Myra and ignored me," she said. "But then, according to what Nana Vernie Sue said when I did something wrong, I was the oops kid. When I asked her what that was, she said it was one that they didn't really plan on having."

Bernie opened the container of applesauce, slid it over to Clara, and put on a pot of coffee. "Life happens."

"Is that another rule?"

"Nope, it's a fact," Bernie answered with a yawn. "So, Vernie Sue and your mama came down on you for working at a bar?"

"Yes, and for not going to church regularly, and for living with my boyfriend without a marriage license, and then for breaking up with him because they thought he was a wonderful man," she answered. "They liked Kent. No, that's not right. They loved him even more than they did me. He proved that he could charm the underpants off a holy woman when he met my family, but that was just an act."

"When did you kick him out?" Bernie asked.

"A year ago, but *he* kicked *me* out, and I will never move in with a man again."

"How in the hell did they not know for a whole year?"

"It's a long story, but the short version is that I didn't go home or call very often. There was always tension in the air while I was there, like maybe I had cooties that would jump off on them," Clara said with a shrug. "Can I have the coffee and aspirin now?"

Bernie filled a mug with coffee, shook a couple of pills out into her hand, and set both in front of Clara. Then she picked up her half-empty cup and sat down across from Clara. "I'm awake now and in the mood for a story, so talk to me."

Clara opened her eyes and took the aspirin with a sip of coffee. "I moved in with Kent and knew by the next week I had made a mistake. He was the jealous type and hovered over me until I could hardly breathe. But…" She added two spoonsful of sugar to her coffee. "This is really strong."

"It's coffee. Anything less is just murdered water," Bernie said. "Go on with this thing about Kent."

"We worked together at an oil company in Amarillo. We had already moved in together when he went home with me to the family reunion a year ago. Mama and Grandma loved him. He lied and said that we went to church regularly and belonged to a young adult group. I didn't correct him because I wanted them to like him— and me, too, for that matter."

"Was he religious?" Bernie asked.

"Not in the least, but he really sucked up to them both. Then I lost my job and went to work bartending from six in the evening to two in the morning. One of Kent's friends knew about a dancing job in a strip joint, and Kent was determined I would take it because it paid better than what I was doing, and I was letting him control our joint bank account that he insisted we set up when we moved in together. I refused and he kicked me out."

Anger boiled up from Bernie's toes to the tips of her dyed red hair. "Did you tell your mother and grandma about that?"

"I did," she nodded. "They jumped on a soapbox and declared that I was probably the one that asked him to live with me because I was so much like you. They said I was lying about a good Christian man like him asking me to work as a stripper. Then Grandma said that she bet he had proposed several times, and I was too stubborn to marry him. He really had done a snow job on them, and they wouldn't even listen to me when I tried to explain that he had lied."

The boiling hissy fit inside Bernie got so hot that it came out in her tone. "That's when you drove all the way out here?"

Clara nodded. "Yes, it is. I need a job and a place to stay until I can get on my feet. I'll follow the rules and promise to never get drunk again."

"You've got a roof over your head and you can work for me." Bernie pushed back her chair, stood up, and opened the door when she heard a yip at the door. Pepper pranced in like he owned the place and stood up on his hind feet.

"He's begging for food," Clara said. "No telling when he ate last or had anything to drink. I got the feeling that the old guy who stole him for you hadn't done much with him."

Bernie filled a bowl with water and set it on the floor. "What do I feed him?"

"Kent browned a little hamburger and scrambled an egg into it for his dog. I miss Brutus far more than I ever missed him," Clara said with a long sigh. "Brutus was always glad to see me, but Kent usually started in on me about something I'd done wrong the minute we got home."

"Where did you live for a whole year after Kent kicked you out?" Bernie took a package of hamburger out of the fridge and tossed a handful into a skillet.

"With one of my friends, but then she moved to Alabama, and I was barely making rent before the bar where I was working closed up and I didn't have a job," she answered. "I had a little savings, and I qualified for an unemployment check, but it wasn't enough to pay rent. I looked for another job, but…"

"But what?" Bernie asked. "Everywhere I go I see Help Wanted signs. Never mind, you are here now, at least for six weeks. If everything works out with Nash, I will most likely sell the bar to him at the end of that time."

"Where are you going?" Clara asked.

"Your aunt Mary Jane has offered to let me bring a travel trailer and park it at her place in Spanish Fort. How long has it been since you've seen her or your cousins?"

Clara finally smiled. "A long time. Probably right before she moved from the city to that brothel. Mama doesn't agree with Aunt Mary Jane writing trashy romance books, and Grandma really preaches against it."

Bernie cracked an egg and added it to the browned meat. "Have you read her books?"

"Every single one of them," Clara replied with half a giggle. "I especially love the ones she wrote about the hookers that worked out of the Paradise."

Pepper barked twice and ran around Bernie's feet like

a little whirlwind. "Settle down, boy. It would burn your tongue out of your mouth if you tried to eat it before it cooled down a little bit. When we get this animal's breakfast done, we are going to have bacon and eggs, then we're going to get dressed and go to town for groceries for us and food, collar, and leash for this critter."

"Then what?" Clara asked.

"After that, we are going to come home, clean up last night's mess in the bar, and decorate it for Independence Day," she answered.

Clara's blue eyes popped wide open. "You are open on Sunday?"

"Nope, that's my one day off each week, but we're going to put up the decorations and open up tomorrow at six like usual," she answered, "but that's after we get back from the store."

Tears streamed down Clara's face. "I can't believe you are doing this for me, without even giving me a long lecture."

"I need an inside person to give me the lowdown on Nash. Is he really serious about buying my bar, or is he out to get it and then resell to a developer who wants to put in another convenience store and gas station on the spot?"

"I can be a spy," Clara declared with a nod. "Or a bartender, or a dog walker, or I can even clean up the place after hours."

"Rule number two for you." Bernie held up two

fingers and set the plate of food down for Pepper. "Always turn out the lights and go home when the bar closes down. Then take care of mopping and polishing glasses and beer mugs the next day when you aren't worn to a frazzle."

"Yes, ma'am." Clara finally grinned so big that it reached her bloodshot eyes.

———

Bernie had just washed her hands in the Walmart bathroom in Duncan when her phone rang. She saw that the call was coming from her sister, Vernie Sue, so she hit the accept icon and took the call out into the store where her cart waited.

"Hey, how was church this morning? Did you get dehorned, saved, and sanctified for the whole week, or do you need a revival to get your soul in order for the judgment day?" she asked as she sat down on a nearby bench.

"Bernadette, you are going to hell for talking that way," Vernie Sue scolded in her best self-righteous voice. "It's past time for you to be thinking about where your soul will spend eternity."

"I figure you've prayed enough for me through the years that I've got a good fightin' chance of gettin' my foot in the door. Once that happens, I can talk my way inside." Bernie chuckled. "I haven't heard from you since you told me to leave the last family reunion I came to.

Why are you calling today?" She heard a long, loud sigh and then nothing for several seconds, and pulled the phone away from her ear to see if her sister had ended the call.

*I miss the old landlines where you got a loud click in the ear when someone hung up on you,* Bernie thought.

"Is Clara there?" Vernie Sue asked bluntly. "She told me and her mother that if she was going to get the name of being like you, then she would have the game. So, did she come to that horrible bar or not?"

"Why do you want to know?" Bernie shot back.

"Just answer the question…please," Vernie Sue said.

"Since you said 'please,' I would guess that the preacher's sermon this morning was on loving your neighbor, which can translate to loving your sister unconditionally."

"Is she or not?" Vernie Sue raised her voice a notch.

"Again, why do you want to know? Is she lost or has she been kidnapped? Have you filed a police report? You tell me what is going on."

"She threw a hissy fit, a lot like you used to do when you were mad. Anyway, she showed up here yesterday morning, and when her mother and I tried to talk sense to her, she stormed out. We haven't heard a word since then, and whether we agree with her decisions or not, we would like to know where she is," Vernie Sue said.

Sucking on a lemon couldn't have taken the smile off Bernie's face. "What did *you* say or do to make her that angry? Did you get out the soapbox and preach at her? Or did you open up your arms and tell her that you loved her?"

"Okay, okay!" Vernie Sue shouted. "She could show up at your place in the next couple of days. Would you call me if she does?"

Bernie hesitated so long that she could imagine her twin sister tapping her foot on her perfectly polished hardwood floors—in the house that she inherited from their parents.

"Well?" Vernie Sue finally said.

"No, I won't. Not until you tell me the whole story as to what you did to upset her." Bernie waved at Clara who passed by on her way to the ladies' room.

"She's been working in a bar, and got fired, and packed all her stuff in that old rattletrap of a car of hers and came back up here to Fritch looking for a place to live until she could get on her feet," Vernie Sue answered and then there was a long pause.

Bernie thought of Vernie Sue's daughter Mary Jane, living in an old brothel in an almost-ghost town. She had brought her two youngest daughters back home when one of them needed a change, let them live in the Paradise rent free, and even got them jobs teaching at a nearby school.

Vernie Sue finally went on. "Her mother and I had a talk with her, and it didn't set well. She said that she would come to Oklahoma and see if you would give her a job. Don't you dare take her in!" she warned in the bossy tone that Bernie remembered all too well.

Bernie laughed out loud. "That ship already sailed. One twin sister's trash is another sister's treasure. She will be working in my bar and living with me."

"You can't do that," Vernie Sue screamed.

"A bad time to tell someone that they cannot do something is when they already did it," Bernie said. "Y'all come on over to Ratliff City and see me some time, but only for the next six weeks. After that, I will be living in Spanish Fort in Mary Jane's backyard with my new attack dog, Pepper."

Vernie Sue gasped so loudly that Bernie thought she might have stroked plumb out. "Don't you dare die over this," she said, "or I will wear a red sequin dress to your funeral that's cut down to my belly button in the front, and up to my hip on the right leg."

"I cannot believe that we came from the same parents. Mama would be so ashamed of you," Vernie Sue scolded.

"I recognize a guilt trip when I hear one, and I'm not interested in going on one at my age. You have a wonderful day, Sister Vernie Sue. I see Clara coming out of the bathroom, and we have a lot of shopping to do today to get ready for our big July Fourth bar bash tomorrow. You and Marsha should come over and join us. I'll give you the friends and family discount on all your drinks."

"I'd rather eat dirt," Vernie Sue snapped.

"Then, darlin'…" Bernie dragged out the last word in such a sarcastic tone that it even gave her chills. "I pray that whatever you scoop up in the backyard for Sunday dinner hasn't been used for a litter pan by one of your cats." Bernie knew she was irritating the hell out of her sister, but it felt so good that she didn't care. "Bye now, and remember you are always welcome at my place, even if you wear a religious T-shirt."

# Chapter 3

CLARA AND BERNIE STOPPED at a great little steak house for lunch, and while she had been eating two huge pork chops, Clara thought of the day before when she had used her last dollar bill for a package of peanut butter crackers at the convenience store. That and what was left in her water bottle were what she had had to eat all day when she reached Ratliff City. She had pulled into the parking lot on an empty stomach, with a desperate prayer, bald tires, and a flood of tears that she couldn't control. Less than twenty-four hours later, she was sitting in a nice restaurant with the great-aunt who supposedly had been spawned by the devil himself.

"I feel like I stepped into a fresh cow patty and walked away smelling like a rose," Clara said.

"Proving that not all bad experiences produce horrible results," Bernie told her.

"Never thought of it that way," Clara said, "but it's the truth. Some lead you down the right path. That makes me wonder what will happen next now that I'm on one that feels like it could be *the one*."

"Never know, but if you keep walking on it, you might find happiness," Bernie replied. "I can sit right here at the age I am and attest to the fact that I certainly did."

"I hope so," Clara said. "I've been at odds with everything in my life for so long that it seems to me like the other shoe will drop any minute."

"That will pass like your hangover did." Bernie chuckled. "Finish your pork chops so we can go home and get to decorating."

"I haven't been out to eat in so long that I'm savoring every bite," Clara told her.

"Savor it faster. We've got milk and ice cream in the truck. Granted they are in a cooler, but there's just so much a person can ask of one little ice pack in this miserable heat wave."

"For ice cream, I will get a move on," Clara declared. "I haven't been able to afford a luxury like that in over a year."

The waitress came around and refilled both of their tea glasses. When she had gone, Clara looked across the table at her octogenarian aunt and asked, "I can understand putting up stuff for Christmas, but why for July Fourth? We put up the tree after Thanksgiving and leave it until New Year's Eve. That's more than a month. Why go to all that trouble for one day?"

"I didn't get married and have kids like my sister did," Bernie answered and finished up the last bite of her baked potato. "I was more or less pitched out of the family when I decided to live my life on my terms. When I became owner of this bar, I decided to make it my family. The family has tolerated me on a few occasions, but to love me unconditionally is out of their reach. What does any family do for holidays?" Bernie asked. "They put on costumes and have a good time."

"We did that for Christmas, but we only wore costumes to the church program," Clara answered.

"In the Chicken Coop family, we have fun on every holiday, and I always dress up," Bernie said.

"Are you serious?" Clara asked.

"Very, and it's a lot of fun. You'll see when we get back to the bar and get everything out of the storage room."

"Why did you name the bar the Chicken Coop?"

"I didn't. The previous owner did. Story has it that a family lived on this land and a tornado blew their house away. All that was left was a chicken coop, and years before it had become a landmark for directions. 'Turn left at the old chicken coop' kind of thing. He built the bar and named it the same thing," Bernie explained.

Clara turned up her glass of sweet tea and downed more than half of it. "I'm done. Let's go home, and I love that idea of keeping the name."

Bernie slid out of the booth and smiled. "You've been here one day and you're already calling it home?"

"Yes, I am," Clara answered.

===========

"What is all this stuff anyway?" Clara pulled out a chair in the bar, eased down into it, and stared at half a dozen boxes she had dragged from the storage room that afternoon. Less than twenty-four hours ago, she had wondered if she might be living out of her car, and now not only did she have a home, but also a job that started with decorating the Chicken Coop.

"If it has a big number four on the boxes, that means it's for July Fourth," Bernie explained.

Clara took a long drink of her tea and asked, "Are we going to use everything? That seems like a lot."

"Yes, we are. There's lots of stuff plus our costumes for July Fourth. Each year, I switch out what I wear, so there's half a dozen or more for us to choose from. We're about the same size, so you won't have any trouble finding one that will make you feel good." She opened a box and pulled out a short red-and-white-striped skirt and a royal blue peasant blouse with stars printed on it.

"This is for you. I wore it several years ago before my varicose veins took control of my legs. That's what I get for working in spike heels for years. Another rule to remember is to always wear good shoes at work, like the ones you have on now." She held up a pair of socks with lace around the tops and a headband with tinsel and stars attached to it.

"You really want me to wear that getup?"

"Yes, I do," Bernie answered. "You should see what I wear for Mardi Gras!"

"Aunt Bernie!" Clara tried to scold, but her giggle defeated the purpose. "This is not New Orleans."

"It most certainly is for one weekend of my choosing, and we have beads and the whole nine yards," Bernie argued.

Clara raised an eyebrow. "Do you show your boobs, too?"

"Nope." Bernie shook her head seriously. "Gravity done claimed those things years ago. To show the customers my cleavage would cause a stampede out of here."

Clara's giggles turned in a guffaw.

Bernie shook a bony forefinger at her. "Don't laugh. Mister Gravity will come for you someday in the future, and there won't be a thing you can do about it. Of course, a man created gravity and even named it. Other than big, old beer bellies, men don't suffer from the damn thing like we do. A woman would have better sense than to make something that would claim her boobs, her butt, and even her face, but getting back to this holiday. Independence Day is downright poetic for you, don't you think?"

Clara's smile turned into a frown. "Why do you say that?"

"Think about it," Bernie told her. "You have declared your independence by coming to Ratliff City to stay with me, haven't you?"

"Absolutely," Clara agreed.

"Then this can be your best holiday, even better than

Christmas or Valentine's Day. And, honey, I do it up right with red, white, and blue everywhere, from sparkling garland to the songs on the jukebox."

"What are you wearing?" Clara asked.

Bernie pulled out a pair of sequin-covered pants. One leg was blue with stars. The other was red and white stripes. "This and this," she held up a vest that matched. "I'll also have a necklace made of stars that light up."

Clara held up the short skirt and shook a few wrinkles from it. "I'm glad that I'm not as tall as my cousin, Ursula. If I was, this skirt wouldn't even cover my underwear."

"You really haven't been to see your relatives since you were a little girl?" Bernie asked.

"I haven't ever been to Spanish Fort. Grandma and Mama told Aunt Mary Jane if she moved into an old brothel in a ghost town, they were washing their hands of her. I asked them why they were so against that area since they had lived there back until Mama and Aunt Mary Jane both finished high school. They wouldn't answer me," Clara said.

"Vernie Sue and I graduated from the old high school in Spanish Fort," Bernie said. "She hated that part of Texas because I embarrassed the family so much when the free love movement hit. The talk about the twin sisters—one all sweet and righteous and the other a hellcat on steroids—died down years ago. Most of the gossips of that day are in the cemetery, but the thought of Mary Jane moving back there was more than she could handle."

"When I saw them last, Luna and Endora were cute little blond-haired girls. I think I'm about the age that Rae and Bo are. That was before Aunt Mary Jane got divorced and moved. Grandma shudders when she even says the word 'Paradise.' She treats it like a swear word that by uttering it, she is bound for hell on a rusty poker. I guess folks really must have made fun of the house when she was a kid, right?"

"Yep, they did," Bernie said with a smile.

Clara mimicked her grandmother for a second time. "'How could my daughter live in a house of ill repute? I moved away from that area to get away from the stigma of living in a town where brothels had been the normal thing, and now she's moving right back into that den of evil. And worse yet, she has raised her seven little girls in that place?'"

"You sound just like her, and you are funny. If you can do other voices, we could put you on the stage to do stand-up comedy. But speaking of the Paradise, let's go one afternoon this week." Bernie chuckled. "Not tomorrow though. We'll be too tired after all this work. We can spend the afternoon and be home in time to clean up for opening sometime."

"Aunt Bernie!" Clara exclaimed for the second time in less than an hour. "Do you have a private little plane parked out beyond those trees?"

"Why would I need one of those?" Bernie asked as she ripped open another box.

"There's no way we can go to Spanish Fort and back in one afternoon. I drove most of yesterday just to get here, and Aunt Mary Jane lives somewhere back in Texas," Clara reminded her.

"Spanish Fort is right across the Red River. It's only a couple hours' drive from here," Bernie informed her.

"I would love to go, but didn't all the cousins move away?" Clara asked.

"You are really behind times." Bernie began to put centerpieces on all the tables. "Yes, your cousins all moved away. Matter of fact, a couple of them didn't live so very far from your folks in Fritch. One is a police-woman, and the other is a teacher."

"They never came to see us, or if they did, Mama never mentioned it," Clara said.

"They most likely didn't even know they were close to kinfolks, since your mama and grandma more or less shunned Mary Jane, like they did me. The youngest set of twins, Endora and Luna, are teachers now, and…"— she stopped and pointed to another box—"open that up and take the garland behind the bar. We'll hang it up above the liquor shelves."

Clara set her beer to the side and ripped the tape from the box. "You were saying about Luna and Endora."

"Endora had a very bad breakup with her boyfriend a year ago. A couple of teaching positions came up in a little school south of Spanish Fort, so she and Luna moved back to the Paradise. She's had a rough time adjusting. She's not as tough as you and me. Having company might be a boost for her," Bernie explained. "I'll get the ladder out from the storage room. Neither one of us is tall enough to put up the garland without it."

Nash poked his head in the door. "Hey, what's going on in here?"

"Decorating for the holiday," Bernie said.

"Need some help?" Nash asked. "Since I plan to buy this place, I need to learn all the ropes. There's more to running a bar like this than pouring a double shot of whiskey or drawing up a mug of beer. I can do those things already, but the rest I need to be taught."

Bernie motioned him inside with a flick of her wrist. "I never turn down help, and you *will* have to dress the part tomorrow. Show him what you are wearing, Clara."

Clara fought back a blush when she held up the skimpy skirt and shirt. She'd seen Nash only in a glance through a veil of tears the night before. Hershal with his dead goldfish and tiny dog had sat next to her. Now that she could really see Nash in good light and without tears, her heart pitched in an extra beat, and her pulse jacked up halfway to the ceiling.

"Well, then..." He flashed a brilliant grin and combed back his thick hair with his fingertips, "I guess I'll drag out my patriotic overalls that only come to my knees, and my matching cowboy hat. Shirt or no shirt?"

"Whatever feels good," Bernie answered. "Will you get the ladder from the storage room and help us put up the garland and ceiling decorations?"

"Absolutely." Nash closed the door behind him and headed across the room. "Do you do this every year?"

"Yes, I do, and the customers love it. I fix this place up for every holiday, and if things begin to slag or get boring, sometimes I even make up a day for celebration," Bernie replied. "One year we celebrated the International Day of the Chicken. We didn't promote compassion and respect for the bird like some folks did since we enjoyed buffalo wings and chicken salad sandwiches that evening, but we had a wonderful time doing the chicken dance. I even have a costume in one of the boxes in the storage room and pictures to prove I'm telling the truth."

Nash laughed so hard that he had to wipe his eyes with a paper napkin. "What else do you get all fixed up for?"

"On October twenty-eighth, we celebrate the end of Oktoberfest and have a beer-drinking day where all draft beer is buy one, get one free. I have all of the celebrations written down." She pointed toward a calendar hanging on the wall beside the door leading back to the storage room.

"No wonder this place has been here since Grandpa Hoot was a young man," Nash said. "It's not just a bar. It's a fun place to go."

Clara snuck a few side-glances toward Nash and

visualized him with no shirt. The room got at least twenty degrees hotter even though the air conditioner vents were shooting down cold air. She sure wished that she had one of her mother's church fans with a picture of Jesus on one side and an advertisement for a local funeral home on the other.

Men like Nash had always been her kryptonite, especially those with arms the size of hams and a ripped abdomen that strained at the seams of his snug-fitting knit shirt. He dang sure did not look like a lawyer. He could have posed for the covers of those sexy bodice-ripper romance books that were taboo in the house where she grew up. She mentally gave herself a come-to-Jesus talk. Getting a major hot flash over a man she didn't even know was ridiculous. Nash probably had a girlfriend, or maybe even a fiancée, waiting in the wings. Worse yet, he could be controlling and jealous like Kent.

*If you like a man who looks like Nash, why in the hell were you ever with Kent?* The voice inside her head asked. *He had thinning blond hair and his shirts hung on his frame like they would on a skinny scarecrow.*

"In the beginning, he was funny and sweet. That was what I was looking for, but he turned into a control freak. And besides, it's not right to compare one person to another," she muttered.

"What was that?" Bernie asked.

"I was talking to myself." Clara slid another long look at Nash when he returned with the ladder.

"That's another way that you are like me. I talk to myself all the time and solve a lot of problems that way," Bernie said.

"I've done it all my life. Myra and Luke were older than me and didn't have the time or inclination to listen to what I had to say about anything. What do I do with all these red and blue bowls?"

"Line them up on the bar," Bernie told her. "We'll put pretzels and peanuts in them tomorrow just before we open."

"You were telling me about Luna and Endora," Clara said as she worked.

"Endora was engaged and found out that her feller was sleeping with her best friend," Bernie said as she held up the garland for Nash to attach to the wall right below the ceiling. "The woman and Endora's fiancé both worked at the school where she and Luna worked. It was quite a mess, and Endora isn't over it even yet. She's sworn off all men and declares she will be an old-maid aunt and enjoy all her sisters' kids," Bernie explained.

"So, some of the girls are married?" Clara asked.

"Nope, not a single one of them. Mary Jane ain't gettin' any younger, and she's ready for grandbabies," Bernie said as she opened another box.

"Who are Endora and Luna?" Nash asked.

"My cousins that I haven't seen in years. Aunt Bernie is filling me in on what I've missed." Clara wondered where they would find room to put anything else, but Bernie brought out more garland. Not that Clara minded. Watching Nash up on that ladder was like a trip to the candy store with unlimited finances. Even if he might be in a committed relationship, there was no law against looking.

"Ursula is trying to break into writing romances," Bernie went on to spill more tea. "Mary Jane has almost got her convinced to come back to the Paradise for a year to work on her first book. If she does, she'll be home for Thanksgiving."

Clara opened up three more beers and passed one up to Nash. Their fingers brushed against each other's in the transfer, and sparks danced around the room like fireworks. She reminded herself in a scolding inner voice that she would be working with this guy, and that her own *rule number one* was that she didn't mix business and pleasure. Not anymore. Not after the experience with Kent. Besides all that, she would probably be without a job again in six weeks if and when Nash bought the place—unless he hired her to keep working there. That was a possibility, albeit a slim one, that she wouldn't mind thinking about.

"Where did those women get such strange names?" Nash asked.

"Their mama, my niece, is a famous romance author," Bernie explained. "She named all seven of her girls after whatever character was in the book she was writing at the time of their birth. So, the first three are

Ursula, Ophelia, and Tertia after heroines in historical romances. She thought she was finished having kids, but then she had twins, Bo and Rae—one was named after a singer and the other one for a cop in a couple of contemporary stories. Then she got a surprise when they were still in diapers and she had another set of twins, Endora and Luna, named after a couple of characters in a paranormal book."

"And you are *just* Clara?" Nash asked and locked eyes with her. "Was your mama writing a historical book?"

"My mother worked for the FBI when I was born, and you are right. I'm *just Clara*, plain old name that she got from a colleague's grandmother who brought cookies to the office every couple of weeks," she answered.

"I like it," Nash said. "And honey, if anyone ever tells you that you are plain, send them to me and I'll take them to the eye doctor."

"That is sweet. Thank you." There was no fighting the blush that time. She whipped around and tore into the last box, hoping that he didn't see the fire in her cheeks.

"Just tellin' it like I see it."

————

"Well, look who has decided to make an appearance," Bernie said when the bar looked like an explosion of red, white, and blue.

Pepper wandered into the bar from the storage room

and barked at Bernie. "Are you hungry, or do you want to go chase squirrels again?"

"Looks to me like he would cross his legs if he could." Nash chuckled. "I promised Grandpa and Granny I would be home in time for supper, so I'm going to leave you ladies to it. See you tomorrow evening at five, right?"

"Nope, make it a quarter to six. Place is clean, so we're ready to open," Bernie answered. "The only thing left to do is pour up the pretzels and peanuts. Clara, will you please put the new collar and leash on Pepper and take him out back for a walk?"

"Yes, ma'am," she answered.

When they were gone and the bar was empty, Bernie sat down at one of the tables and propped up her aching feet on an extra chair. "This is a Danny Glover situation: 'I'm too old for this shit,'" she said, quoting a line from the *Lethal Weapon* movie. "It's time for me to retire and let some younger folks run the place."

Her phone rang and she groaned. She didn't want to talk to her sister or to Clara's mama, Marsha. She jerked the phone from her shirt pocket, saw that it was neither of them calling, and answered on the fifth ring.

"Hey, Mary Jane, I was just talking about you today," Bernie said. "What's going on over on your side of the Red River?"

"You sound tired, Aunt Bernie," Mary Jane said. "Why don't you close up the bar tomorrow and come celebrate the holiday with us?"

"Thank you for the invitation, but we just finished decorating the place for the Fourth," Bernie replied and covered a yawn with her hand. Four hours of sleep wasn't enough for anyone—much less a woman who was pushing seventy. Okay, okay! So, she cheated about a decade when it came to her age.

"Well, you know that you're always welcome. We keep looking for a call from you saying that you've sold the bar and are on your way down here to the Paradise. Please tell me you haven't changed your mind about that. I worry about you," Mary Jane told her.

"No, I have not, and it's possible I have a buyer, and you'll never guess what happened last night. A sexy man, a bawling great-niece, and an old lover with a dead gold-fish and a Chihuahua dog walked into my bar," Bernie said with a giggle.

"Is this one of your bar jokes? And which of my daughters is in Oklahoma with you? Is it Rae or Bo, and are they all right?" Pure old unadulterated worry was in Mary Jane's voice. "Tell me which one it is, and I'll be on the way soon as I put on some shoes and get my purse."

"It's not one of your girls. It's Marsha's youngest one, Clara," Bernie quickly explained.

"Whew!" Mary Jane let out a long breath. "Send her down here if she needs help. I'll take her in."

"I've got everything under control," Bernie assured her. "And, honey, I thought that sounded like a bar joke too, but it's the bona fide gospel truth." She went on to tell her favorite niece about what happened. "So, now I have a prospective buyer who is willing to work for free for six weeks, and Clara needs a job, so I hired her to help him." She stood up and headed back to the apartment. "I was wondering if you and the girls have plans for Tuesday or Wednesday. We'd love to drive down and visit."

"Either day is great. Maybe talking to Clara will perk Endora up a little. God knows she needs something to shake her out of the doldrums."

"I'll do my best to help with that when I get all moved in down there," Bernie offered.

"That would be wonderful."

"Hey, can we not tell anyone that I've moving down there?" Bernie asked. "I want to surprise Ursula."

"No problem, and right now it looks like she'll be here right before Thanksgiving," Mary Jane said. "I'm not sure the twins and I can keep a secret that long, but we'll try. Come in for lunch. According to the weatherman, it's going to rain both tomorrow and Tuesday."

"Then Wednesday it is," Bernie said. "But what is going on with this stupid weather? Rain in July in these parts is as scarce as hen's teeth."

"Who knows? Maybe it'll clear off enough that we can have our usual fireworks show here at the Paradise. What did my mama and sister have to say about Clara working in a bar?"

"Use your imagination," Bernie answered, and filled her in on the situation.

"No wonder it's going to rain. Lord have mercy! It might even snow," Mary Jane gasped.

"Yep," Bernie said. "Those were my thoughts exactly. We'll be there on Wednesday unless between now and then Marsha sends a late tornado to tear down my bar. And I sure don't want to drive in a storm in case lightning comes with that rain. Don't want to take any chances on it hitting me for taking Clara in."

"See you then." Mary Jane laughed out loud. "Be safe."

"I hope that only applies to my driving," Bernie teased.

"Yes, ma'am," Mary Jane said in a serious tone. "To tell you to be safe in other areas would be a waste of breath."

"You have always been the smart one in the family," Bernie said and ended the call.

"Was that Mama?" Clara asked. "I've been expecting her to call me all day."

"Nope, it was not your mother or your grandmother," Bernie answered truthfully. "Are you disappointed that you haven't heard from her?"

Clara shook her head. "Not really. If she does call, it will be to yell at me or make me promise to go to that religious rehab place where I will repent for all my past sins and get my wings and halo at the graduation in three months." She stopped long enough to take a breath. "Right now, I'm grateful to be here, but like I told you earlier, I keep feeling like the other shoe is going to drop any minute."

Bernie had not talked to Clara's mama, but the fact that she *had* talked to Vernie Sue was about to put her in a leaky canoe and send her down crap creek on a guilt trip. If she expected to get any sleep that night, she had to 'fess up and tell Clara the truth. "Your grandmother called me when we were shopping. They know you are here, and they are not happy," she blurted out and felt better. "I wasn't going to tell you because you've already had enough of their threats and demands, but there it is."

"I'm glad to know. Now I don't have to talk to them," Clara said.

"Right then, I was talking to your aunt Mary Jane. We're going down there for lunch on Wednesday," Bernie said.

Clara covered a yawn with her hand. "I really do feel like I've won the lottery."

"Just remember that folks say the lottery is cursed, and winning it is not a good thing. Enough about the lifestyles of the self-righteous in Fritch, Texas. Let's order a couple of pizzas to be delivered, open two beers, and watch some television until bedtime."

"You don't have to twist my arm one bit," Clara agreed. "But I might fall asleep long before dark."

"I'll wake you if you snore," Bernie said.

# Chapter 4

Thunder that rivaled the noise of a heavy metal band awoke Bernie on Monday morning. Lightning zigzagged through the sky so close to her bedroom window that she was sure it almost parted her red hair. She threw a pillow over her head and shook her fist at the ceiling. Without a doubt, her pious sister had called down rain from heaven to ruin the fireworks shows in southern Oklahoma and northern Texas to punish her for taking Clara in. In between bouts of rain slamming against the window, she could hear Pepper whining not far from her ear.

"For once the weatherman could have been wrong," she muttered as she threw back the covers. "Dog, you really do *not* want to go outside, but if you do, know that I'm not going with you. If you want to brave this storm to add more water to a bush, then you are on your own."

She padded down the hall in her bare feet with Pepper right behind her. The electricity blinked off when she reached the kitchen, leaving the apartment in near-total darkness, but she didn't need light to find her way outside. She had lived in the place long enough that she could get around with her eyes closed, even after drinking one too many double shots of whiskey. She reached for the doorknob and stepped on a slug at the same time. The slimy little booger squished up between all the toes on her left foot, and she let out enough cuss words to blister the pale-yellow paint right off the walls. She tried to shake the gooey mess off, but evidently it had a healthy dose of superglue DNA in its system.

"Aunt Bernie, are you all right?" Clara's high-pitched voice cut through the next blast of thunder.

"I'm fine, but there's a dead slug between my toes." She walked on the heel of her foot to the back door and opened it.

Pepper ran out like his little tail was on fire, and another flash of lightning lit him up when he hiked his leg on one of the patio chairs. Bernie didn't even have time to grab a paper towel to wipe the slug away before he scratched on the back door to be let back inside. She stood on one leg like a flamingo, or maybe it was an ostrich, and got off-balance when she tried to open the door. When she took a step, a second slug went to meet its maker. She backed up and plopped down in a chair and let out another string of swearing that could have easily peeled the drywall right off the studs.

"Sit still, and I'll bring paper towels and a warm washcloth," Clara said as she came into the room with a flashlight.

"I hate anything that crawls," Bernie declared, "and these miserable things are at the top of my list. They can't possibly serve a purpose in life, except to test what little Jesus I have inside my soul. Check the floor before you come in here. Where's there's one, there's usually half a dozen leaving a trail of shiny slime all over the floor."

Pepper ran over, sniffed Bernie's foot, and growled deep in his throat. Then he shook from his eyeballs to the tip of his tail, leaving water that smelled like wet dog on her feet.

"Why didn't you chase them off before they wound up between my toes?" Bernie snapped. "You are a lazy mutt, but then Hershal didn't ask for your résumé or your pedigree when he stole you, did he?"

"Here you go." Clara handed her a roll of paper towels, then shined her flashlight around the floor. "Looks like those were the only two."

Bernie jerked off several sheets and swiped at her feet, shivering the whole time. "If these things smelled as bad as they feel, they could run a skunk some serious competition. Lord, I hate this. It feels like glue mixed with snot on my skin."

Clara shivered. "That is gross!"

"That doesn't begin to describe it." Bernie scrubbed at her feet with a warm, soapy washcloth. "This is definitely not starting out to be my favorite Independence Day."

"No matter what happens, it will always be the best

one in my eyes," Clara said. "Even with the thunder, the rain, and the slugs, it beats where I was last year."

"Then next time you can deal with the slugs, and we'll see if that changes your mind."

———————

The rain stopped and the sun came out at noon, but by four o'clock dark clouds had rolled in from the southwest. Nash arrived a little early and came inside the bar with water droplets clinging to his silver hair.

"The weatherman gets a gold star for being right," he said.

"Or a bullet from folks with whining kids because they couldn't go outside and shoot off firecrackers all day," Bernie grumbled.

Clara stopped putting peanuts and pretzels in the colorful bowls and stared at Nash with wide eyes. He wore a sleeveless muscle shirt under a pair of short overalls with red-and-white legs and blue stars on the bib, black cowboy boots, and a hat that had been created out of plastic wrappers with Budweiser logos.

Bernie nudged her on the shoulder. "Pretty sexy, huh? His hair says he's older than thirty-five, but his body and that getup tell a different story."

"I have never seen anything…" Clara's gaze traveled from Nash in his short patriotic overalls to Bernie and then down at her own short skirt.

The rooster crowed and two of Bernie's regular

customers dashed inside. "Happy Fourth," one of them growled.

"I don't know why you are so grumpy," the other one said as he led the way to the bar. "We have always spent the holiday right here. Don't matter if the sun is shinin' or we're dodgin' tornadoes. And we're never disappointed. Look at all the decorations and… Oh, my! Bernie and whoever this delightful little lady is she has working tonight are both a sight for sore eyes."

"Amen to that," Nash said. "What can I get you guys?"

"A pitcher of beers and some good music," Mr. Unhappy answered.

"Coming right up," Nash said.

Bernie picked up a whole roll of quarters from beside the cash register and headed for the jukebox. She plugged in the maximum amount and began to push buttons. She started with Billy Ray Cyrus's song, "Some Gave All," and then went on to choose a couple by Toby Keith. When the machine told her to add more money, she went back to the bar.

"I can't believe you still have one of them old jukeboxes that play real records," Nash said as he filled pitchers and set them on a tray along with beer mugs.

"If you buy the place, are you going to trade it in for a digital one?" Bernie asked.

"No, ma'am," Nash said. "Does a man still come around to change out the records?"

"Nope," she answered. "When he retired, I bought the records I wanted from him for a quarter each and made him teach me how to change them out. If I retire, I'll show you how it's done."

"That is a jewel that I would never get rid of," he vowed.

Clara picked up the tray and carried it back to the table where the first customers were seated. Bernie noticed that Nash seemed frozen with a bar towel in one hand and a dreamy expression on his face as he watched her walk across the floor.

"She's pretty cute in that getup," he said.

"Yes, she is," Bernie agreed.

"Is she in a relationship?" he asked.

"Are you?" Bernie fired back at him.

Nash wiped down the already clean bar. "No, ma'am. Eighty-hour weeks didn't leave much time for dating."

"No, she is not seeing anyone," Bernie answered.

The rooster crowed again to let it be known that more customers were on the way. By the time Toby Keith had finished singing "Made in America," the place was half-full and more people were steadily coming in. Most usually Bernie was busiest on Independence Day after the local fireworks shows had all finished, but not that night. From the time the doors opened at six o'clock until she figured it was about time to turn on the television above the jukebox, the tables were full, the small dance floor was crowded, and the barstools were all taken.

Bernie put the jukebox on pause and yelled, "Our fireworks display here in Ratliff City has been rained out, but that doesn't mean it's raining in New York City. Everyone put your hats or your hand over your hearts and sing with me. It doesn't matter if you sing off-key or out of tune, just show your appreciation for this great county that we are privileged to live in." She started singing the national anthem, and when they reached the "rockets bursting in air," she hit the remote's play button. The television screen lit up with a brilliant array of fireworks being shown live from the East Coast.

"That was impressive," Nash said.

"She's amazing," Clara agreed. "Are you really still thinking about buying this place?"

"Not only am I thinking about it, but I'm going to write Bernie a check the minute she gives me the green light. I was happier than I had been in years on Saturday night. And that wasn't a flash in the pan, so to speak, because tonight has been even more fun," he answered.

When the fireworks show ended, Bernie started up the jukebox again. "Letters from Home" by John Michael Montgomery was playing when she went back to the bar. She expected most of the people to call it a night, but several couples made their way to the dance floor for a slow country waltz.

"I'm almighty glad you are both here," she said as she made a half-dozen margaritas and set them on a tray. "This has been my biggest night in the history of the bar."

"When's the next big shindig?" Clara asked.

"Labor Day weekend. I usually do that one on Saturday night and have Sunday to clean up the place," she answered.

"That's after the six weeks is up," Nash said.

Bernie handed Clara the tray and pointed to a table in the corner with six middle-aged women. "Yep, so this could be my last big hoorah. If it is, I couldn't ask for a better send-off!"

"Do you think Clara will continue to work for me?" Nash asked.

"That's between y'all," Bernie told him. "The apartment has two bedrooms. If you offer her the room she's staying in right now as part of her bonus package, she might consider it. My advice is that you should wait a while to even talk to her, to be sure that you can stand to work together six days a week. I tried hiring a few helpers. Some were lazy. Some had trouble taking orders. Others were consistently late to work. I finally gave up."

"Sounds like good advice." He took four bottles of beer from the cooler and hurried down to the other end of the bar.

Clara brought back an empty tray and wiped it down. "I'm sure glad you told me not to wear high heels."

"I'm smarter than your grandmother gives me credit for." Bernie chuckled.

"There was never any doubt about that," Clara told her as she drew up four mugs of beer.

Usually there were a couple of hangers-on when Bernie flashed the lights to let anyone left in the bar know that it was closing time, but that night more than twenty customers started toward the door.

"Fantastic party, Bernie," one of them called out when he set his empty mug on the bar. "My friends and I were going to the Duncan fireworks show, but when it got rained out, someone mentioned driving over here."

Another one of his group winked at Bernie. "And I got a date with a beautiful woman out of the deal. Sparks flew all around us, and if things work out, by this time next year she may be my wife."

"If she is, you remind Nash here of the fact you met her here and he will give y'all the first round of drinks on the house," Bernie told him.

"You won't be here?" he asked.

"Probably not," she replied.

"How about that gorgeous red-haired bartender?" The third one in the group pointed at Clara.

"Come back and find out," Bernie teased, amazed that she had a bit of humor left in her after the hectic night.

"Oh, I will," he said and flashed a bright smile toward Clara.

Bernie locked the door behind the last of the customers and sat down in a chair at the nearest table. "I would love to have a double shot of Jameson on the rocks, if one of you will bring it to me. My butt is dragging so badly that we probably won't even need to sweep the floors."

Clara fixed the drink, took it to Bernie, and then sat down across the table from her. "Thank goodness we don't have to clean up tonight. I'm almost too tired to breathe."

Nash set a beer in front of her and dragged over another chair. "This might help restore enough energy to get you to bed."

"I wish every night would be just like this one." He twisted the top off his beer and took a long gulp. "That was the fastest eight hours I've ever spent."

"Me too," Clara agreed. "But I'm not so sure I want every night to be like this. How did you ever manage all alone, Aunt Bernie?"

"You do what you have to do," Bernie answered.

# Chapter 5

CLARA WAS STRUCK SPEECHLESS when Endora came out to the truck to meet her and Bernie. There was no doubt that they were cousins, with the same blue eyes and face shape. Clara might have been slightly curvier than Endora, but still it was one of those uncanny almost doppelgänger moments. Then the front door opened, and Luna waved from the porch.

"It's like looking in the mirror and seeing two more of me wearing blond wigs," Clara whispered.

"We've got the same DNA flowing through your veins. I remember when we were little, and you came to visit. I loved your red hair. A couple of my sisters got it, but Luna and I both got this straw-colored stuff," Endora said. "Come on inside. Y'all are just in time for lunch."

"I remember us playing together with your Barbie dolls, but that was in a big city," Clara said.

"Yep, it was, and those dolls came with me to this house. I'm so glad that you are here. I can just barely remember you and your sister and brother coming to see us before we moved to the Paradise." Endora looped her arm into Clara's and led her to the house. "Let's have lunch and then catch up on our lives. I hear that you are working at Aunt Bernie's bar."

"Yes, I am, and I love it," Clara said.

"Mama, they are here," Luna called out and then gave Clara a hug. "It's been too long, girl. Come on in the house, where it's cool. I swear, this has been one crazy summer. If it's not hotter'n blue blazes, then it's raining. The heat we expect. The rain not so much, and we're not used to this muggy feeling in the middle of summer."

Mary Jane gave them both a hug and then motioned toward the table. "Welcome to the Paradise. I'm so glad to get to see you again, and that you are helping Aunt Bernie. I've been worried about her overdoing. I'll be glad when she's living close by where I can keep an eye on her. We made a hot chicken casserole, salad, and fresh yeast rolls."

Bernie gave her another hug. "The one with potato chips on the top?"

"I remembered that was your favorite," Mary Jane said. "It's ready, so let's all five sit down at the table and visit while we eat. Joe Clay says to tell y'all hello. He's off helping the pastor of our church put a new roof on the parsonage."

"You go to church?" Clara asked and then wished she could cram the words back into her mouth.

"Of course." Mary Jane grinned. "And Aunt Bernie will go with us when she moves down here."

"I don't know why that would surprise you," Luna said.

"But those amazing books you write…" Clara snapped her mouth shut and wished she could hit a button and delete the words.

"Even the preacher's wife can't wait to get her hands on Mama's books when they come out," Endora said.

"Wow!" Clara exclaimed. "I want to go to a church like y'all do."

"Nash's grandpa, Hoot, and his grandma, Darlene, would probably welcome you," Bernie said. "I'm a CEO Christian and have sat on the pew with them a few times."

"What is that?" Luna asked.

"Christmas and Easter only," Bernie answered as she pulled out a chair and sat down. "I have to show the good Lord on occasion that I still appreciate his house of prayer."

"Mama, can I be that kind?" Endora asked.

"Nope," Mary Jane answered, "and neither will Aunt Bernie be when she moves to the Paradise."

Bernie put a couple of big scoops of casserole on her plate. "But I won't be living in the Paradise. I will be staying out in the backyard in my trailer."

Luna had taken a swallow of cold sweet tea and spewed it all down the front of her shirt. Endora tossed an extra napkin her way and laughed out loud.

"Well, Sister," Luna said as she wiped at the wet spot. "That was worth it if it made you laugh."

"Oh, hush!" Endora scolded and passed the casserole over to her sister. "Be glad you didn't already have food on your plate, and what was so funny anyway?"

"I think it was Aunt Bernie's tone more than what she said," Luna answered. "She even did a little head wiggle. The underlying message was that she would go to church if she wanted to, but that since she didn't officially live in the Paradise, she didn't have to attend with us."

"The trailer is like Las Vegas," Bernie informed them. "What happens there stays there, but I don't mind going to church at all once in a while. I can sit with the family and think about Sunday dinner."

"That's what I do. If God really loved me, He wouldn't have put me through that horrible time with my ex," Endora said.

"Maybe He is testing the Jesus in you to be sure you are worthy for the next person He tosses over the fence for you to meet," Bernie told her.

"He can keep whoever it is, or give him to someone else," Endora declared. "Burn me once, shame on you. Burn me twice, and you can go to hell."

Luna laughed out loud. "I don't think that's the way the saying goes."

"It is in my mind," Endora snapped.

After all that Clara had heard about the infamous Paradise, she could hardly believe how comfortable and relaxed she was in the house. The aura surrounding her here wasn't unlike the one at Bernie's bar. She felt as if she had finally found peace and happiness.

*Don't get too comfortable or happy. Don't come running back to me when the shine wears off this new ridiculous job of yours and when you figure out that my sister isn't what you think she is.* Her grandmother's voice popped into her head.

Clara took a deep breath and shoved food in her mouth to keep from arguing with her.

———————

"Why don't you girls give Clara a tour of the house, and y'all have a visit. I'll help Mary Jane take care of cleanup," Bernie said in an attempt to run the cousins out of the kitchen when everyone had finished lunch. Clara could use a therapy session with someone who had essentially been through similar experiences. From what Endora had said, she could definitely benefit from comparing notes with her cousin. And besides all that, Bernie wanted time to talk to Mary Jane without all the girls around.

"I don't mind helping," Clara said.

"We only have so much time before we have to start back. You girls need to make the most of it," Bernie said.

"No argument from me," Luna agreed, and led the way out of the kitchen.

Mary Jane pushed her plate back and refilled both her and Bernie's tea glasses. "Now, tell me about this fellow who is willing to work for free to get a chance at buying your bar."

"I've known his grandparents for years. Hoot, that's his grandpa, comes in the bar every week when his wife is at her quilting meeting at the church. Nash is their grandson, and he seems to be a good fit for the bar." Bernie pulled her phone from her shirt pocket and scrolled down through it. "Here's a photo I shot of him and Clara on Monday night."

"Good-lookin' fellow," Mary Jane said, "but isn't he a lot older than Clara?"

"Nope, only about five years. Seems that he got premature gray hair. Downright sexy, don't you think?"

"Oh, yeah," Mary Jane answered, "and Clara looks happy. I feel bad that I've missed so much of her life."

Bernie cut a brownie in half and ate it with her fingers. "That's not on you. Maybe someday Marsha will grow up and realize how much family means to a person."

"It's been more than twenty years since I moved into the Paradise," Mary Jane said with a long sigh. "It's just a house that quit being a brothel over a hundred years ago. I can't understand why they were all so against me living here. Or writing romance books, either. It's what I do, not who I am."

"Add that to the anger they have at you for not throwing me out with the trash and continuing to let me be a part of your life, and you might have an inkling of their excuses and reasons for the way they treated you,"

Bernie told her. "Changing the subject here. I'm worried about all three of those girls. Clara and Endora have been through tough times, but something is off with Luna. She seems happy and sad at the same time."

"She and Endora are the kind of twins that share each other's emotions," Mary Jane explained. "Luna feels guilty if she's happy because Endora can't get over the betrayal. Her fiancé snowed us all. We thought he hung the moon and stars, but all that was fake."

Bernie nodded the whole time Mary Jane was speaking and thought of another fellow by the name of Kent who was pretty much the same, even if he was an abuser in a different way. "Sounds an awful lot like the story Clara told me about the fellow she was living with up until a year ago. Too bad Marsha didn't stand up for her like you have done for Endora." She went on to tell Mary Jane about the controlling relationship Clara had gotten out of. "I think all three of them need to find a man who would walk a mile over hot coals and through a tornado to bring them a bouquet of wildflowers."

"You got that right, but I think the last man who would do that might have been Joe Clay Carter, and I married him more than twenty years ago," Mary Jane said.

"I'm a pretty good reader of people, and I think Nash might be one of the few." An idea floated through Bernie's mind that she could possibly be a matchmaker for all her great-nieces. She could practice on Clara, and then move on to all seven of Mary Jane's girls once she had moved to Spanish Fort. Of course, Ursula and Luna would be first on the list. Endora would need to see that her sisters could have a happy-ever-after, and that all men weren't like that sorry sucker who did her so dirty.

"What are you thinking about?" Mary Jane asked. "You look like you are about to chew up railroad ties and spit out Tinker Toys."

"Endora," Bernie admitted. "I could take that fool that caused her pain into the woods behind my bar and leave his carcass there for the coyotes."

"I'd help you drag him," Mary Jane said. "Maybe we could make it double fun and do the same with Clara's ex."

"Now you are talking," Bernie agreed.

---

On one hand, Clara hated to see the afternoon end. On the other, she couldn't wait to talk to Bernie about her twin cousins on the trip back across the Red River. Bernie had driven down the long, tree-lined lane and was back on the road leading out of town when she finally spoke.

"What do you think of the Paradise now that you've visited your cousins and aunt?"

Clara gazed out at the pale-blue sky without a single cloud in sight. "It's kind of like that," she answered.

"Like what?" Bernie frowned.

"The sky. No dark clouds. No bad omens. Just peace and a beautiful day. But I got to admit I'm worried about the twins. We talked a lot about Endora's and my exes. It's been about a year for both of us, but she hasn't moved on like I have. We both don't know if we can fully trust another man enough to enter into a relationship again, but I'm willing to try. It will be a very long time before Endora has reached that place," Clara answered.

After that comment, Bernie figured that she might have a little success fixing Clara up with her happy-ever-after, but she would have to really put forth some effort with Endora. Maybe it would be best to start with Ursula. Seemed fitting since she was the oldest, and it would only be right that she get married and give Mary Jane her first grandbaby.

"What are you thinking about so hard?" Clara asked. "We are going to get back in time to open the bar on time, aren't we?"

"Yes, we'll be there in plenty of time," Bernie answered. "I asked Mary Jane and the twins to keep the fact I'm moving to Spanish Fort a secret. I want to surprise Ursula."

"That's what you were thinking about?"

Bernie put on her best smile and told one of those white lies that does not keep a person out of heaven. "Of course, and wondering if I should have asked them to keep such a big secret."

"So, you are really selling the bar?"

"I am," Bernie answered. "If not to Nash, to someone

else. Now that folks know someone is interested, they'll start coming around with offers. It's kind of like being engaged. I've seen it time and time again in the bar crowd. Once a guy is taken, then the women decide that maybe they weren't giving him a fair shake, and they begin to flirt with him."

"I don't understand," Clara said.

"I'm an excellent judge of character, and I'm ninety percent sure that I'll sell the bar to Nash, but if either of us changes our mind, then I'm not worried. There will be other prospective buyers." Bernie really wanted to hatch her plan to do a little matchmaking between Clara and Nash, not talk about selling what had been her home for decades.

*Trying to fix your great-nieces up with a happy-ever-after is just an excuse to keep you from thinking about moving away and leaving the bar behind,* the pesky voice in her head scolded.

"Maybe so," she whispered.

Clara had been staring out the side window, but suddenly she whipped around with tears streaming down her face. "Like the old saying goes, if it wasn't for bad luck, I'd have no luck at all."

"What are you talking about?" Bernie asked.

"I find a place like the Chicken Coop that I love, and an aunt who's been good to me, not to mention…" She grabbed a napkin from a fast-food place from the glove compartment and blew her nose. "Not to mention cousins that I fit right in with, and now in a few weeks, it's all going to be gone."

Bernie swallowed twice but the lump in her throat wouldn't disappear. "Clara, I will not leave you out in the cold. You've got my word on that. Nash has already asked me if I thought you would be willing to work for him if he buys the place. So, there's an option. Plus, did you see all those empty bedrooms at the Paradise? Your aunt Mary Jane would gladly put you in one of them and probably find you some kind of job. So, there's a second idea. This side of the family takes care of its own."

"Are you sure?" Clara's tone said that she needed more assurance.

Bernie reached across the console and laid a hand on her shoulder. "I'm positive sure, and I never go back on a promise. No more worrying about the future. I've got you covered."

"Thank you," Clara whispered. "I'll do my best to make you proud."

"You already did," Bernie told her. "Now let's get on home and let Pepper outside. I bet his little bladder is close to bursting and he is cussin' us in dog language right now."

———

Clara couldn't even see Nash yet when she and Bernie were in the storage room, but that tingly feeling on the back of her neck told her that he was already in the bar.

"I hear Nash whistling, Aunt Bernie. How did he get inside before us? I swear that I locked up after closing last night."

"Of course you did," Bernie said. "I gave him a key before that in case we had a flat tire or ran out of gas. How did you know he was here?"

Clara crossed her fingers behind her back like she did as a child when she was telling a lie. "I heard someone rattling around in the bar and figured it was Nash. If I'm wrong, then we've got a burglar who is probably drinking all our top-shelf liquor."

Bernie slung open the door, peeked outside, and whispered over her shoulder. "Nope, it's just Nash. No whiskey stealers there." She raised her voice and yelled, "Hey, I see you've already started the cleanup. Thanks for that."

"You are welcome," Nash said as he walked toward the storage room. "Did I hear something about someone stealing whiskey?"

"No, Clara thought we had a burglar. She didn't know you had a key," Bernie answered as he got nearer.

"I thought someone had broken into the place," Clara answered, and fought down a little disappointment that he was allowed to come and go at will, but Bernie had not offered to give her a key.

Nash came on inside and grabbed the mop and the galvanized bucket. "I've got a load of beer mugs in the dishwasher, and another one rinsed and ready to go in when that finishes. I've already swept, and now I'm ready to mop."

"That's good," Bernie said. "Clara and I will get the cooler restocked and make sure that any empty whiskey bottles are thrown out."

As usual, Nash's T-shirt hugged his body like a glove, and his muscles strained the sleeves. Clara had a devil of a time keeping from drooling. She went to the storage room and brought back a case of beer and caught another glimpse of Nash through her peripheral vision.

*Never work,* the voice in her head chuckled. *That would be mixing business and pleasure. If things went south, you sure wouldn't have the option of working for him when Bernie left. If you are ready to settle down in this area, choose another. There's lots of proverbial fishes in the sea.*

"Let me help you with that," Nash said so close behind her that she could feel the warmth of his breath on her neck.

"Thank you." She handed him the case of beer and, with trembling hands, took a step back. He set the case on the bar and stood there for a moment as if he was trying to figure out what to say or do next. "I'll help you get these put in the cooler in a minute."

The way he was fidgeting, she expected him to tell her that his girlfriend was coming by that evening. "I'm usually not this backward. I'm used to standing in court and talking a jury's ears off, but I'm a little gun-shy right now."

"About what?" Clara asked.

"I want this bar so bad I can taste it." He chuckled and raked his fingertips through his hair. "That's something my grandpa says when he really, really wants something—like a new tractor. But it's the truth, and since Bernie gave me a key after only a few shifts, I think I've got a good chance at getting it. But I know I can't run it by myself, and truth is, I don't want to. I probably shouldn't spring this on you, but I can't wait any longer to ask you."

She held her breath in anticipation, halfway hoping that he was about her ask her out, even though she would have to say no. At least, she would know that the attraction she had wasn't one-sided.

"Would you consider staying on when Bernie is gone and helping me?"

"I would," she answered without hesitation. The only emotion she should have felt was one of absolute relief. Since she refused to date a coworker, the decision had been made for her. But there was a little disappointment mixed in there, too.

"Great!" he said and then picked up the case and headed out of the storage room.

"Huh," she muttered. "Now I really need to get over this infatuation because he will be my boss."

*You damn sure got that right,* the annoying voice in her head agreed.

Bernie popped her head into the room, did a scan

of the liquor shelves, and said, "We need two bottles of Jack Daniel's Black Label, one of Jameson, and one of Patron Silver."

"You got it."

"I had chicken pox when I was fifteen," Clara muttered again, "but I got over them, and hardly ever even think about the itching. So, that proves I can get over my crush on Nash. I may have to work at it, and calamine lotion won't heal it, but if I'm strong enough to stand up to my mama, I can do this."

But somehow this was more bittersweet than being a five-year-old with itchy bumps all over her body.

# Chapter 6

BERNIE HAD A GOOD feeling about trying out her match-making idea when she could practically see the sparks flying between Nash and Clara from the time they saw each other that evening. She'd been around long enough, and seen vibes between couples long enough, that she could recognize the attraction from a mile away. The only thing that worried her a little were Clara's long sighs, but that could be because she was tired from the trip down to Spanish Fort and back that afternoon. The plan she came up with was to leave them alone in the bar as much as possible. Someone in her past had said that the best way to get to know someone was to work with them, so she would give them plenty of space to do just that.

"The rooster has crowed, so that means it's time for a drink," Hoot chuckled as he crossed the room and claimed a barstool. "Bernie, can you believe that we got rain this time of year? Not that I'm complainin'. A rancher never gripes about rain, no matter when it comes down on us, but my gauge says that we got four inches."

Bernie hopped up on a stool right beside him. "It's

a strange thing for sure, especially at this time of year. What can we get you?"

"I'll have a beer. Whatever is on tap, long as it's cold," Hoot answered.

"Comin' right up, Grandpa," Nash said.

The rooster crowed again, and more than half a dozen customers came inside. One of the guys removed his hat, pulled a red bandanna from the bib pocket of his overalls, and wiped sweat from his forehead. "It's hotter'n a two-dollar pistol out there. I need something cold in a bottle. You ever realize that this place is a lot like that old television show where everybody knew everyone's name? What was it called?"

"*Cheers*," Nash replied. "You want Coors?"

"That's right. I always liked that show. They don't play good stuff like that anymore. Coors will do just fine, and don't wipe the dew off the outside," he said. "Bring us six. We're going to sit over there under the ceiling fan. It's the only way we can catch a breeze in this stinkin', steamy weather."

Nash uncapped the bottles, set them on a tray, and nodded toward Clara. The way that he watched her walk across the floor until the rooster told them more folks were coming inside did not escape Bernie's eye. She felt like rubbing her hands together like a little girl. Yes, sir! All she had to do was give them a little push, and presto! Wedding bells would ring out all over Ratliff City and her very first attempt at matchmaking would be successful.

"I think Nash might have a little crush on Clara," Hoot whispered out the side of his mouth.

"I see the same thing," Bernie said in a low voice. "Any reason either of us shouldn't like the idea?"

"None that I know of," Hoot answered. "He said something to me and his grandma this morning at breakfast about having asked her to stay on if you sell him the bar. He seemed all excited about the idea. You know that he is serious about buying it, don't you?"

"Anyone that works six weeks for free has to be sincere," Bernie replied and squashed the feeling that she should get behind the bar and help out.

"Trust me, he is." Hoot picked up his mug and joined two other men about his age at a nearby table.

The next group that arrived was Loretta and Dolly. "Thank God for air-conditioning," one of them said as they headed to a table.

"What can we get you this hot night?" Clara asked.

"Two margaritas," Loretta answered.

"Y'all pulling an extra shift this week?" Bernie called out over the buzz of several conversations.

"Yep, one of the weekday gals is getting married tonight and several of the others wanted off to attend the wedding. Who ever heard of having a wedding on Wednesday night? But hey, that means extra money for us," Loretta answered.

Bernie smiled and figured the mention of a wedding was an omen. She was definitely getting all the feels that she was on the right track. Ursula, Luna, and Endora could get ready to sit back and watch her work her magic this fall. Then, of course, she would talk Tertia and Ophelia into coming back to Spanish Fort and help to get them in committed relationships. She rubbed her hands together like a little girl when she thought of how happy Mary Jane was going to be to have all her girls back at the Paradise.

*What about Bo and Rae?* the aggravating voice in her head asked.

She set her mouth in a firm line and drew down her brows. *They will be the tough ones for sure, but after I've gotten some experience with the others, they'll be a breeze. I have a mission, and I will not fail. Mary Jane is good enough to let me move onto her property and be a part of her family, so I will help her get a houseful of grandchildren.*

Clara nudged her on the shoulder on her way back from taking margaritas to the nurses. "You look like you are arguing with someone."

"I am, and it's with myself," Bernie told her. "And for the record, the voice in my head can't hold a candle to the real me when I set my head to do something."

"There was never any doubt of that," Clara said.

Sometime around ten o'clock, Bernie noticed that the temperature had risen in the place and turned the thermostat down a couple of degrees. Figuring it was all the warm bodies in the bar, she wasn't a bit concerned until thirty minutes later. She went back to the thermostat to find that it was now eighty degrees.

"Well, hell's bells!" she groaned.

"Hey, Bernie, if you want us to leave, just say so," a guy in the back corner yelled. "Don't try to fry our brains."

"Air conditioner is on the blink," she said. "I could open the doors, but the thermostat says that it's over ninety degrees outside, so that won't help."

"Figure up my tab," another customer said. "I'm going home where it's cool, even if the wife is making me sleep on the sofa."

"You shouldn't have bought that new fishin' boat without askin' her," Loretta yelled across the room.

"She'll come around, and when she does, I'll still have my boat." He chuckled and headed to the bar to pay his bill.

Bernie figured it up, made change for the bill he gave her, and used a bar rag to wipe away the beads of sweat popping up above her lip. "What do you kids think? Should we close down early or stay open until the right time?"

"We still have customers," Clara answered.

"If it was already your place, what would you do, Nash?" Bernie asked.

"I'd stay open until the last customer left. When I first came back to Ratliff City, I hauled a bunch of hay for Grandpa. I can take the heat," he said.

"Okay, then, that's what we'll do." She found the remotes for the ceiling fans and turned them all on high speed. "Maybe that will help a little. The man who works on the A/C can probably get out here tomorrow morning, but it's too late to call him tonight."

"Long as it is fixed by opening, we should be fine. How old is the unit anyway?" Nash asked.

"Had it installed two years ago. There's a separate one for the apartment," she answered.

"Praise the Lord," Clara said.

———

"Now would be a good time for a cool-down thunderstorm," Nash said when the next bunch of people came into the bar.

"Be careful what you wish for." Clara's tone was grumpy in her own ears. "You might get a tornado right along with that."

"Not at this time of year," Nash said. "Since business is slow, we might as well gather up the empty mugs and get the dishwasher going."

Clara locked eyes with him. "You aren't the boss yet."

"You've been testy all day. Is it the heat or are you mad at me?" he snapped.

"What makes you think I'm angry?" she shot back.

"Honey, you've been in a mood ever since we were in the storage room. Did I do something to upset you?" Nash asked.

"I'm not your honey," she said in a low growl, "and the world does not revolve around you just because you look like sex on a stick. Maybe I'm upset over something that has nothing to do with you or this bar." She didn't even bother to cross her fingers behind her back.

He flashed a brilliant grin. "So, you think I'm sexy?"

"Don't flatter yourself," she said and took a tray to the other side of the room to gather up dirty mugs. She'd loaded six on a tray before she realized she had done exactly what he'd asked her to do and got angry all over again.

*Stop this childish behavior,* she scolded herself. *Be honest and tell him why you are upset. He didn't do anything but help you carry cases of beer out of the storage room.*

She drew in a long breath and held it until her chest tightened before she let it out between clenched teeth. She needed time to think about how to approach her attraction to him before she talked to Nash. This wasn't the time or place—not with Aunt Bernie so close by and with customers lined up at the bar.

———

Bernie made the decision to close up the bar at midnight. There was only one customer left and the thermostat had jumped up two more degrees. "See you tomorrow, Nash," she said as she followed him to the door and locked it behind him.

He held out the extra key that she had given him,

and Bernie shook her head. "Keep it in case you ever need to open up for me. We're going to Duncan tomorrow to look at a trailer I can pull behind my truck. We should be back by five, but if we aren't, you can take care of things. Oh, and tomorrow is also the day that the beer delivery guy comes in. You can sign for my regular order, but don't let him talk you into that cheap brand. He always tries to pawn a case or two off on me, and it does not sell."

"Got it," Nash said with a nod. "See y'all then. Do you know what's wrong with Clara?"

"Nope, but I did notice that y'all had a few words," Bernie answered. "She's had a tough year. Give her some space to work things out."

He picked up his cowboy hat and settled it on his head. "I can do that. If you decide to stay on a few more years, will you consider hiring me to work for you?"

"I will give it some thought. Good night to you, Nash," she said.

"Thank you, and good night to you, Miz Bernie." He tipped his hat toward her.

Without even realizing it, he had just given her the proof of love that she wanted for her bar. He liked it so much that he was willing to work there if he couldn't buy the place. Now if she could figure out what bee had gotten stuck in Clara's bloomers, things would be great.

Clara had already left the bar, so Bernie turned off the fans and flipped the light switch. There was something about the end of the day when the bar was dark that brought out a whole slew of memories, but she didn't take time to dwell on them. She picked up two bottles of beer, twisted the tops off, hurried on back to the apartment, and sighed when the cold air hit her in the face.

"It feels pretty dang good, don't it?" Clara had kicked off her shoes and stretched out on the sofa. "Pepper didn't take long to do his business, and he's flopped out on the cool kitchen floor."

Bernie handed one of the beers to Clara, sank down in her recliner, and popped the footrest up. "I'm worn plumb out. How about you?"

"Not as much tired as hot," she answered.

"And aggravated about something, right?"

"Yep, but I'd rather talk about anything else," Clara answered. "Like why are you planning to live in a trailer? Why don't you just take over one of those bedrooms up in the Paradise?"

"Several reasons," Bernie answered. "Sometimes I might want to put a little Jameson in my morning coffee. What Mary Jane don't know won't hurt her on that issue. And a cigar helps me figure out something when I'm worried. I would never smoke in the house, but still, I would have to be careful. That's enough right there, but then there's Pepper. I can't ask Mary Jane to let me bring a dog into her house. She has a sassy cat that is twice his size, and that vicious critter would probably kill him. But the biggest reason is that I need my own space."

"Good reasons," Clara said, "but you could just leave Pepper here. I've kind of gotten attached to him."

"Can't do it." Bernie chuckled. "Hershal could possibly go to hell for stealing the dog for me. I wouldn't feel right if I didn't take him with me. If Hershal ever comes back into the bar, I'll pretend that I would have rather had the dead goldfish. But truth is I've wanted a Chihuahua my whole life. My sister claimed to be allergic to cats and dogs, so I could never have one."

As if the dog understood what Bernie said, he hopped up on the edge of her chair and whined. She picked him up, and he licked her chin and then curled up in her lap. "Poor little guy was lonesome. He'll be happy when he doesn't have to stay alone every night."

"Well, if you change your mind…" Clara said.

"And if you decide you want to talk about whatever has put you in a grouchy mood, I'm here. I'm a bartender, and that makes me an excellent listener," Bernie said.

"I like Nash, but after Kent, I vowed never to date a coworker again," she admitted. "So, we will have to keep our relationship totally professional."

"And that makes you all grumpy?" Bernie was more than a little disappointed that her matchmaking wasn't going to be a smooth ride.

Clara was quiet for several moments before she spoke. "Yes, it does. It's like having one of those maple-sugar-topped doughnuts laid out in front of me and being told that I can't even smell it, much less take a bite."

"I've walked a mile in your shoes a few times," Bernie said with a smile. "But what if Nash is the one?"

"How would I know that after less than a week?" Clara asked.

"My advice to you is to listen to your heart, not your mind, but don't get in a rush." Bernie wasn't happy that the Universe decided to put her first-ever attempt at matchmaking in jeopardy. She had read somewhere that most couples didn't meet, sit down on a blanket under a shade tree, and fall in love. No, sir! They had to overcome all kinds of obstacles, but Mama Fate could have been nicer to Bernie since this was her virgin cruise in the new field of happy-ever-after business. It didn't have to put her first couple on a high limb in that big, old scrub oak tree and lob rocks at them.

Clara finally ended another long moment of silence. "That sounds like a line from one of Aunt Mary Jane's books."

"It probably is, but it doesn't make it any less real," Bernie said. "I'm going to take a shower and go to bed. At least now that the new laws have passed, the smoke doesn't hover around the ceiling like dark clouds. I used to have to come home every night after closing and wash that smell out of my hair."

Clara took a couple of long drinks from her beer. "Any form of tobacco was outlawed before I even started bartending," she said and then groaned, "Why couldn't you have found an ugly bartender?"

"That was an abrupt change of subject." Bernie chuckled. "If you will remember, I didn't find Nash. He found me, and I'm pretty sure I'm going to sell to him. But the way you are feeling, it might be best if you go to Texas with me, rather than staying here."

"Maybe so," Clara agreed and stood up. "But tonight I have decided to not think about Nash anymore."

"Take your empty beer bottle with you and put it in the recycle bin," Bernie told her.

"Yes, ma'am."

"Sweet dreams. Maybe they'll even be about Nash and help you decide whether to stay and fight or to take flight and go with me to the Paradise."

"I hope I don't dream at all. I need a rest from all things that involve decisions." She stopped and sat back down. "Before I go, tell me about you and Hershal. He thought you were in love with him and even risked going to jail for stealing for you. What's the story?"

"It's a short one," Bernie answered. "We were in our early forties, and he was a regular at the bar. We flirted. We slept together. I went on one short truck run with him that lasted from Saturday night after work until about noon on Monday. He wasn't the only one in my life back then, and I had no idea that all these years later he would even remember my comment about that little dog we saw on the trip. He still came into the bar occasionally, but the fire had gone out in our little romance. The end."

"Been there. Done that. Have the memories to prove it." Clara stood back up. "I'm going to take a quick shower after you're done so I don't get the bedsheets all sweaty. Good night, Aunt Bernie."

"Good night, my child," Bernie said.

# Chapter 7

THE AROMA OF BACON drifting down the short hallway and into her bedroom awoke Clara the next morning. She inhaled several times before she opened her eyes to be sure that she wasn't dreaming. She threw back the covers and padded barefoot to the kitchen.

Bernie handed her a mug of steaming-hot coffee and motioned toward the table. "Want your eggs fried or scrambled?"

"Scrambled is good," Clara said. "You didn't have to make breakfast for me. What can I do to help?"

Bernie cracked half a dozen eggs into a bowl. "It don't take any more time to cook for two than for one. Besides, I had an ulterior motive. I wanted you to wake up and go with me to Duncan today, and I figured the aroma of coffee and bacon would wake you up. You can help by staying out of my way. Sit down and have a few sips of coffee to get your eyes open."

"So, you are serious about looking at a trailer today?"

"I am. The folks that have the place told me that it belonged to their parents who seldom used it. The old folks are in a nursing home now, and they are cleaning out the house and garage. It should be in good shape and will be cheaper than buying a brand-new one."

Clara obeyed Bernie's order and sat down at the table. She usually just had a bowl of cereal or a piece of toast for breakfast. A full meal was a luxury that she couldn't afford except on payday, when she treated herself to the special at a local diner—two eggs, two pieces of bacon, and a biscuit with gravy. "All you had to do was knock on my door, or even yell my name down the hall, and I would have been here as fast as I could get awake."

"You would have been in a horrible mood all day if I disturbed a sexy dream about Nash." Bernie chuckled. "But if you woke up from a dream that he was making you breakfast after a night of wild passionate sex, that would put a smile on your face and make you subconsciously happy all day."

"How did you get so smart?" Clara wasn't about to admit that she had been dreaming about Nash. She was still in shock that her aunt took her in so quickly, gave her a job, and seemed glad to have her live in the same apartment, but some things were personal and best kept hidden away close to the vest, so to speak.

Bernie loaded two plates, brought them to the table, and took a seat across the table from Clara. "I don't consider myself smart. I got through high school by the skin of my teeth. If I have any intelligence at it, I got it by tending bar since long before you were born. If you listen to people's problems and stories that long, you'll be able to read folks, too."

Clara picked up her fork and tried to concentrate on her food, but it didn't work. She kept mulling over what Bernie had said about Nash taking over her dreams. Did Bernie have the magical ability to walk right into Clara's fantasies about a man that she could never have? A shut bedroom door meant that someone should at least knock—even in a dream.

"When you worked with Kent, what was your…" Bernie took a sip of coffee and frowned. "I'm trying to think of what you kids say today, but it's not coming to my mind."

"Job description?" Clara offered.

Bernie snapped her fingers. "That's it. What was the actual thing that you did?"

"I sat in a cubicle all day and input data, or information, into a computer," she answered. "Kent had, and still has, a small office where he talks to prospective clients about oil well products that the company sells. When the pandemic hit, I worked from home for a while. Those were some miserable days for sure, having to spend twenty-four seven with Kent in the same room. Then when everyone went back to the office, the company had taken a hit and had to downsize. I got a pink slip and went to work at the bar."

"Where were you happiest?" Bernie asked.

Clara took a moment to try to figure out why her

great-aunt was asking so many questions. Was she merely making conversation, or did she have an agenda? "I hated that cubicle so much that some mornings I actually had chest pains on the way to work, and then being home-bound with Kent was even worse."

"And when you had to leave the house to go to the bar where you worked?" Bernie asked.

"Kent got home about fifteen minutes before I left," Clara answered.

"What does that have to do with…" Bernie started.

Clara interrupted before she could finish. "I realized this very moment that I looked forward to leaving the apartment every evening to escape being around him. By the time I got home after three most mornings, he was asleep. I usually sacked out on the sofa to keep from waking him."

"Okay, then, but what has that got to do with how you felt when you were at the bar?" Bernie asked.

"I was very happy at the bar and around lots of people. I actually got claustrophobic in that cubicle. Then when we worked from home, I prayed that we could go back to the office so I could at least have a little distance from him," Clara admitted. "I wasn't sure if it was because I wasn't working near Kent where he could watch my every movement and criticize me if I even spoke to a male coworker, or that I wasn't shoved into a cubicle, or if it was that he stayed on me constantly to produce more work when we were working from home."

Bernie finished off her food and took her plate to the sink. "That means you are a people person, and the bar was a perfect fit for you. Too bad the place in Amarillo went out of business, but I'm glad that door closed so that the one to my place could open for you."

"Thank you, Aunt Bernie," Clara said. "That means a lot to me. And thanks for making me realize what makes me happy."

"Once you figure that out, it don't matter if you dig ditches or are the president of the USA. You are a success, because your job makes you happy," Bernie told her. "Finish up your breakfast and get dressed. We're burnin' daylight," she said, chuckling.

"Granny says that when she wants us to hustle," Clara said.

"It comes from an old John Wayne movie called *The Cowboys*." Bernie smiled. "Watching that was one of the few good memories I have of me and Hershal. We have to cherish those times."

"Amen to that, because there aren't many of them," Clara agreed.

———

Not even a wispy white cloud had taken up residence in the clear blue sky when Bernie and Clara started out for Duncan. When they first drove away from the parking lot, Pepper had been all excited and looking out the side window, but by the time they reached the end of town, he had curled up in Clara's lap with a paw over his nose. Bernie had wanted to know if Clara was in the bartending business as a stopover to something better, or if she was truly happiest when she was in the middle of people. She really hadn't wanted to hear any more about Mr. S.O.B. Kent that morning when she asked her great-niece about what made her happy.

*But it does seem that every bit of information I get from the conversations with Clara makes me understand her better, even if it involves that sorry sucker,* Bernie thought as she drove west toward Duncan.

"You sure are quiet," Clara finally said when they reached the outskirts of town.

"I was wondering if somewhere in our past, maybe more than a hundred years ago, if there was an ancestor who didn't care what other people thought of their choices in life, and if maybe you and I got some of their genes," Bernie admitted. "And then my mind jumped to that sorry sucker you lived with. I would like to squeeze that fool's neck until his eyes popped out of his head and rolled around on the floor like marbles."

"I like that visual." Clara giggled. "If there were genes that were that independent, I'm afraid that they got watered down a lot when it got to me."

"Not from what I've seen," Bernie disagreed.

Clara shifted positions and Pepper growled at her. "Hush and go back to sleep."

The dog actually sighed and closed his eyes.

"If anyone got a healthy dose of sassy DNA from our ancestors, that would be you," Clara said. "I've got this soft spot in my heart that wants to please people. I always wanted to be like Myra—all rainbows and unicorns. I tried really hard to follow her example, but no matter how hard I worked at it, I couldn't pull it off."

"You'll get over that attitude." Bernie remembered all those years when she and her twin were growing up, and how badly she wanted to make her mother smile like Vernie Sue did. "One day you will wake up and figure out that you have to be true to yourself first and foremost. It's a tough job in the beginning, but it gets easier with age."

"I hope so," Clara whispered.

"Turn left at the next stop sign," the GPS lady's voice said.

"Ever wish that the powers that be would use a sexy man's voice instead of that tinny-sounding woman?" Bernie chuckled.

"If that happened, we would deliberately make mistakes"—Clara grinned—"because we'd want him to talk to us, even if all he said was, 'Reroute, reroute,' or maybe, 'Make a U-turn at the next intersection.'"

Bernie made the turn. "Yep, for sure. I hope this trailer is what I want so I don't have to run all over the country trying to find one."

"According to Granny, 'What will be, will be,'" Clara quoted.

Bernie stopped at a house with a huge garage sale going on. "And the rest of the story is: what won't be, might be anyway."

Clara unfastened her seat belt, attached Pepper's leash to his collar, and opened the door. "Is that the trailer over there beside the house?" She set him on the ground, and he promptly hiked his leg on the front tire.

"Must be. I don't see another one. It looks pretty fine from here." Bernie followed Clara to the porch where a lady had set up a table to collect money. "Hello, I called earlier about that trailer. Is it all right if we just go inside to look at it?"

"Sure, help yourselves. You must be Bernie. I'm Clarisse," she answered. "It goes as is. We don't want to clean out all the dishes, linens, and all that, but the price is not negotiable. We won't take less than what I quoted you on the phone when you called."

"Fair enough," Bernie said with a nod. "Got a problem with me taking my dog inside it?"

"Not at all, long as he doesn't make a mess," the woman answered.

An elderly man brought a pair of lamps to the porch and set them down. "That's a cute little dog. Want to sell him?"

"No, he was a gift from an old friend," Bernie answered.

"My granddaughter would sure be good to him," the man pressured. "Her birthday is tomorrow, and her mama says I can get her a dog if it's a small one."

"You might check the animal shelter," Clara suggested.

The guy laid a bill on the table. "Never thought of going there. Thanks for the tip. I'll take Amanda with me so she can pick out whichever one she wants."

"You missed your chance. Hershal would never know that you sold the dog." Clara teased on the way to the trailer.

"No, I didn't." Bernie picked Pepper up and carried him up the three steps to the front door of the trailer. "Now I can remind this feller that he has a price on his head if he doesn't behave."

Clara stepped back to let Bernie enter first, and then followed her. "Wow! This is amazing. Nice-sized refrigerator, and a cute little love seat. Are you going to find some good-lookin' feller and make use of that?"

"Honey, I would have to buy one of those how-to books if…" Bernie went on back down to the bedroom area.

"Don't you be giving me that line of crap," Clara scolded. "I bet you've forgotten more than I'll ever know about entertaining a man in the… That's a queen-sized bed! I didn't expect to see one that big in a trailer."

"Me neither," Bernie said, "especially for the price she quoted me. I'm buying this, but I'm going to have to get a bigger truck to pull the thing to Spanish Fort. You can have the little one I'm driving now. Your old car has seen better days."

Clara shook her head.

"You don't want it?" Bernie asked.

"No, I'm not sure I heard you right," Clara whispered.

"I didn't stutter," Bernie said. "I don't need two vehicles and you can use an upgrade."

"But…but…but…" Clara stammered, and tears welled up in her eyes. "You've already given me a place to live, food, and even a job."

"Family takes care of family. Let's go tell the lady that I'll be back later today to get the trailer, and ask her if she wants cash, or maybe a cashier's check. Then we'll drive to the dealership and buy a new truck to pull it with. I'll call Joe Clay this evening and tell him that I'll bring it down Sunday afternoon. He said he would have it plumbed and maybe even build a small front porch for me when I move down there." She patted Clara on the shoulder. "This is happening. I'm glad you are here to share in my last days before retirement with me."

"Thank you," Clara muttered and wiped at her wet cheeks. "I'm glad I'm here, too. In less than a week, I've figured out what makes me happy, and I owe that to you."

"That's just the first step," Bernie said. "Happiness is a journey, not a destination. Enjoy the trip, and never look back with regrets."

———

Bernie hadn't been joking around when she said she was going to buy a new truck. Not only did she pick out a fancy one, but she also whipped out her checkbook and didn't bat an eye when she wrote out the amount to pay for it. Then she went to the bank, got a cashier's check, and called the lady who owned the trailer and asked if she could pick it up on the way home.

Now Clara was driving Bernie's old pickup truck—hers in a couple of days when the title was transferred—and following behind her aunt's new rig toward Ratliff City.

Her thoughts spun around like they were on a merry-go-round, making her dizzy as they jumped from one scenario to another and played the what-if game all the way to the bar. What if she stayed at the bar and worked for Nash? Could she keep the attraction for him at bay? Would she eventually give into it, get her heart shattered, and be bitter like Endora? What if she didn't fight it, and she and Nash wound up together, then it went sour?

"Looks to me like I'll end up with a broken heart no matter which what-if is in play," she muttered as she parked the truck in its usual parking space. "With my luck, there's only about a ten percent chance that things could go right."

Nash pulled his vehicle in right beside her and raised an eyebrow. "Looks like y'all have been on a buying binge."

"We have," Bernie said. "It's a beauty, ain't it?"

"The trailer is nice, but that truck is gorgeous," Nash answered. "I wanted a candy-apple red one, but decided to go with the white since it was on sale that day."

"When you retire, you can have a new red one," Bernie told him.

"I'll put that on my bucket list," Nash said. "Does this mean you are really going to sell the bar to me?"

"It means most likely," Bernie told him, "and that I like what I'm seeing in you. It will take a while for you to get a loan all done through the bank, so we'll…"

Nash held up a palm and butted in. "I don't need a loan. I'll be paying cash. I know this is what I want to do. When you get ready to make it official, just let me know and I will write you a check, or we can go to the bank and simply do a transfer from my account into yours."

"After we close tonight, meet me and Clara out behind the bar. We'll have us a cigar and talk more about all this," Bernie said. "Right now, we need to get inside and clean up before we open for business."

Clara had never smoked a cigar in her life, but if that's what her aunt wanted to do, then she would give it a try. Who knew? Maybe that was the icing on the cupcake that made Bernie so successful.

In all the excitement of the day, Clara had forgotten that the AC had been on the blink, so she was shocked when cold air rushed out to meet them. "I've never been so glad to see air-conditioning."

"Amazing what a new fan motor and thermostat will do," Nash explained.

"Yep, the repairman was here first thing this morning, before I even started making breakfast for you, Clara. Nice thing is that the unit is still under warranty, so the parts were covered. All I had to pay out was for the labor," Bernie said. "Now, Clara, you can clear the tables and start the dishwasher with the first load. I'll wipe down the tables, and Nash can put the chairs up on them so we can sweep and mop. It's almighty good to have help."

"You think we can run this place without Bernie?" Nash asked Clara.

"We can give it our best shot," she answered. On one hand, she was excited that she wouldn't have to leave the Chicken Coop. On the other, she felt as if the merry-go-round was going way too fast. Still, she had two options in front of her—the bar and living in Spanish Fort. That was more than she'd had when she first walked in the place.

She had loaded a tray with mugs and was on the way to the dishwasher when Nash touched her on the arm. "You looked excited over the cool air, but now you look worried, or maybe sad. Want to talk about anything?"

She set the tray down on the bar and opened the dishwasher. "Last week I had nowhere to go. Now I have decisions to make, and I don't want to look back with regrets on whatever I wind up doing."

"That's understandable," Nash said. "I was in the same aggravating spot until I came home to my grand-parents' ranch and they told me about this place. I'm excited now, and happy that I don't have to go back to three-piece suits and an office in a thirty-story building."

"I'm glad to hear that," Bernie said. "Looks like

we're about done with this, so let's sit down and rest our feet for a few minutes." She unlocked the door and had barely gotten settled into a chair when the first rooster crow echoed through the empty place.

Hoot came inside and let out a long sigh. "Man, it's good to be in out of the heat. I thought I'd be the first one here tonight, but it looks like someone beat me." He glanced around the place. "Where's the owner of that new truck and trailer out there?"

Bernie raised her hand. "Sittin' right here. It's a beauty, ain't it?"

Hoot removed his cowboy hat and sat down in the last empty chair around the table. "Yes, ma'am, it is. Nash, I need a beer so cold that it makes my throat hurt, and bring Bernie a double shot of Jameson on the rocks to celebrate her first step in retirement. Put them both on my tab, and I'll settle up before I leave."

Nash nodded and pushed back his chair. "Coming right up."

"So, you are serious about selling the Chicken Coop to Nash?" Hoot asked.

"I am," Bernie answered. "He's proved himself this past week, but I've been here a long time, and it will take a while to sort through my stuff."

Clara overheard the conversation between Hoot and Bernie, but then the sound of vehicles out on the gravel parking lot drowned out anything else they said. The rooster crowed again, and three couples came inside and ordered six mixed drinks. The women went straight to the jukebox, and music soon filled the place. Clara poured up Bernie's whiskey, then added an icy-cold bottle of beer to the tray and carried them back to the table.

"Anything else?"

Bernie took a sip of her drink. "Nope. We're going to sit here and visit a while unless it gets so busy that I need to come help out."

"Just holler if you need a refill," Clara threw over her shoulder and made her way through the new customers who had arrived.

"Looks like it might be a steady night for a Thursday," she told Nash as she made half a dozen piña coladas for the three couples.

"Yep," he agreed. "If things are like they were at the place I worked when I was in college, then Wednesdays are slow because of church night most usually. Then Thursday picks up a little, but not as much as the weekend crowd."

She lined the drinks up on the bar and tucked a bar rag into her hip pocket. "That's the way it was in the place I worked at in Amarillo, too."

"I tended bar at a country club on nights and weekends in Austin for a few months, and then worked downtown at a place like this a while," Nash said. "Do you think Bernie will really retire, or will she back out?"

"I wouldn't bet on anything this early in the game,

but she sure seems serious," Clara answered, and quickly mopped up a beer spill. "What do you think?"

Nash started unloading the dishwasher. "I'm trying not to, but I'm sure hoping a lot. What's this about smoking cigars after work?"

"She says that sometimes helps her sort things out."

Clara brushed against his arm as she walked past him to get to the far end of the bar. The vibes were still here. Someone out there should develop a relationship calamine lotion that would stop the romantic itch when a woman couldn't have what was standing right beside her.

# Chapter 8

BERNIE'S ABILITY TO CROOK her forefinger around a lit cigar and hold a highball glass with a triple shot of Jameson in the same hand completely mesmerized Clara. Her great-aunt could even sip the whiskey without setting her red hair on fire and take a drag from the cigar without spilling the liquor down into her bra. She could make a mint if she went on the road with that trick and told bar stories starting with the night a man walked into the bar with a dead goldfish and a Chihuahua. She wouldn't even have to embellish or exaggerate all that much.

Clara pictured her tiny little aunt wearing her July Fourth getup on the stage in Las Vegas. Or maybe teaching a class on using one hand to drink and smoke, and keep the other one free to wave around while she told stories about what had happened in the Chicken Coop. She wouldn't get in trouble or get sued for talking about the past. After all, what grown, self-respecting person would admit that they'd been drunk at a bar with such a strange name? There wasn't a policeman or a judge in the whole world who wouldn't laugh that right out the court doors.

"Are y'all ever going to light your cigars?" Bernie asked.

"Of course," Nash bit off the end of the cigar and lit it, took a puff, and blew the smoke out. "Tell me again why we are out here."

Clara followed his lead and coughed when she tried to inhale the smoke from the first puff.

"Darlin' girl, you don't inhale." Bernie chuckled. "You just want the sweet taste in your mouth. It goes right well with whiskey, and when you are young, the kisses from a sexy man afterwards is downright intoxicating. And Nash, this is like a therapy session only you don't have to write a check to pay for it when we are finished."

"Kind of like a group thing?" Clara asked.

"That's right, and it don't cost a dime," Bernie agreed. "The cigars were a gift from a friend who snuck them out of Cuba, and the whiskey is right off the top shelf from the bar, so sit back and relax with the finest therapy tools on the market. Your whiskey will be gone when we finish here, but you should save what's left of your cigar for next time. I do not believe in wasting anything, especially imported, illegal cigars. I'll go first this time, but next week, one of you will have to do it."

"Fair enough," Nash said. "Please show us how it's done. I've never been to a therapy session. How about you, Clara?"

"Nope, but my mother and grandmother wanted to send me away to a church rehab-type thing for someone to preach Aunt Bernie out of me," she admitted. "Does almost being committed count?"

"Comes pretty close," Bernie said and picked up Pepper. "But here goes on my story. My name is Mary Bernadette Marsh. My twin sister is Vernie Sue. My folks thought it was cute to give us rhyming names. To say that we are as different as fire and ice would be a major understatement. I jumped from job to job until I was well into my twenties, and for the most part lived out of my ten-year-old car. I was sitting in a game of Texas Hold'em one night. Right here in this very bar. I was down to my last twenty bucks, and the owner of this place hadn't had much better luck all night. He didn't want to be put to shame by a sassy red-haired woman, so he bet his bar against me. Told me that I was bluffing, and that he would take my crumpled-up twenty-dollar bill and buy himself a new fishing rod with it. You could get a fairly decent one back in those days for that amount."

"Are you serious?" Nash asked.

"I am," Bernie took a puff on the cigar and blew out smoke rings. "And soda fountain soft drinks were a dime, and an ice cream cone sold for the same."

Clara's smoke came out in a fog, not in perfect little circles.

"Evidently he lost, but what kind of hand did you have?" Nash asked.

"He had a straight flush and reached for my money, but I laid down a royal and took the Chicken Coop from him," Bernie answered with a chuckle.

"That was lucky," Nash said. "Have you played much since then?"

"Oh, yeah," Bernie replied, "If I won, I banked the profit for a rainy day, and that amount has grown into a goodly sum. But I never, not once, put my bar up for collateral."

Clara had been listening to the whole story, but she had also been staring up at millions of stars. Weird things were supposed to happen on the nights when a full moon was out, and it was big and beautiful that morning.

*And they are happening in your life,* the voice in her head whispered.

She tuned back into the conversation when Nash asked, "Is this what therapy is? Just telling our life story?"

"Nope," Bernie replied. "Therapy is talking about whatever comes to a person's mind. As I think of selling the Chicken Coop, it brings back memories of what might have happened if I hadn't drawn that hand. I might have gone back home to Fritch, Texas, and fell into a rut—one that wouldn't have brought me nearly as much happiness as this place has."

"Like marriage, kids, and grandkids?" Clara asked.

"Maybe, but the Universe smiled on me that evening, and like that old song says, 'I did it my way.' I don't have a single regret about my life."

"Not even that our family has been so ugly?" Clara asked.

Bernie took another puff and blew out more smoke rings that disintegrated as they floated up into the trees. "Nope. Had they let me live my life my way and loved me unconditionally, I might have never ended up being as happy as I have been. I have a lot of wonderful memories. And now I'm going to move to Spanish Fort and make more. Mary Jane and her girls need me," she said.

To Clara's way of thinking, the night really did get stranger with each passing moment. She hadn't expected to ever be Bernie's favorite niece, but she needed her as much or more than anyone at the Paradise did. She couldn't tell her that she didn't want her to leave Ratliff City—not when she seemed to be set on retiring. Bernie had done so much for her that to beg her to stay would be beyond selfish.

*Endora needs her worse than you do.* Evidently the voice in her head had a different opinion. *That cousin of yours needs some sass in her life to bring her out of the depression.*

Nash took a sip of his whiskey. "This is a peaceful place back here, and I hope that sometime in the middle of August, I can call it home."

"You've certainly proven yourself the past week," Bernie said, "but you have to give me your word, both verbally and on paper, that if you ever sell the bar, I get first chance at buying it back. It's an institution in these parts, and I don't want it sold to someone who will tear it down and put in a gas station."

"You've got it, and I'll sign the papers saying so," Nash promised.

"Okay, then, that is taking a step forward. Next Saturday night you can have a turn, Clara, at telling us whatever is on your mind," Bernie nodded toward her and stubbed out her cigar on the ground. "Right now, I'm going to bed. You kids can stay up and visit until the cigars or the whiskey or both is gone, but don't come crying to me if you have a hangover tomorrow morning, Clara." She set Pepper on the ground and stood up. "You might want to keep that smoke going until you are ready to call it a night."

"Why?" Clara asked.

Bernie tossed back the last of her drink and set the red plastic cup on the chair. "The mosquitoes that cross the Red River from Texas are only slightly smaller than buzzards, and if they gang up on someone as small as you are, they could carry you away faster than an EF5 tornado. But they hate any kind of smoke, but especially that from cigars. Don't forget that we are taking the trailer to Spanish Fort tomorrow, and we're supposed to be there by noon. See you Monday evening, Nash. Come on, Pepper, it's way past our bedtime."

"I'll be here at five o'clock," he said. "Have a good time tomorrow and be safe."

"I always have a good time at the Paradise, but I've

never been accused of being safe." Bernie chuckled and went inside the apartment.

Clara took one more puff of the cigar and stubbed it out on the ground. "I'll take my chances with the mosquitoes. I know you were a lawyer, and that you got tired of long hours, but are you getting a dose of culture shock? Moving from a city the size of Dallas to this place has to be quite an adjustment."

"In Dallas, I never had time to do anything other than sleep and go to the office," Nash said. "Most of the time I even ate there. I used to wonder why I even paid rent on an apartment. There was a gym and a shower at the workplace, and I could have kept my clothing in a locker."

"Even during the pandemic?" she asked.

"I used the apartment during the time I worked from home, but the hours didn't slow down much if any. What about you? Is coming here a culture shock for you?" he asked.

"Oh, yes!" she said with a giggle. "And that's a joke. I left behind the small town of Fritch with a population of less than two thousand to come to a place that doesn't even have a hundred people living in it. The only thing here is cows and the Chicken Coop, from what I can see. Fritch does have a couple of businesses and a few stop signs."

"That means we are working at the most prosperous establishment in the whole town of Ratliff City," Nash told her.

She covered a yawn with the back of her hand. Her mind said it was well past the time to get some sleep. Her heart told her that she wanted to stay and talk to Nash for a while longer. "Churches, bars, and post offices hardly ever go out of business. So, I don't think that the bar will suffer when Aunt Bernie takes wings and flies across the Red River."

"Never thought of it that way," he said. "I have a question. You don't have to answer if it's too personal or painful, but why were you so upset when you arrived here?"

"It is very personal and painful, but here it is," Clara said. "There seems to be a pattern in my family. Sisters who are very different, and at odds with each other most, if not all, of the time."

"Aren't they all?" Nash asked.

"This family takes it to the extreme. Aunt Bernie owns a bar. My grandmother is super religious and condemns Bernie for her lifestyle. Aunt Bernie had no children, but Nana had three—a son, and two daughters. Mark, Marsha, and Mary Jane. If I ever have kids, I'm not going to give them all names that start with the same letter. Marsha is my mother, and she is a chip off the old block. She and Nana are very quick to pass judgment. Believe me when I say it's either their way or the highway, and I'm living proof of that statement."

"Hold on a minute and let me get this straight. I can see where Bernie and her sister would be very different, and there would be hard feelings there, but what has that got to do with you?" Nash asked.

"I'm getting to it," Clara answered. "You heard Aunt Bernie's story of how her generation of two sisters have always been at cross horns. Then my mother comes along, and she and her sister are wildly different. My mama was an FBI agent until she retired and got all wound up in the church with Nana Vernie Sue. Her sister, Mary Jane, lives in an old brothel called the Paradise, and she writes steamy romance books. In each generation there is a set of sisters. One is a pretty white sheep, and the other is a coal-black one."

"I'm beginning to see what you are talking about. What about you?"

"I have a sister, Myra, who is married to a preacher," Clara answered. "It doesn't take a genius to know which one of us…"

"No, it doesn't," Nash butted in. "But I'm still in the dark as to why you were so upset."

"I lost my bartending job in Amarillo and waited until I was on the verge of living in a shelter before I swallowed my pride and went home to Fritch. I needed a place to stay until I found a job, but when my mother and grandmother found out what I had been doing, they really did want to send me off to that rehab place I told y'all about. I hadn't seen Aunt Bernie in years for all the reasons I just told you about, but she was my last hope."

Clara stopped and stared out over the wooded area.

She drew in a long breath and went on. "I half expected her to tell me to hit the road, but she has showed me nothing but love and compassion from the time I walked into her bar. I was crying because I was angry, humiliated that I had to come to her for help when the family had treated her like a pile of steaming cow manure, and I was quite literally broke and hungry. Twenty-eight years old, third-generation black sheep, and needing help."

"That kind of situation would bring a grown man to his knees," Nash whispered.

Clara was so sleepy that when she blinked, she had trouble opening her eyes. "Thank you, and now I suppose we had better call it a night. I've got to go to the Paradise with Aunt Bernie tomorrow. I hope you were serious about me working here if you buy the place."

Nash put out his cigar, stood up, and extended a hand toward her. "Very serious, and I appreciate that you shared your story with me."

She put her hand in his, felt that familiar zing, and could almost see the sparks competing with all the stars in the sky. "Thank you for listening and for offering me a job."

She let go of his hand and stumbled over the chair when she took a step. She grabbed for something to break her fall and had a split-second visual of breaking her neck as she pitched backward. Suddenly Nash's strong arms wrapped around her body, and her chest was pressed tightly against his. Her pulse had jacked up so high that her heartbeat pounded like a rock band's drums. She intended to move away from him and make a joke about being clumsy, even though she felt so safe right where she was. But when she pulled away and looked up into his eyes, she froze.

He moved his hands from her waist, tucked her messy red hair back away from her face, and cupped her cheeks in his big hands. Desire shot through her body when his thumbs made lazy circles on the soft spot below her ears. For the first time, she truly understood the old saying about being putty in a man's hands. The song that had played on the jukebox that evening ran through her mind. The lyrics asked if he would lay with her in a field of stone, and would he still love her when she was down and out.

Everything, including doubts, fears, songs, and adages left her mind when she saw his thick dark lashes flutter, his eyes close, and realized that he was going to kiss her. She moistened her lips, tiptoed, and moved her hands up from his chest to wrap them around his neck.

For the next few moments, she and Nash were the only two people on earth in a vacuum-sealed bubble. His lips on hers and the passionate kisses gave them life, and if they ever stopped, she felt as if she would evaporate into nothing but a vapor.

But then the bubble popped, and reality hit her like a wrecking ball.

"That was a mistake," she muttered.

"I disagree," Nash said with a smile.

"We can't… We work…together," she stammered.

"We can, and we do, and we are adults. We can compartmentalize our work and personal lives." He grinned as he drew her close for a hug and then kissed her on the forehead.

"Good night, Clara," he whispered.

His warm breath melted all the determination to not get involved with him right out of her heart and soul. Who would have ever thought that cigar and whiskey breath could make such fiery-hot kisses? Or was it the tickle of his soft beard on her face? Then he walked away into the darkness, leaving her shivering even though the temperature was still in the high eighties.

# Chapter 9

NOT ONLY HAD BERNIE never pulled a trailer behind a vehicle, but she also hadn't had time to get the hang of driving a new truck with all the bells and whistles that the newer models had. She didn't even turn on the radio for fear that the noise would distract her. Driving in deafening silence gave her mind plenty of time to think about the next phase of her life.

Item number one on her roller coaster of thoughts was the difference in Clara that morning. She had seemed both excited and sad at the breakfast table, not totally unlike what Bernie had seen in Luna. The mixed emotions were still in Clara's expression that morning as she stared out the front window. Bernie chalked it up to her having jumbled feelings about putting down roots in a town the size of Ratliff City.

*She has found something that makes her happy, but she has to want it bad enough to grab on to it with both hands and hang on for dear life,* Bernie thought as she crossed the Taovayas Indian Bridge over the Red River and into Texas.

*What are you going to do about it?* The pesky voice in her head asked.

*I'm going to fix it,* Bernie growled in her mind and then smiled at the next idea that popped into her head. She could sell Nash half of the Chicken Coop and give the other half to Clara. That way her niece would never be beholden to anyone again. She had always planned to leave the fortune she had amassed over the years to Mary Jane's girls, but since Clara had come to her for help, it would be only fair that she also got a little inheritance.

Bernie nodded in agreement with her decision, but decided to mull it over for a while before she made her final decision. It would bind Nash and Clara together and make them a business couple, but in time, if she gave them plenty of time alone, it would develop into something personal, too.

"Yes," she muttered.

"What was that?" Clara asked.

"I was agreeing with an idea I had," Bernie answered. "You've been awfully quiet."

"Taking the trailer to the Paradise seems so final, and I already miss you," Clara answered.

"Girl, I'm only an hour away from you, and since the cops seldom ever patrol this back road, you can get here faster if you keep a sharp eye out for a stray highway patrol." Bernie wiggled her eyebrows and grinned. "Since you and Nash will be sharing the apartment, maybe he will make breakfast for you."

"I'll most likely be doing that myself," she said.

"Do you think that he'll be so good in bed that you are the one making a thank-you breakfast?" Bernie teased.

"I don't expect that I will ever know," Clara said. "Like I've told you before, I'm not getting involved with a coworker—and especially not with my boss. That could create all kinds of problems."

"Yep, it could," Bernie agreed, "but what if he wasn't your boss, what then?"

"Maybe, but not likely. He's got enough money to pay cash for the Chicken Coop. I have a check in my purse for what I made last week, which I shouldn't even cash."

"Why not?" Bernie asked. "You earned every dime of that money."

"You gave me a home. You feed me. You love me unconditionally. I should be working for free. I came to the bar in a hot mess, and you took me in." She stopped and took a long breath.

"Been fun, hasn't it?" Bernie said.

"More than words can describe," Clara answered.

"Then stop looking back. The past is gone and only the memories remain. Choose the good ones and throw out the bad. The future isn't guaranteed, so make the most of this day. Now, back to Nash. Money is only dirty paper with dead presidents printed on it. Nash's heart has no idea if he has a million dollars in the bank or he doesn't have two pennies to rub together. And neither does yours."

*Holy hell, this matchmaking job is harder than I thought it would be, but I'm not giving up on Clara and Nash. I can see the attraction growing faster than I even thought was possible. I've still got a few weeks before I turn the bar over to them,* Bernie thought as she made the final turn toward the Paradise.

Clara sipped a glass of icy-cold sweet tea and set the rocking chair in motion with her foot. The afternoon sun was hot, but a nice little breeze fanned across the wide porch. Luna sat in a matching chair on her left, and Endora in one on her right. She imagined the women who worked in the Paradise when it was a brothel sitting on the porch and having mint juleps. Her aunt had described the way that Madam Raven ran the place so well that Clara wondered what it would have been like.

"What's on your mind?" Endora asked.

"Actually, I was thinking about…" She stopped and asked, "Have y'all read your mother's books about the ladies who worked here when it was first built?"

"Of course," Luna answered. "It's a great story."

"I've been thinking about what it must have been like," Clara said. "Those women did have more independence than the married women in the area. Many of them had regular lovers, too, and managed to teach the men how to please them. My ex was one of those slam-bam, snoring-in-two-minutes type of guys." She was glad she could talk about such personal things with two women who were close to her age.

"Oh no, that's terrible," Endora declared. "But since I'm off men forever, I'm changing the subject. Are you still happy working for Aunt Bernie? I don't think I could ever work in a bar."

"Very, very happy," Clara answered. "And I also love that we are reconnecting and I can't wait to see my other five cousins."

"Me too," Endora said. "Mama never told us what happened to make her side of the family so mad at us."

"She lives in a former brothel," Clara whispered and shifted her eyes around in a dramatic gesture, "and she writes romance books."

Endora giggled. "Those are crazy reasons."

"There seems to be a division among sisters that goes way back on the family tree," Clara said and explained the differences from Aunt Bernie and her sister, all the way down to Clara and Myra.

"I'm glad we didn't have that kind of thing among us seven," Luna declared. "We argued and even had some hellacious fights out in the yard, but when it came to unity…"

Endora butted in and finished the sentence. "If someone crossed any one of us, or hurt our feelings, they were in for a battle with all seven of us."

"That's because you lived in a brothel and your mama wrote romance books," Clara said with a giggle. "You are the lucky ones. You broke the mold."

"Were there any cheating men in all that history of the sisters?" Endora asked.

"I'm sure there were," Clara answered. "When Aunt Bernie moves down here and you are lucky enough to get her full time, you should ask her about her love life."

"Lucky?" Endora asked with a puzzled expression on her face.

"Why are you asking that?" Clara frowned.

"Aunt Bernie gets into everyone's business," Luna whispered. "For some reason, she doesn't want Ursula or the other sisters to know that she's moving here. Mama practically brought out the Bible, made us lay our hand on it and swear we wouldn't say a word to them."

"That's for two whole months," Endora groaned. "I have trouble keeping a secret for two days. Thank God that Luna knows, or I would explode trying to keep from telling her. We share everything."

Clara noticed that Luna squirmed a little in her chair and didn't make eye contact with her sister. There was a whole pot full of gossiping tea to be spilled there for sure, and it had nothing to do with telling the other five sisters that Bernie was moving to Spanish Fort.

"Speak of the devil," Luna whispered with a grin.

Bernie opened the door and poked her head out. "Y'all want to go see where Joe Clay parked my trailer?"

"Sure," Clara, Luna, and Endora all chimed together.

"We really could be sisters rather than just cousins," Luna said.

"I like that idea," Clara said. "Our names end the same way, so we could pull it off. Clara, Endora, and Luna."

They followed Bernie through the kitchen, and Clara smiled when Mary Jane picked a floppy, straw hat off a hook beside the back door as she passed by and crammed it down on her head. "Got to keep the sunspots at bay as much as possible."

"Mama fussed at me and Myra if we even mentioned trying to get a tan, but Nana Vernie Sue was even more vocal about it," Clara said and then wondered if she shouldn't have even brought her mother's name up.

"Marsha was right about that," Mary Jane said. "I always discouraged my girls from tanning, too."

*Well, how about that?* Clara thought. *She said something nice about her sister, and I've never heard Mama say anything sweet about Aunt Mary Jane.*

————

The hands on the clock seemed to go in warp speed the rest of the week. Bernie looked at the date on her phone on Friday and couldn't believe that four days had passed since she took her trailer to the Paradise.

"Aunt Bernie, Nash and I can do this cleanup if you will change out the jukebox. It's time to get some different music on there," Clara suggested when they were walking through the storage room.

"Time has gotten away from me," Bernie admitted. "You are so right. I need to remove all the Fourth of July songs, so I'll take you up on that offer. Go on and get busy"—she stopped and pulled a storage box of records from a shelf—"and I'll get the change done."

Clara took the container from her. "Let me take that for you."

"Thanks," Bernie said. "Next time around, it will be y'all's turn to do this."

Nash came into the storage room and hoisted a large cardboard box of beer onto his shoulder. "Do what?"

"Change out the jukebox records," Clara answered. "I've never done that. Have you?"

"Nope, but I'm willing to learn." Nash set the beer on the bar and then turned to Clara. "That looks heavy. Let me carry it for you." He took the box from her and put it on the floor beside the jukebox. "Do we clean up the place first, or learn how to do this?"

Bernie scooted the jukebox out far enough that she could get behind it. "I reckon you better learn this first. You already know how to sweep, mop, and restock, but since I won't be here next time this needs to be done, you had best learn the process."

She carefully removed the back of the jukebox, pulled out records, and slipped them and the tabs with the name and artist into empty paper sleeves. Then she reversed the process until every slot was filled—mostly with country music, but she did add a little Creedence Clearwater Revival and Etta James for flavor.

"And that's all there is to it," she said when she finished and filed the records she had removed into the box behind the Fourth of July tab. "I change them every holiday, and sometimes in between, but y'all can figure out how often you want to do the job. I think I'll go through some of the stuff in the storage room this evening. Y'all have been doing most of the bar business all week anyway, but if you need me, just holler and I'll come running. Or maybe I'll just walk real fast."

"Does this mean you are about ready to draw up the contract to sell the place to me?" Nash asked.

"Just about, but you promised me six weeks, and I'm holding you to it," Bernie answered. "It will take that long for me to go through everything and decide what Pepper and I want to take, and what we'll be content to leave behind. I've already told him that there's lots of squirrels on the Paradise property, so he can't even ask about taking some from here."

"I'll gladly work the six weeks and learn all I can about how you do things," Nash said with a grin and glanced over at Clara.

Bernie fought the urge to do a little jig right there beside the jukebox. The looks they had exchanged all week said she was making progress—even if it was in baby steps. She could easily pack up and be ready to leave by Monday after she visited with her lawyer, but she needed more time to convince them that they belonged together.

*What if you are wrong?* her sister's voice scolded. *She should be finding her soulmate in church like her sister did.*

"I've run a bar for decades, and I know when two people belong together," Bernie muttered, then glanced around to be sure that neither Clara nor Nash heard her.

# Chapter 10

Bernie had always known the time would come when she would have to hang up her bar rag, but now that it was almost here, she found it to be bittersweet. Change wasn't easy for a middle-aged woman who had lived with a six-to-two routine for too many years to count.

*Middle-aged, my hind end.* Her sister's annoying voice popped into her head. *Accept that you are old as dirt and that it's time to age gracefully.*

"You can have that crap about aging," Bernie growled. "When I die, I'm going to slide into heaven right after my last breath, and I'm going to have used up every moment of the life the good Lord gave me. I won't have wasted a single moment of it."

Vernie Sue would never set foot in a bar, so why was she sending her spirit to argue with Bernie that evening? Sure, her sister had done her fair share of mental aggravation through the years. But if Bernie wasn't allowed at the family reunion, then Vernie Sue should keep her sanctified butt on the front pew in church and off a barstool in the Chicken Coop.

She set the box of records on a table and pulled up a chair to go through the selection for the next time the jukebox needed to be changed out. The millennials and Gen-X folks didn't give two whoops and a holler about old records, so through the years she had managed to get her hands on whole stacks of them from online dealers.

"The kids could possibly draw a few younger folks to the bar, and they won't even know who Merle Haggard and Willie Nelson are," she muttered and wiped a tear from her eye.

She had vowed that if the right buyer came along, she would not get emotional when she gave up her life as a bartender. But the one lonely tear flowed down her cheek and dripped onto her T-shirt said that wasn't going to happen. She was quickly wiping it away with the back of her hand when the door between the bar and storage room opened.

Clara came in and picked up two bottles of whiskey from a nearby box. "We are low on Jim Beam and Jameson. Is that the records we are supposed to use next time we change out the jukebox? I would be glad to help you go through things on Sunday afternoon."

"I'll get it done," Bernie told her.

"Do you have a turntable?" Clara asked.

"What?" Bernie frowned.

"A… What do you call them? One of those things that you…" Clara shooed away a fly that buzzed around the room.

"A record player or a stereo?" Bernie chuckled. "Answer is no. I haven't had one of those in years."

"Maybe you should get one and then take a few records with you so when you get lonesome for the bar, you could play them," Clara suggested.

"Darlin', I can play anything I want on my phone," Bernie reminded her great-niece.

"Yes, you can," Clara agreed.

*See there, I'm not getting old,* Bernie sent thoughts northwest toward her sister. *Can you even use all the apps on a cell phone?*

"Besides"—Bernie shrugged—"I'm not taking much of anything with me. Since the trailer is furnished, it will give me a brand-new start. I will want to take my box of pictures and personal things from my bedroom. But I'm not loading up my truck with stuff that will have to be stored."

"What about all your costumes? Don't you think the folks at the Paradise would love to see you all dressed up for holidays?" Clara asked.

"I will take some of them, but I promise to leave at least one for you to wear at each celebration," Bernie said, "and you are right. Dressing up makes me happy, and I should share that with Mary Jane and her girls. Did I tell you that Joe Clay has my trailer all ready for me and Pepper to move into? And from what you have been saying with your actions as well as your words, you do not plan to go with me to the Paradise."

Clara set the bottles on the worktable and hugged her. "That's right. I didn't see a single bar in Spanish Fort, and you have helped me figure out that this kind of work is what makes me happy. So, I'm staying right here, but are you sure about this? Sometimes, you look so sad that I have my doubts that retirement is what you are really ready for. You've still got a few weeks to change your mind, and Aunt Bernie, living and working with you has been awesome beyond what words could say."

"I'm not ready at all, but I'm positive that it's time. I didn't realize how frazzled I was until you two kids came along to help me," Bernie answered with a long sigh. "I want to have some quality in my life between now and the time I drop dead. Plus, Endora needs me to pull her up out of the doldrums, and Mary Jane needs at least one member of her family to show her some love."

"Luna needs you, too," Clara said. "I believe that she's got some secrets that she doesn't want Endora to know about."

"Yep." Bernie nodded. "I got the same feeling."

Clara picked up the bottles and headed across the room. "It's the end of an era, but the beginning of a new one for both of us."

"And Nash, too," Bernie said. "Remember, tomorrow night is our cigar and whiskey therapy session."

"Yes, ma'am, I'm looking forward to it." Clara nodded and left the storage room.

Bernie pushed back her chair, left the records on the

table, and looked around the storage room. "I'll miss all of this, but that's normal. I made the decision to keep this bar even through the tough times, and the Universe sent me a loud omen when Clara and Nash both walked into my bar the same night. If I ignore that, then I might never get another sign," she said as she headed back to the apartment. She walked down the hallway and into her bedroom, where she opened her closet door. She had to drag a ladder-back chair across the room and climb up on it to reach the boot box marked "Pictures" in fading ink on the end.

"I bet you can't hop right up on a chair without falling on your chunky butt," she fussed at her sister who was almost three hundred miles away. "So, don't be telling *me* that I'm old as dirt."

She carried the box to the kitchen, set it on the table, and made a pot of coffee.

"There is a whole lifetime right there in a box that once only held a pair of cowboy boots," she told Pepper. "And we are going to look at them tonight. Then we're going to put them in the take-with-me pile of stuff. I'll add to the pictures as life goes on, but for tonight, I will enjoy the past memories."

The dog stretched out on the floor under the table and went to sleep.

"Lot of help you are," she said as she poured a cup of coffee, added a shot of Jameson, and then removed the lid from the box. "I haven't done looked through these in years. The least you could do is keep your eyes open and listen to the stories I planned on telling you. Right along with photos of my sister up until I won this bar, I have a picture of every one of my lovers, and some of those who wanted to be, but I just didn't feel the attraction. Then there's all the school photos that Mary Jane sent me of her girls, and the good times when we had our holiday celebrations here at the Chicken Coop."

Long after midnight, she put the box away and headed back to the bar at closing time to check on Nash and Clara. She hummed along with Alan Jackson's "Livin' on Love" as she crossed the storage room and peeked into the bar. If there had been a few stragglers left behind, she planned to hang back until they were all gone. But the place was empty except for Nash and Clara, each with a mug of beer, sitting close together at the bar. The scenario looked so intimate and sweet that not even the angels could have pushed her into that room. She eased the door shut and went back to the apartment.

———————

Friday and Saturday nights were always busy times in a bar, but not that evening. There were only a handful of customers coming and going from opening until closing. Clara would much prefer being so hectic that she almost had to make an appointment to catch her breath. Being slow meant she had more time to relive that kiss that she'd shared with Nash a few days before—and get all tingly just thinking about the effects it had on her hormones. That kind of thing did not help her keep the vow she had made to *not* date a coworker, and especially a boss who held her future in his hands.

"Won't be much in the way of cleanup tomorrow," Nash said when he flickered the lights fifteen minutes before closing.

The last customer paid his bill and left without a fuss. Clara locked the door behind him and crossed the room. She hiked a hip on a stool. Nash drew up two mugs of beer and set them both in front of her. He rounded the end of the bar and sat down beside her— so close that their shoulders were barely inches apart. Sparks sizzled between them like miniature lightning streaks. This had to be an omen that she should go with Bernie to Spanish Fort. Her willpower had bottomed out just sitting beside Nash. There was no way she could work with him every day and quite possibly live in the same apartment with him and win the war against the attraction.

The sounds of the Pistol Annies singing "I Feel a Sin Comin' On" filled the room. Down deep in her soul, Clara could relate to the lyrics saying that she had a shiver down to the bone and a buzz in her brain.

"What's so funny?" Nash asked.

"Just a few thoughts in my head that would make me blush if I talked about them," she admitted.

He took several sips of his beer, slid off the barstool,

and held out his hand. "May I have this dance, please, ma'am?"

Clara recognized the song as soon as the piano prelude started to "Rest Your Love on Me." She put her hand in his and let him lead her to the middle of the small dance floor. He sang along with Conway Twitty and began a slow country waltz. She had always believed in everything happening for a reason. With that in mind, was this song telling her to listen to the words that said for her to lay her troubles on his shoulder and put her worries in his pocket? Could it possibly be that Nash was *the one*?

The song ended and she tried to take a step back, but he hugged her to his chest even tighter. "One more, please," he whispered softly.

Again, she recognized the tinkling piano music when it introduced "A Picture of Me (Without You)," an old Lorrie Morgan song. If it was true that things happened for a reason, then the lyrics had to be telling her that she would be as lost as heaven with no angels singing if she had decided to leave the bar and Nash behind. If she did, she had no doubt that she would always have regrets at not giving the attraction between them a chance.

Fate had brought her to Ratliff City for a reason, and the Universe had answered the questions that plagued her through the songs on the jukebox. Nash stepped back, brought her hand to his lips, and kissed her knuckles. "Thank you for a perfect ending to this night."

She raised her head and got lost in his eyes. They were mossy green with gold flecks in them, and she sank into them. His dark lashes fluttered, and she barely had time to moisten her lips before his mouth closed in on hers. Just like the last time he kissed her, she could feel his heart pounding and keeping time with hers through her palms that were pressed against his chest. When the string of kisses ended, they were both panting like they had crossed the finish line in a marathon race.

"Anything that wonderful can't be a mistake," he said.

"But what if the heat plays out with time?" she countered and thought of what Bernie had said about the fire being gone between her and Hershal. "A flash in the pan is hotter'n blue blazes for a few minutes, but then it dies and leaves nothing but cold ashes in its wake."

"Then"—he shrugged and slung an arm around her shoulders—"I guess we'll have to keep that steam going by kissing even more. My grandma says that a gentleman walks his date to the door, and…"

"This wasn't a date," she argued.

"And," he went on, "my grandpa says if you get a good-night kiss, it is a date. So, technically this is our second date."

"What happens on the third one?"

"We will see if we want a fourth one," he answered.

The voices in her head shouted for her to walk away, even if she had to go back to Fritch. Her heart yelled much louder that she should ignore everything and take a chance on Nash. She blocked the first one and listened to the second. "I'll see you tomorrow night at six then, but it's not a date. It's called showing up for work."

"That depends on whether there's a good-night kiss involved after our cigar and whiskey therapy." He chuckled as he walked her through the storage room to the door leading into the apartment.

He brushed a soft kiss across her bee-stung lips and said, "Good night, beautiful. I'll be dreaming of you."

"Is that a pickup line?" she teased.

"Only if it works." He flashed a bright smile, turned, and walked out of the room—whistling the tune to "Rest Your Love on Me."

# Chapter 11

MEMORIES OF THE LAST time Bernie wore her Mardi Gras costume flooded her mind as she carefully folded the flamboyant outfit, put it in a box, and added a dozen strands of beads and a lot of bangle bracelets. She hummed the jazz music that she always put on the jukebox for the Friday and Saturday nights when the Chicken Coop celebrated the holiday. Etta James with her "At Last" and Louis Armstrong singing "Hello, Dolly!" and "Georgia on My Mind" were some of her favorites.

"Can't leave out Ella Fitzgerald and sweet, sweet Ray Charles," she said with a sigh. "I could have shown that man a really good time if I'd ever met him in person."

She shook out the Christmas outfit she intended to take with her—a green sequined dress that had a side slit so high that she had to go commando when she wore it. "My Christmas present to me was a firefighter the first year I wore this. Lord have mercy!" She fanned herself with the back of her hand. "It was a wonder we didn't set the mattress ablaze that night."

Her phone rang and jerked her right back to the present, but when she checked the caller ID and saw that it was Clara's mama, she hit the decline option on the screen. She was too deep in dragging out her memories to listen to a bunch of crap about convincing Clara to go to Fritch so Marsha and Vernie Sue could talk her into going to a save-thy-soul rehab center.

"I believe in God, and I pray every night, but I also believe that He supports unconditional love," she muttered.

She ignored the phone when it rang five more times. "No thank you," she hissed.

The third time it started the incessant noise, she figured she had better answer it—just in case Vernie Sue had had a cardiac arrest or maybe a stroke and was having trouble talking her way into heaven. Maybe they had her sitting at the gates waiting to get Bernie's opinion on the matter. Marsha had already said at multiple reunions that her mother deserved gold stars and diamonds in her halo, but Bernie decided that she would get Mary Jane's thoughts before she gave Saint Peter the green light.

"What do you want?" Bernie answered.

"That's a fine way to answer the phone," Marsha huffed.

"You never call unless you want to yell at me about my lifestyle. Well, like the country song says, I'm happy being me, and I think Clara has found her place in life right here in Ratliff City," Bernie snapped.

"You exasperate me." Marsha groaned. "And Mama too, for that matter. Was there ever a time that you two got along?"

"Probably not," Bernie answered. "She's always been too high and mighty to accept me for who I am, and I refused to change. I will not give up my happiness to please her narrow mind. Are you calling today to try to get me and your mother to call a truce? Will she let me wear my *I love Jesus but I drink a little* T-shirt to the reunion in the fall?"

"Probably not, but that's not the reason I'm calling," Marsha said.

"Then spit it out so we can say goodbye." Bernie could hear the bitterness in her own voice. She didn't like it, but dang it all anyway, her sister's side of the family aggravated the hell out of her.

"I feel convicted," Marsha said in a low voice. "I've tried to pray about it, but God won't talk to me."

Bernie laid the Mardi Gras costume on the table and sat down with a thud. "If you can't love your own child unconditionally, then how can you expect Him to love you the same way and open the door to visit with Him?"

There was a long pause and then Marsha asked, "Do you love your sister unconditionally?"

"Yep, I do," Bernie answered. "I support her religious beliefs, and according to what Jesus taught, I have to love her, but there's not one place in the Good Book that says I have to like her. So, what have you done that God has turned his back on you?"

"I was wrong to treat Clara the way I did, and I should have stood up to Mama and told her to butt out," Marsha admitted.

Bernie held the phone out from her ear and stared at it for a long moment. Surely that shot of whiskey she had had to give her enough courage to go through her costumes hadn't dulled her hearing. Neither Vernie Sue nor Marsha had never admitted being wrong about a single thing in the past.

Bernie glanced out the kitchen window at the sky. Stars flickered around the moon, so there wasn't a late tornado about to hit Ratliff City. "Would you repeat that?" she asked as she returned the phone to her ear.

"Are you getting deaf as well as cantankerous?" Marsha snapped. "You and Mama both should get fitted for hearing aids."

"I am not getting old, and there's not a thing wrong with my ears or my eyes," Bernie answered in an icy-cold tone. "Were you also wrong in the way you have treated your own sister? Mary Jane has never talked ugly about you, but I can't say the same for you about her. And while we are discussing family, Vernie Sue has an even dozen grandkids, nine of them granddaughters. But she only acknowledges the three boys and Myra, probably because that girl is a preacher's wife. She even set you against your own sister from the time y'all were young. Is that any way for her to act?"

Marsha sighed again. "Mama will have to answer for her own choices, Aunt Bernie. She tried to talk Mary Jane out of getting a divorce. If she had to leave Martin, then she should have come home to Fritch and gotten a decent job."

"Sounds to me like you aren't willing to take a step toward really reconciling with either your sister or your daughter, unless they do things on your terms," Bernie told her.

"I am willing to start with Clara, but she won't even talk to me," Marsha said. "Will you *please* help me convince Clara to come home? I promise not to preach at her or make her feel like she doesn't matter."

Bernie shook her head and set her mouth in a firm line. "Have you ever watched that old movie *Steel Magnolias*?"

"Yes, I have—more than once. What has that got to do with anything?" Marsha growled.

"The women in that movie should be an example to all of us. They didn't all come from the same social world, but they accepted each other with no holds barred. This conviction you have should include more than just Clara," Bernie told her.

"I'll start with my daughter, and even that won't be an easy job with Mama living right next door to me," Marsha said.

"You won't get any victory unless you extend it further," Bernie said. "If you want Clara to come home, ask her yourself. But in my opinion, you need to love her for who she is right where she is—not just if she comes back to Fritch and buckles down to your rules. But hey, what do I know about all this sister feuding stuff? Vernie Sue and I have been at it longer than you and Mary Jane, and we sure ain't been much of an example for the two of you."

"You are right, Aunt Bernie, but I'm hoping that even though I'm past fifty, I can do things differently," Marsha said.

"It's possible, but only if *you* work at it. This whole thing has parked on your shoulders, and it's kind of hard to teach an old dog new tricks," Bernie told her.

"But not impossible," Marsha said. "It might even work between you and Mama if…"

"Don't even go there," Bernie warned.

"Okay, then I'll just say good night and have a great Sunday, if you even acknowledge the Lord's Day." Evidently, Marsha had too much of her mother's DNA flowing through her veins to leave things alone and not have to get in one last little dig.

"Darlin' girl. I acknowledge God every day, not just when the church doors open. Good night to you, too." She tapped the end icon on the screen of her phone. "I understand Hershal loving his goldfish so much now. Crazy as it sounds, that was his confidant, like you are mine, Pepper."

The little dog wagged his tail.

"I figured at first I would take you to the nearest animal shelter, or maybe give you to one of the customers, but you have proved your worth. You don't talk back when I tell you my secrets, and I'm about to tell you a big one," she whispered.

Pepper seemed to glare at her.

"Your cute little face will freeze, and you won't be able to eat or get a little sip of my Irish coffee in the morning if you don't smile." She could have sworn that she saw the dog's expression change. "I just talked to Marsha, and can you believe that she wants me to…" She ranted and raved about the phone call until she figured out that the bar would close in ten minutes. "Enough about that. Thanks for listening, but right now, the kids should be closing up the bar, and we have to get the whiskey poured up so that we're ready for our Saturday night therapy session."

"Aunt Bernie?" Clara's voice floated through the apartment. "We need you in the bar. Someone is in crisis and won't leave until she talks to you."

"I'll be right there," Bernie grumbled. "What are they going to do without me? Maybe I got too hasty about selling out and moving to the Paradise. I'm needed here."

*But you are needed more in Texas,* the annoying voice in her head reminded her.

"I'm going to miss this," she whispered to Pepper as she headed across the room. "But it'll be a small price to pay if I can get all seven of Mary Jane's girls settled down and starting a family. I want to live long enough to see

Mary Jane's grandchildren running around in that big old house. I've got more years behind me now than I've got in front of me, so I have to get busy."

Viola, a regular customer for the last thirty years, was sitting in the corner with at least four empty shot glasses on her table. Mascara had turned her tears into black streaks running down her cheeks. "Oh, Bernie, what am I going to do?" she sobbed.

Bernie pulled a chair close to her, sat down, and draped an arm around her shoulders. "The first thing you can do is talk to me," she said.

Viola left a smear of black across her cheek when she swiped the tears away. "He's finally done it, Bernie."

"What did he do? Drop dead? Did he leave behind an insurance policy?"

"Hell, no!" Viola hiccupped. "I wouldn't be crying if he'd died. He left me, and not even for a younger woman like he always said he would. He kicked me out of the house and moved Darlene Branan in with him. She's got to be seventy years old if she's a day, and from what I hear she's got money from her dead husband's insurance. Poor man ain't been dead but a month, and she ain't got the sense God gave a rock. Claude will have that money in his bank account within the week."

"When did all this happen?" Bernie asked.

"When I came home from working a double shift at the café in Duncan," she answered. "I've got nowhere to go, and he's even cleaned out our joint checking account."

"Did you do what I told you to do a couple of years ago?"

Viola nodded. "I have been putting all my overtime money in a separate bank account."

"Then you put on your big-girl panties, pull up your bootstraps, and go find a cheap motel for a couple of nights. Rent your own place over in Duncan and move on with your life. You are only sixty years old, girl. It's not time for you to lie down and die over a cheating bastard like Claude Wilson. You gave him twenty years of your life. That's enough, and when he comes crying to you because he can't make rent or buy a six-pack of beer on his salary, tell him to go to hell," Bernie told her. "Unless his new woman is willing to support his expensive tastes, he's going to have to get a full-time job."

Viola stood up and nodded. "I know that's what I need to do, but I just needed to hear you say it. I can stay with a friend a couple of days until I find a place. And if I ever even think of getting married again, shoot me with that sawed-off shotgun you've got under the counter. I'll write up a permission slip saying I made you do it, so you won't have to go to jail."

"I don't imagine it will come to that," Bernie got to her feet and gave her a sideways hug. "You've learned your lesson. Now it's time to prove to yourself and to him that you are independent and strong without a man."

"I do tend to fall in love too fast, don't I?" Viola

sniffled.

Bernie walked her to the door. "Yes, you do, but now you know what your problem is, you can tackle it."

Viola blew her a kiss and left with a smile on her smudged face.

"Okay, kids," Bernie said as she locked the door. "It's past time for our Saturday night therapy session. I was about to pour the whiskey when this little problem came up."

# Chapter 12

CLARA KICKED OFF HER shoes on the way through the apartment, picked up the remains of her cigar from the night before, and sighed when she sank down into one of the chairs in the backyard. "Before you leave, will you teach me how to take care of problems like Viola?"

Bernie sat down beside her. "Nope, but you will learn it as you go. Listening to others and helping them if they ask for your advice is part of a bartender's job. Sometimes they just need to talk, and you don't have to say or try to fix anything at all. The trials you have been through in your own life have given you the understanding of other folks, and also the knowledge to say the right things to help them through any crisis. Just lean on the emotions of how you have felt in any given situation."

"Those are some good thoughts," Nash said.

"Thanks, but it comes from years and years of listening to folks' problems," Bernie said and lit up her cigar. "Any bartender worth his salt should be given a complimentary license to practice psychiatry after their first year."

Clara nodded in agreement. "I sure heard some stories—both sad and happy. Looking back, they were probably the very thing that helped me when Kent tossed me out. I figured if those people could survive through their deepest pain and talk to a stranger, then I most definitely could do the same. But I didn't count on my own family telling me that I had to meet their demands before they could lend me a helping hand. Thank you again, Aunt Bernie."

Bernie blew a puff of smoke out into the air before she spoke. "What made you think they would help you?"

"To begin with, I'm family," Clara answered with a shrug. "And then when Myra wanted a big wedding last year, I cleaned out my savings account so she could have the dress she wanted."

"Honey, that taught you a valuable lesson," Bernie said.

"And that is?"

"Money can buy material things, but it cannot buy love," Bernie answered.

"I thought the parents paid for their daughter's wedding," Nash said.

Bernie frowned and took a sip of her whiskey. "Why would your folks let you do that?"

Clara shrugged a second time. "Nana and Mother said that the wedding should be simple, since she was marrying a preacher. There was a lot of talk about being humble and setting an example for other young women."

Bernie chuckled. "I can hear it all now, but I bet Myra had champagne taste on a Kool-Aid budget when it came to the dress."

"Yes, she did, and when we went shopping for it, Mama refused to pay for it. Since she graduated from college, Myra has been working as the church secretary, and with her tastes, she barely makes it to the end of each paycheck. When she tried the dress of her dreams on, she cried when she saw the price tag, so I bought it for her as her wedding present. I thought that would surely carry a little weight when I needed help."

"And you found out real quick that giving your older sister the money for that dress did not mend one of the fences between you and the rest of the family, didn't you?" Bernie asked.

Clara swallowed down the lump in her throat and swatted at a fly buzzing around her face. "Too bad cigar smoke doesn't chase away these pesky critters as well as mosquitoes. To answer your question, Aunt Bernie, no it did not fix anything between us. Mama was mad at me for buying the dress. Myra said thank you, but she didn't ask me to be a part of the wedding party. I got an invitation two days before the event, and I went, but the reserved pews were too crowded with all their church family, so I was seated near the back with the less fortunate folks."

"I can't imagine having kinfolks like that," Nash said. "It hasn't been all wonderful with my folks. They divorced when I was a little boy, and Granny and Grandpa had a big hand in raising me, but if I needed a place, my dad and stepmother or my mom and her husband would take me in."

The heat of the last of Clara's whiskey traveling from her mouth to her stomach was nothing compared to the sparks she felt coming from Nash. He was at least a foot away from her, but that didn't stop the electricity between them. "It would take a pure miracle to change the attitudes of angels against those who don't have wings," she finally said.

"Amen," Bernie agreed and stood up. "I'm going to turn in. You kids be sure you lock up. Good night."

"'Night," Nash said.

"I think she might be trying to play matchmaker between us," Clara whispered when Bernie had gone inside.

"My grandfather is doing the same," Nash said out the side of his mouth. "Shall we humor them a little? After all, they are all getting up in years."

"How do you propose we do that?" Clara asked.

"Well, to start with, you could go to church with me and my folks tomorrow and then have Sunday dinner with us at the ranch," Nash replied.

Clara took a hit off her cigar and blew out the smoke. "Are we just pretending, or is this a real date?"

"Depends on whether I get a good-night kiss," he teased.

Clara turned to face him. "That would mean we would spend the *whole* day together."

"If you get tired or bored, it could be a good-afternoon kiss." He flashed a brilliant smile toward her. "Can you be ready to go at ten fifteen? Our services start at ten thirty and are over in an hour."

"I don't date coworkers, and definitely not someone who will probably be my boss," she told him.

"Then we won't call it a date," Nash said. "It will be going to church with a friend and having dinner at his grandparents' house."

"That sounds like the beginning of a relationship to me," Clara argued.

"If you don't go out with me, will you regret it in a year, or even six months?" he asked. "And why won't you date coworkers?"

"I've told you about my ex," she answered. "And he wasn't the first person I dated from a job. Not a single one of them ended well."

"Don't judge all experiences by the bad ones in the past. This one might be like grabbing the golden ring at the carousel."

"It will make things awkward if our relationship…" she started.

Nash laid a hand on her arm. "But what if it turns out to be awesome?"

"Why would you want to date me anyhow?" she asked bluntly.

"Because I like you a lot, and there's been chemistry between us since we first met," he answered.

"When I was blubbering like a two-year-old who didn't get her way?" Clara shot back at him.

"Yep, and I thought you were beautiful even then, but the feelings I have got even more pronounced every time after that. Didn't you feel the same?"

"I did, but…"

He gently squeezed her arm. "I won't beg, Clara. If you don't want to take this any further, just say the word and I will back off. But know that I feel something that I haven't ever experienced before, and I really want to spend more time with you."

"Okay, then," Clara agreed, "but if we're going to wake up and be dressed that early for church, we had better call it a night."

"I agree." Nash put out his cigar and downed the last sip of his whiskey. He bent at the waist and brushed a sweet kiss across Clara's lips. "I'm looking forward to tomorrow," he whispered before he disappeared into the night.

In an attempt to cool her whining hormones, Clara took several deep breaths and let them out slowly. Had she just jumped out of the frying pan into the fire, or had she made the best decision in her whole life?

# Chapter 13

THE SKY WAS DIVIDED that Sunday morning with dark clouds rolling in from the southwest and the sun shining brightly in the northeast. Clara could hear Bernie and Pepper both snoring as she had a bowl of cereal and a cup of instant coffee for breakfast. One loud noise that sounded like a constipated elephant, and then a tiny little snort that was almost like a sneeze from an aristocratic lady. She made a mental note to tell Mary Jane to be grateful that Bernie would not be living in the Paradise.

She finished eating and tiptoed to her bedroom, got dressed, and wrote a short note to Bernie telling her that she was going to church and afterward to dinner with Nash and his grandparents. When Nash knocked on the back door, she had just finished setting the piece of paper up beside the coffeepot.

She opened the door and Pepper ran out ahead of her, chased a squirrel up a tree, and hiked a leg on a nearby bush. "Good mornin'," she said with a sheepish grin.

"It is now." Nash's eyes traveled from the hem of her

denim skirt, up to the lacy western shirt she had chosen, and on to her long, red hair that she'd twisted up into a messy bun on top of her head. "You look amazing. I should have brought a big stick with me."

"Do people take sticks to your church?" She wondered what she had gotten herself into, and if she could back out. If Pepper didn't come back in a few seconds, could she use the excuse that she had to chase him down to skip the strange services that required the member of their congregation to bring such things into the building?

"No, darlin'." he chuckled. "But I might need one to beat off all the young guys who want to ask you for a date. I guess I can use the hymnal if things get out of hand."

"Thank you for that, but what you probably need is a new set of contact lenses," she teased, but was inwardly grateful that the place didn't require anything weird.

Pepper ran back into the house, and she quickly closed the door.

"I have twenty-twenty vision, and I call it like I see it." He looped her arm into his and slowed his stride to match hers.

The parking lot seemed empty with Nash's truck parked beside her old car with bald tires and maybe half a cup of gas left in the tank. On the other side was Bernie's old truck beside the brand-new one. She looked back over her shoulder at her car and Nash's vehicle. They were a testimony to their backgrounds that could easily become an insurmountable obstacle. She tried to brush away the comparison between the two. But the omen in the sky didn't help. One second the sun shone brightly down upon Ratliff City; the next, dark clouds darkened the whole place. Two signs right there that she and Nash came from completely different worlds that more than likely could never find common ground.

*Stop thinking negatively,* the niggling voice in her head scolded. *Enjoy the day instead of fretting about what might happen in the future.*

Nash opened the truck door for her and helped settle her into the soft leather seat. She watched him circle around the front of the vehicle. He looked like he could be a model for the cover of a cowboy romance book in those jeans, pearl snap shirt, and polished boots. The only thing missing was a hat, but if he'd had one on, she wouldn't be able to imagine tangling her fingers in his mop of silver hair.

"Granny and Grandpa are meeting us there," he said as he slid behind the steering wheel. "She teaches the five- and six-year-old kids' Sunday school class. She says she isn't going to retire until I get married and give her some great-grandkids. Grandpa likes to attend the senior citizens' class with his old buddies. I'm not sure if they talk about Jesus, fishing, or how much hay they got off of their acreage, but he's fired up and ready to go every Sunday morning."

"Is that the reason they want you to buy the bar?"

she asked. "So that you'll be close by when you have a family?"

"I suppose it is." He chuckled and turned the truck around. "But they have always said that they'll sell the ranch and move to wherever I'm living as long as it's not in a big city."

"Won't your father inherit the place?" Clara asked.

"He's made his millions." Nash pulled out onto the highway and headed west. "He hated ranching and often said the best day of his life was when he saw cows and hay in his rearview mirror as he left Ratliff City."

"That leaves you," Clara said. "Would you quit the bar to be a rancher?"

"Someday I would like to do both." He slowed down and turned into the church parking lot. "Kids could learn a lot by living in the country and having a big place to run and play. Did you grow up in town?"

"Yep, right in the middle of Fritch, Texas. Daddy works in the oil fields and is gone a lot. Mama worked for the government in data processing. I stayed with my grandma a lot of time until Mama retired. That would be the summer before I started to first grade."

"Did you go to college after high school?" he asked.

"Mama wanted me to like my brother and sister did, but I was sick of school, so Daddy made a phone call, and I went to work in Amarillo for an oil company. I thought he would give me a job like he did Luke, but that didn't happen. It was supposed to be for the summer only, but when fall came, I told my folks I needed a year away from books and tests. That stretched into another year and another," Clara answered. "I kept making bad decisions that landed me on the black sheep list, and my brother and sister made wonderful ones."

"Well, darlin'," he drawled, "you are the prettiest black sheep I've ever seen."

"Is that your newest pickup line?"

"Nope, just the facts, ma'am, just the facts." He wiggled his eyebrows, opened the truck door, and hurried around the front side to help her.

She took his hand and slid off the seat, landed on her feet wrong, and fell right onto his chest. That vision she had of running her hands through his hair became reality when he gazed into her eyes, cupped her face with his big hands, and kissed her right there in the church parking lot. A streak of lightning zigzagged through the sky at the same time she closed her eyes and tangled her fingers in his hair.

He took a step back and wiped his forehead in a dramatic gesture. "I guess we aren't supposed to be making out in this place."

"Probably not," she panted.

Folks were milling around visiting with each other when she and Nash entered the sanctuary. The children ran helter-skelter around the pews, and the whole place had the feel of a family reunion rather than a serious church service. The menfolks wore cowboy hats or caps with a John Deere logo or with something about a feed and seed store or being a Vietnam vet, but not a single woman had donned a fancy hat to match her outfit.

She was reminded of the lyrics in Miranda Lambert's song that said that it wasn't her mama's broken heart. "Only instead of a broken heart, this sure ain't my mama's church," she muttered and then looked around to be sure that Nash had not heard her.

Clara had been told her whole life not to compare one person with another. Not that her mother or grandmother stuck to their own advice. But that notion left her mind when she thought of Nana Vernie Sue and her mother attending services that morning in their cute little hats that matched their straight skirts and matching jackets, it sure wasn't an easy rule to follow. Not when the women around her were mostly dressed in jeans and T-shirts.

"Hello, I'm Nash's grandmother, Darlene," a woman said and laid her hand on Clara's shoulder. The woman was short like Clara, had lots of gray in her dark hair, and eyes that seemed to look right into Clara's soul. "We are so glad you came with Nash this morning and that you're going home with us for dinner afterwards. Come with me, and I'll show you where we sit. Hoot will keep Nash talking until the bell rings."

"Pleased to meet you," Clara said and let go of Nash's hand.

He glanced down at her and smiled. "Be there in just a minute."

She nodded and followed Darlene to the third pew on the right side. She wasn't sure what the bell ringing had to do with anything. In the Fritch church, everyone went inside after Sunday school, sat down, and waited quietly for the song director to tell them what page to turn their hymnals to. Then the preacher delivered his sermon. After the benediction, the folks stood up and began to visit somewhat like they were doing right then.

*Dark clouds and sunshine*, she thought as she sat down beside Darlene, and Nash squeezed into the end space right beside her. Clara jumped when a lady picked up a small brass bell and rang it several times.

"That's just calling the folks to their seats and telling them to be quiet," Nash whispered.

"The Bible tells us to make a joyful noise," the lady who was evidently the song leader said when everyone had taken a seat and gotten quiet. "It doesn't say that we have to sing on key or carry a tune. God is looking for happy people with a good spirit, so let's raise the roof this morning as we sing number three hundred in the hymnal, 'Love Lifted Me.'"

*Signs are popping up all around me,* Clara thought.

Nash took a hymnal from the back pocket of the pew in front of them, opened it to the right page, and shared it with Clara. Darlene beamed and Hoot's smile lit up the whole church. Even in the place where she attended services with her family, sharing a songbook with a guy meant they were a couple.

Nash had a lovely deep voice. Darlene made a joyful noise all right, but she couldn't have carried a tune in a galvanized milk bucket. Other than in the shower, Clara had not sung in so long that she wasn't sure where she stood in the mix. And it wasn't an easy job to sit so close to Nash that their shoulders and hips touched and think about Jesus at the same time.

Clara heard the first few words of the sermon—something about the love of God in the heart could and would change a person for the better, and how forgiveness encouraged that love. She disagreed with that statement. She had no doubt that her grandmother loved God, but it sure hadn't sweetened up her spirit. She refused to dwell on her family, but instead thought about Nash, Bernie, and even Pepper.

She came back to the present when the preacher asked Hoot to give the benediction and then all but tip-toed to the back of the church so he could shake hands with the folks as they left. Hoot stood up, bowed his head, and said a short prayer, followed by a loud "Amen" that everyone in the congregation echoed.

Then all chaos broke loose again. Folks seemed to make a determined effort to shake hands with Nash, who in turn introduced them to Clara. Not a single one of them threatened to haul her outside and tar and feather her when they found out she was Bernie's great-niece. Instead, most of them sent greetings to her.

"I'm starving," Nash finally said. "Let's sneak out the

side door like Granny and Grandpa did a few minutes ago. She made pot roast for dinner, and she's got a big pan of hot rolls risin' to go with it."

"I might have gained five pounds from thinking about all that," Clara said.

Nash tucked her hand in his and led her through the thinning crowd to a side door. She giggled when she realized his truck wasn't twenty feet away.

"What's so funny? Haven't you ever slipped out of church without shaking the preacher's hand?" he asked.

"Yes, I have, but my car was never parked this close. I feel kind of like I've robbed a bank and that's the getaway truck," she said.

"Did you listen to every word of the sermon?" Nash picked up speed and hurried her over to the passenger's side of the vehicle.

She hopped up on the seat and shook her head. "No, I did not. I tuned out right after he started talking about the love of God in our hearts. Does that mean I robbed the Lord, and this really is a getaway truck?"

"Depends on what you were thinking about instead of listening," Nash declared. "Want to share your thoughts?"

"That, darlin','"—she dragged the last word out into several syllables—"is between me and the good Lord."

*Maybe it's not between you and God at all,* the voice in her head said. *As hot as your thoughts were, they might have been between you and Mister Lucifer.*

# Chapter 14

THE DARK CLOUDS THAT had been blowing up from the southwest had thrown a shadow over the backyard that Sunday morning when Bernie went outside with Pepper. A gentle breeze cooled the area and shook the leaves of the pecan and oak trees. Bernie sucked in the aroma of honeysuckle blooming somewhere out there in the wooded area. She sat down in a lawn chair and sipped her coffee that had a little kick of Jameson added to it. Had it been possible, she would have patted herself on the back. Whether they called it a date or not, Clara and Nash were together, and that was the first step in falling in love. Church had let out at precisely eleven thirty. That meant her niece was in one of those vehicles that Bernie could hear driving down the road and hopefully on her way to a happy-ever-after.

The crunching sound of gravel in the bar parking lot told her that someone had forgotten something at the church and was turning around to go back for whatever it was. She chuckled when she thought about a little kid leaving behind one of their tablet things. Back when she and Vernie Sue were little girls, they did not get to take a coloring book or anything to entertain them to church. They were expected to sit still on a hard pew for what seemed like three days past eternity. Their mother preached that children should learn to listen to the preacher's sermon, and if they did, they would grow up to be good girls. Evidently all that holiness danced right past Bernie and landed on Vernie Sue.

She laughed so loud that Pepper forgot about the squirrel he had been chasing and ran back to sit in front of her. "I'm giggling, not crying," she told him.

He cocked his head to one side and growled down deep in his throat.

"You've already put the fear of a Chihuahua into more than one squirrel," she said. "You don't have to convince him that you are as big and mean as King Kong."

The hair on his back stood straight up and he barked several times.

"You've scared them all away," Bernie reminded him, and then saw the shadow of a couple of folks coming around the end of the building. Her first notion was that the church service did not go well, and Clara had refused to go to Sunday dinner with Nash. She hoped that Nash didn't feel obligated to walk Clara all the way to the door, even though they were arguing. He didn't need to see Bernie in her *I love Jesus but I drink a little* T-shirt and pajama pants with Betty Boop all over them.

"Dammit anyway," she swore. She had been so ready

for some good results for her efforts of leaving them together in the bar so many nights.

Then she saw that neither of the two women was Clara. She frowned and sucked air between her teeth when she recognized Vernie Sue and Marsha in their high-heeled shoes, gingerly picking their way around the gopher holes in the yard.

"What the hell? Why are you coming around here ruining my Sunday? It's my only day to do whatever I want," she grumbled and then glared at Pepper. "Why couldn't you be the size of a mountain lion and scare them away?"

He took refuge under her chair and kept a low growl.

"Did y'all get lost on your way to church this mornin'?" she called out.

"No, we spent the night in Duncan last night and attended an early morning service before we came over here. I'm going to ask our pastor if he could start having two on Sunday to give us who want to prepare dinner more time," Vernie Sue said as she sat down beside Bernie without even asking. "You look like hell, and I hate that shirt."

"This is my place, not yours, and it's not a family reunion where you are the queen bee. I will wear what I damn well please. Now I understand those storm clouds." Bernie snapped.

"What is that supposed to mean?"

"Aren't you afraid that lightning will shoot down

out of the sky and strike you dead for sitting so close to a bar?"

Marsha eased down into the third chair and sighed loudly. "Can you two be civil long enough for us to have a discussion? We have driven all the way down here, so be nice."

"I'll try if she will," Vernie Sue agreed. "You got old and wrinkled since I saw you last, but then you have always lived a rough life."

"Have you looked in the mirror lately?" Bernie snapped without taking her eyes off her twin sister. "We are identical twins except that you got fat and let your hair go gray."

"Oh, for the love of God," Marsha groaned. "We came to see Clara and to apologize for the way we made her feel when she needed help."

"Marsha, darlin', sometimes it's too late to do what you should have been doing all along," Bernie scolded.

"What's that supposed to mean?" Vernie Sue asked.

"If you can't figure it out, then you aren't even as smart as I thought you were," Bernie told her.

"Well," Vernie Sue huffed, "I'm smart enough to know that we've been sitting here at least five minutes, and you haven't even offered us a drink of water. Have you lost all the manners our mother taught us?"

Bernie held out her mug. "This is my coffee, and it has a little kick of Jameson in it. The kitchen is right through that door, so help yourself to whatever you want.

Refrigerator has food in it. You are family, not guests, so I'm not obligated to wait on you. Coffee is in the pot, but you can have a sip of mine if you are dying of thirst. I would never want you to die behind a bar. That might keep you from going to heaven."

Vernie Sue reached for the half-empty mug and then shook her head. "I can smell whiskey in it all the way over here."

"A sip or two might loosen you up a little," Bernie said.

"Are you calling me…" Vernie Sue started.

"That's enough, Mother," Marsha said in an icy-cold tone. "We didn't come all this distance for you and Aunt Bernie to argue. Where is Clara? We really do want to talk to her and maybe, hopefully, even take her home with us."

"I'm surprised that her old car even made it this far," Vernie Sue said.

Bernie took a sip of her lukewarm coffee and decided that when she refilled the mug, it would fill it to the brim with Jameson. She deserved no coffee in it at all if she was going to have to put up with her sister until Clara came home.

"Y'all might as well come on in my apartment. It's getting hot out here, and the mosquitoes are starting to buzz around." She hoped that they declined and went on back to Duncan.

Vernie Sue crossed her arms over her chest. "I will not go into a beer joint."

"I didn't invite you into the bar. I don't want you in there spreading your condemning aura all over it," Bernie said. "There's a storage room between the Chicken Coop and my apartment. I don't want y'all in my place of business, but out of family courtesy, I will let you come into my apartment and let you make yourselves a sandwich. I'm more hospitable than y'all are."

"I'm very welcoming," Vernie Sue argued.

"You threw your own sister out of the family reunion if I remember right," Bernie reminded her.

Vernie Sue shook her chubby finger at Bernie. "That shirt, the very one you are wearing now, was and is sacrilegious. And for your information, people come to my house all the time, and I always offer them something to drink, and most of the time I even give them some homemade cookies or a slice of pie."

Bernie stood up and took a step toward the back porch. "I ain't got pie or cookies except for the store-bought chocolate chip ones, but I'm hungry so I'm going inside where it's cool to make myself a sandwich. Y'all can sit out here in the heat all afternoon if you want, but Clara is out on a date, and most likely won't be home until dark."

"Who…what…where…" Marsha stammered.

"She went to church this morning with Nash Murphey, the guy who is going to buy the Chicken Coop, and after the services she was going to his grandparents' house for Sunday dinner. Nash is a good man, and he really likes Clara. From what I see, she likes him, so y'all are wasting your time trying to get her to leave Ratliff City."

"Church!" Vernie Sue fumed and then she saw Pepper and put up both palms. "Get that thing away from me. You know I'm allergic to cats and dogs."

"Not to Chihuahuas. They are the only dog that folks with allergies can have," Bernie told her. "Pepper lives with me and Clara. So, get over yourself, Vernie Sue. And Clara has even asked for him. I'm leaving a note in my will that if I die before Pepper does, she will inherit him. Are you sure you want her to live in Fritch with a sassy little dog?" She marched into the house and closed the door behind her. Let them both sit out there and suffocate in their fancy church clothes, high-heeled shoes, panty hose, and possibly even a girdle.

"Dammit!" she swore again as she got all the sandwich makings from the refrigerator, along with store-bought potato salad and coleslaw, and brought paper plates and chips from the pantry. "I only get one day a week to relax, and they have spoiled it. I hope those Texas-sized mosquitoes come up over the Red River and carry them away. Allergic to dogs, my royal hind end." She fussed and fumed the whole time she made herself a plate.

She had just sat down at the table when the back door opened and Marsha came inside. "Thank you, Aunt Bernie, for the offer to stay in a cool house and make ourselves a bit of lunch. We had planned to take you and Clara out to a café, but there's not much of a place here, is there?"

"Only pizza at the gas station. They deliver if you want to call in an order," Bernie answered. "Help yourself to whatever you can find. I have left the sandwich makings on the table in case Vernie Sue decided that she could bear having a Chihuahua around her for a few hours. There's a bundt cake one of my customers brought me a couple of days ago under the dome over there." She pointed in the general direction, but didn't tell them that it was butter rum with extra liquor in the icing.

Marsha opened a cabinet door and took down two paper plates. "Thank you. We ate breakfast in the hotel, but I'm starving."

Bernie sat down at the table and felt the heat from her sister's glare when she came through the door and glanced around the kitchen. "What?" she asked.

"Don't you say grace?" Vernie Sue asked.

Bernie bowed her head. "Thank you, God, for giving me a full, happy life and letting me make enough money to buy this T-shirt, and for this bologna and cheese sandwich with mustard, pickles, onions, and all the other fixin's. Amen."

"That was pure sacrilege," Vernie Sue mumbled. "But then I should have expected it from someone like you."

"Mother, that is enough," Marsha scolded her.

"Whose side are you on?" Vernie Sue demanded.

"Why do we have to take sides?" Marsha asked. "I wish I had stayed in the FBI and moved the family to Washington, DC, and I'm thinking about moving my membership to that new all faith church that just opened up on Main Street in the old clothing store."

Vernie Sue smeared mayonnaise on two slices of bread and added smoked ham and cheese. "If you do that, I'll be the laughingstock of the whole town. Our family has been hardcore members of the Community Church since all three of you kids were born. And just who would have raised Clara for you if you had moved that far from me? I did all I could for that girl to give her a proper upbringing, and look who she turns to when we don't support her wild ways."

Bernie took a bite of her sandwich and chewed slowly to keep from slapping her sister right out of the chair she sat in. When she had swallowed and taken a drink from a bottle of cold root beer, she finally had her thoughts under control and could speak. "Just because Clara didn't fit in the perfect little mold you created for her does not mean that she's a bad person. Now, Marsha, why don't you catch me up on what's going on with your other two children."

"Myra and her husband are doing well. She's making a fine little preacher's wife, and they're trying to start a family. She's in her mid-thirties, and her husband wants as many kids as the Lord can give them," Marsha said with a lot of pride in her voice.

"Will that be your first grandchild?" Bernie asked. She could see a little gray sprinkling in Marsha's brown hair, and crow's-feet were taking up residence around her blue eyes. She didn't look happy—not like Mary Jane did.

"No, Luke has two daughters, both teenagers, but they spend more time with their other grandparents than with us."

*I wonder why?* Bernie kept the thought inside her head.

"That's because they live on a farm and don't go to church at all," Vernie Sue growled.

"Mother, you promised that you would be civil and not judge," Marsha scolded.

"It don't make it right," Vernie Sue muttered. "We need to have equal time with them."

"Judging is worse than not being on a hard pew every time the church doors open," Bernie told her. "Why don't you throw out all that self-righteous negativity and replace it with happiness? You've still got a few years left in your chubby little body. Be glad that your grandchildren and those two great-grands are healthy and independent. If they were sick and would follow anything or anyone, you might have something to whine about."

"You have no right to preach at me." Vernie Sue's voice went even colder.

"No, I don't, but by the same token, you have no right to judge me or anyone else on this earth. Let's just take it back a step or two and have a good visit this afternoon while we wait on Clara to come home," Bernie suggested. "After we eat, we can go in the living room and reminisce about the old days, or maybe I can even offer you Clara's bed to have a little nap."

"That sounds fantastic," Marsha said. "It's been way too long since we had a visit, Aunt Bernie."

"How long has it been since you went down to Spanish Fort to see Mary Jane?" Bernie asked.

"Never, but tomorrow we are going to fix that, aren't we, Mama?" Marsha said in a tone that didn't allow room for argument.

"If you say so," Vernie Sue quipped.

Bernie was struck speechless for several moments. "Y'all are going to the Paradise?" she finally asked.

"Yes, we are," Marsha answered. "After we talk to Clara, we plan to drive to Nocona to a hotel and then go see Mary Jane tomorrow morning."

"Does she know you are coming?" Bernie asked.

"Of course not," Vernie Sue answered, "and don't you dare tell her."

"We'd like to surprise her like we did you," Marsha said.

"I promise that I won't say a word." Bernie took a long drink of her root beer.

*But that doesn't mean I won't ask Clara to do it for me,* she thought.

# Chapter 15

"Come on in and make yourself at home," Darlene said when Nash and Clara entered the house through the back door.

Clara stopped and took a deep breath. "Something smells delicious. What can I do to help?"

"Nothing like the aroma of fresh baked bread," Darlene said with a smile. "Thanks for offering. I never turn down help. You can set the table while I whip up some cream to go on the peach cobbler that we're having for dessert."

"Fresh bread and cobbler in one meal?"

"I told you that you wouldn't be sorry you agreed to come have dinner with us." Nash grinned and then kissed her on the cheek. "Need my help, Granny?"

"No, Son, I don't. You can go on in the living room with your grandpa and let us women talk about you." Darlene chuckled.

"Yes, ma'am." Nash smiled again. "But don't believe all the stories that she's going to tell you, Clara."

Darlene popped a dish towel toward him. "Get on

out of here, or I'll tell her some tales that will have her runnin' for the hills."

"I'm going." Nash laughed out loud and dropped another kiss on Clara's cheek. "Don't believe everything she tells you. I wasn't that bad."

"Was he?" Clara asked when he had cleared the room.

"No, honey, just a little on the ornery side like most boys are," she answered. "He was a fairly good boy, and he grew up to be a really wonderful man. We were hoping he would study business and agriculture in college, but his father swayed him over to the law field. But he's found out that's not where his heart is, and we're right happy to have him back here in Ratliff City." She stopped to take down a stack of four plates and hand them to Clara. "Silverware is in that drawer." She nodded in the direction of the sink. "Tell you the truth, we've been wanting to size down the ranch since we are getting up in years. I guess if the good Lord opens a door, we'll be ready to walk through it, but for now, we'll just stick close to our boy."

"He really likes working at the bar," Clara said.

Darlene pulled the hot rolls out of the oven and turned it off, then slid the cobbler inside. "That will warm it up right nice just in time for dessert. And you? Do you enjoy working at the Chicken Coop, too?"

"Yes, ma'am, I really do. Coming to Ratliff City might be the wisest decision I've ever made." Clara wished she could be impolite and ask for a roll while they were steaming hot.

"That's good. I've always enjoyed being a rancher's wife. Enjoying what you do is called success," Darlene told her.

"You sound a lot like Aunt Bernie," Clara said.

Darlene turned on a hand mixer to whip thick cream and talked above it. "That is one good woman right there."

"I think so." Clara smiled. "She's been like a savior to me."

Darlene turned off the mixer and put the bowl of whipped cream in the refrigerator. "Honey, you ain't the only one Bernie has given a helping hand. There's lots of folks in the town that has needed a little something through the years, and she was right there with advice or maybe a handout to pay a utility bill, or lots of other things. A few years back, I told her that the church's old piano was past the days when it could even be tuned. A brand-new baby grand showed up the next week. When I asked her about it, she told me that she had no idea how it got there. She might not be sitting on a pew every Sunday, but she's a fine example of what a true Christian should be. You are lucky to have her in your life."

"Don't I know it," Clara agreed.

———————

After dinner, Clara helped with cleaning up, and then the two older people walked Nash and Clara all the way out to his truck. The sweetest memory that Clara filed away in the back of her mind was the way that the Darlene and Hoot held hands. If she was ever in a committed relationship, she hoped it would last as long as theirs had and that she would still be in love with her partner.

"I would invite you to stick around longer, but Grandpa baled hay yesterday and we really want to get it all in the barn before it rains again." Nash started up the truck and left a trail of gray dust behind the vehicle as he drove down the dirt road toward the bar.

"I've never hauled hay, but I'm willing to learn. Next time you need a hand on a Sunday afternoon, just let me know," she said.

"Thanks," Nash said. "Grandpa still likes to use the small rectangular bales and keep them in the barn. I bet you could drive the truck and trailer really good, so yes, ma'am, I will definitely call you if we get another cutting this year."

The way the time passed when she was with Nash seemed to go in warp speed. Before she could even think to ask about what *another cutting* meant, he had parked his vehicle at the Chicken Coop.

"Man, I could get used to this kind of treatment," she muttered to herself as she watched him walk around the front of the truck and then open the door for her. He kept her hand in his after she slid off the seat and nodded toward the silver SUV in the parking lot.

"Those are Texas tags," she said.

"Think it might be some of your relatives come to haul you back to the Panhandle?" he teased.

"Nope," she answered. "But it might be one of Aunt Mary Jane's girls on their way home for a few days. I would love to see either Rae or Bo. It was like a breath of fresh air to talk to Endora and Luna. I can't wait for you to meet all of them. Maybe we can go down there for Thanksgiving dinner. Aunt Bernie says they all come home for the holidays."

He stopped and kissed her on the forehead. "Darlin', I would be glad to go meet your family, but I'll have to decline for dinner that day. I can't leave Granny and Grandpa alone. How about we have dinner with them, and then supper with your folks."

"Do you think we'll be together that long?" she asked.

"I hope so," he whispered.

"If we are, how about we just combine our families? Darlene and Hoot can go to Spanish Fort with us," she suggested.

"I'd like that, and I think Grandpa and Granny might, too."

"You want to come in and say hello to Aunt Bernie?" she asked.

"I can't stay but a minute. Grandpa was headed out to the fields after he waved goodbye to us," Nash said. "But it would seem rude not to at least speak to her since she let me have you for most of a day."

Clara led him into the living room, stopped dead in the doorway, and stared at her mother and grandmother. Surely she was hallucinating. Even if Myra or Luke died in a tragic accident, they would have called, not come all the way from Fritch to give her the news. "What...how...why?" she stammered.

"They surprised me, too," Bernie said. "They say they are going to the Paradise tomorrow to make nice with Mary Jane. I don't believe them for a minute."

"What are you doing here?" Clara finally got a full sentence out, and then remembered that Nash was still holding her hand. She turned to him and said, "I'm so sorry. This is my mother, Marsha, and my grandmother, Vernie Sue. Mama, this is Nash, who hopefully will be my boss when Aunt Bernie sells the Chicken Coop to him."

"Oh, I'm going to sell the bar to Nash all right, since he's proven that he loves it as much as I do," Bernie answered.

"It's right nice to meet y'all. You have a beautiful daughter, both inside and out. I have to go help get some hay into the barn this afternoon, or I would stick around a while," Nash said and planted another sweet kiss on Clara's cheek. "Darlin', call me later?"

She wrapped her arms around his neck and gave him a long, lingering, and very passionate kiss. "Take that to the field with you and think of me."

Nash grinned and nodded. "I would anyway, but I appreciate that little added bonus there."

When Clara heard the back door close, she crossed her arms over her chest and turned to face her mother and grandmother. "Now what in the hell are you doing here?"

"That is no way to talk to your elders, and don't use foul language when you ask me a question, and you shouldn't be kissing a man in front of us like that." Vernie Sue stopped and sucked in some air before she went on. "You were raised better than that, but I guess Bernie has taught you…"

"Whoa!" Clara held up a palm in protest. "Aunt Bernie has been nothing but kind to me. You are the one that taught me not to depend on relatives." Her blood was nearing the boiling point, and if they bad-mouthed Bernie again, she would show them exactly what kind of blistering hot words could really roll out of her mouth.

"You are unappreciative and…" Vernie Sue started again.

"Shut up, Mama," Marsha said and then stood up, crossed the room, and wrapped her arms around Clara. "I'm sorry about that. I came to tell you that I'm sorry for my behavior, not fight with you. And Mama has gone back on her word to be civil, so I'll apologize for her, too."

Clara's whole body went stiff. She couldn't make herself wrap her arms around her mother and forgive her for the past, no matter how hard she tried.

Marsha stepped back and sighed. "I guess a simple apology isn't enough."

"I told you so," Vernie Sue snapped. "She's just like Bernie—unforgiving and mean."

"Thank you for that," Clara said. "I'll take it as a wonderful compliment."

"Let's go home to Fritch," Vernie Sue said. "I don't imagine we'll get any better reception at that brothel where Mary Jane lives."

"A private word, Clara?" Bernie asked in a quiet voice as she stood and led the way to the kitchen.

Clara followed her but kept going right on out to the backyard. "Aunt Bernie, what is really going on? Why are they here?"

"Your mama feels real sorry about the way she has treated you," Bernie answered. "You need to give her a little consideration. You don't have to forgive her all at one time, but remember, honey, you can eat an elephant a bite at a time. So just take a small bite today, and maybe another one on down the road. She's made the effort to drive all the way from Fritch, so you should hear her out and ignore Vernie Sue."

"I will listen to her because you asked me to, but it won't be easy." She headed back into the living room, pulling a ladder-back kitchen chair behind her. She stopped right beside Bernie's recliner and sat down. "I'm listening to whatever you have to say, Mama, as long as Nana doesn't butt in. But I have a question before you start, and I want an honest answer. What did I ever do to any of you for the whole family to make me feel like I wasn't good enough to even be a servant in it?"

"It's a long story, and one that I hoped I would never have to tell you, but I will be honest." Marsha blushed. "I'll do the best I can to keep it short. It's something I've never told anyone, not even your grandmother."

Bernie sat down in her recliner and popped the footrest up. "I thought you two shared everything—peas-in-a-pod type of thing."

"I was afraid she would throw me to the curb, and I was right because a few years later, she practically disowned Mary Jane for getting a divorce," Marsha admitted.

"You and Daddy almost got a divorce?" Clara gasped.

"That's right," Marsha said. "But when I married your father, I was determined to make it work, even after he retaliated for something that he thought happened by having an affair."

Clara felt like her mind was on a roller coaster that was about to spin out of control. "He did what?"

Vernie Sue clutched her chest like she was about to have a heart attack. "I don't believe you."

"Oh, stop being so damn dramatic," Bernie scolded.

Marsha rolled her eyes and went on. "We had Luke and then Myra, and we were definitely through having children. Myra was five and Luke was eight. We were both busy with our careers and having to depend on your grandmother too often to help us out with the children. Your father had a vasectomy, and a couple of weeks later, I went on a job that kept me away from home for two months. I came home pregnant. He accused me of sleeping with one of my coworkers and didn't think that you were his child, so…" She paused, and tears filled her eyes. "He had an affair with an old high-school girlfriend."

"Sweet Jesus!" Vernie Sue gasped. "Did you?"

"No, Mama, I did not," Marsha snapped, "but for you to ask that question hurts me. Toby thought I did, so he didn't believe me until Clara was born and we had a DNA test done." She looked across the room at Clara. "That's when he went back to the doctor, which was something he was supposed to do not long after the surgery but canceled the appointment. He found out that he was still fertile. Because of his issues, the whole time I was pregnant, he didn't ever bond with you like he did the other two kids, and I was working so much, and…" she shrugged. "That's not an excuse and is barely a reason, but there it is. We didn't want another child, and we didn't do right by you. I'm truly sorry for all of it, but most of all for letting your grandmother warp my mind about Bernie, then about me and your aunt. I hope that in time you can forgive me."

"I did not do that," Vernie Sue declared. "I could see that Clara was the outcast, and I tried to steer her in the right direction."

Bernie chose that moment to speak up. "You should have just given her to me from the beginning. I would have loved raising a little girl, and I would have let her go in whatever direction she wanted."

This was absolutely too much for Clara to take in. It made sense, but it was a bittersweet story. She was the unwanted child, and the very one who had almost split up her parents. "I need to process this, but I thank you for being honest with me, Mama."

"That's fair enough," Marsha said. "I hope it's not too late for us to build a relationship. I promise to be more open-minded about your life choices."

"Well!" Vernie Sue huffed and glared at Marsha. "I'm not so sure it's fair to me. Why didn't you tell me all this when it was going on?"

"Mother, think back to those days. Mary Jane was already having marital problems and you were against her divorcing Martin. I was in the same boat, and you were helping with Clara while I was gone with my job. I had another five years before I could retire, and I was trying to work things out in my marriage. What would you have done?" Marsha asked. "You had practically disowned your own sister for embarrassing you. You don't even have to answer because we both know that you would have done the same with me that you vowed to do with Mary Jane if she got a divorce, kept writing trashy books, and moved into an old brothel. I wanted you to still love me as much as you always did my brother."

Vernie Sue turned and stared at the wall.

Clara expected her grandmother to spew out words like she did when Clara was a little girl and made Nana Vernie Sue angry. She could almost hear them even yet.

*Girl, you are acting just like Bernie, who has disgraced the whole family. If you don't straighten up, I am not going to keep you anymore for your mother. She should have never let her college professor talk her into applying for a job with the government. Her place is being home and raising a family like I did.*

Her chest felt like an elephant was lying on it, and her heart hurt for her mother. She had been through so much, and all she wanted was for her own mama to love her. Clara knew that feeling well.

"I'm sorry you had to go through all this, Mama, but most of all I feel your pain in thinking you had to be good for Nana Vernie Sue. It's a heavy burden. Why did you…"

Marsha held up her right palm and swiped at tears rolling down her cheeks with the other hand. "It took years for your father and me to get past our issues, and I tried to be there for you. I can see now that I made the wrong choices and hope that someday you can forgive me. I can't go back and undo what's happened, but going forward, I will do my best to be the mother I should have been all along."

Bernie chose that moment to reach across the distance separating her from Clara and lay her hand on her great-niece's arm. "Sometimes we are given a set of circumstances that we don't choose, but in the end, they lead us to a wonderful life."

Clara thought about the amazing time she had had

with Nash, not only that day but ever since she first walked into the bar with him. Were all the events that had led her down the path to Ratliff City worth the reward at the end of the journey?

"Yes," she whispered, not only to Bernie's question, but to the one in her own mind.

Vernie Sue finally turned back to face her daughter. Black tears streamed down her wrinkled face, and her chin quivered. "I'm sorry, Marsha, and Bernie, I have not been a good sister or Christian woman. Are we too old to make a clean start? Will you ever be able to forgive me?"

"Like I told Clara in the kitchen, you can eat an elephant a bite at a time. I can forgive, but I'll have to work on the forgetting part. Are you going to throw me out of the next family reunion if I wear this shirt?" Bernie asked.

"I will try my best to accept you as you are," Vernie Sue answered. "But I do have one question. Clara, why are you dating such an old man?"

"He's only thirty-five," Bernie answered for Clara. "He got all that gorgeous gray hair prematurely."

Vernie Sue sniffed the air and snarled her nose. "I'd have to see his birth certificate to believe that."

"And Aunt Mary Jane?" Clara ignored her grandmother. "We heard in church this morning about forgiveness. Jesus didn't judge anyone, so what right do we have to put ourselves on a pedestal and look down on anyone?"

"Yes, I will do better," Vernie Sue nodded. "I've missed a lifetime of making memories."

"Choices and consequences." Clara wondered if she had fallen asleep or been in a trance the past hour. If so, she sure hoped that when she awoke, the past few weeks were real and not a part of the dream. "We make the choices and then we have to live with the consequences," she finally said. "I've got a feeling that this feuding among sisters might go back further than any of y'all can imagine. Did Great Granny have a sister?"

"Three of them," Vernie answered. "And her mother had five sisters."

"I'd say it's time for all of us to break the tradition," Clara said. "Seems to me like it's gone on long enough."

"Out of the mouths of babes," Bernie said.

"I have learned a lot from you," Clara told her with a smile. "I'm glad my path brought me here. I'm happier than I have ever been."

Bernie swiped at a tear with a tissue and then tossed the box across the room. "Vernie Sue, you better go to the bathroom and look in the mirror before you head down to Spanish Fort. You've got black mascara streaks in your wrinkles."

Vernie Sue nodded and stood up. "I may be a mess, but that's minor compared to the disaster that we've all made for the past decades. I won't promise I will change overnight. I'm too set in my ways for that, but I'll give it my best shot to do better. How about we order some of that pizza for supper—my treat—and have a real visit?"

"Why don't you get out that box of pictures that you are taking with you to the Paradise, Aunt Bernie?" Clara asked.

Bernie's blush was as red as her hair. "I guess that would be the ultimate test of whether Vernie Sue will stay in touch with me or if we go our separate ways."

Clara giggled, more out of nervousness than humor. "Bring them on, and no matter what, I'm sticking with you."

# Chapter 16

BERNIE GLANCED AT THE feed store calendar hanging on the kitchen wall that Saturday morning and knew the time had come to give Nash a definite answer. Where had the past three weeks gone? It seemed like only yesterday that Nash, Hershal, and Clara walked into her bar, each of them with a different problem.

The six days since Vernie Sue and Marsha had been there had seemed to speed by so quickly that Bernie got dizzy just thinking about it. She and Vernie Sue had talked on the phone once since her sister had gone back to Fritch, and Bernie figured out really quick that some old dogs couldn't be taught new tricks. Especially Vernie Sue—bless her heart! But at least the old gal had turned her venomous bite toward a couple of women in her church and was leaving Marsha and Mary Jane alone, as well as Bernie and Clara. That was a blessing right there. She and Vernie Sue might never be the sisters they could have been, but Bernie was willing to work with what she had.

"And after all, she lives five hours from me now, and

six when I get moved," she told Pepper as she opened the back door and followed him outside.

He ran off into the woods, and she carefully eased down into a lawn chair, being careful not to spill a drop of coffee from her full cup. "Everything I can't bear to leave behind is packed into boxes, so why wait another three weeks? I called my lawyer yesterday, and he has the papers ready to sign," she muttered between sips of coffee.

Pepper ran across the yard like a mountain lion was chasing him, stopped right at her feet, and barked. She set her mug on the ground and picked him up. "We are going to do just fine in Spanish Fort at the Paradise. I figure you'll have to be on a leash more than you are now, mainly because in the beginning I didn't care if one of those squirrels out there in the woods had you for dinner. But you've grown on me, and you are a damn fine listener. I promise to take you for a long walk every day and not let Mary Jane's cat claw your eyes out."

The dog curled up in her lap and went to sleep. Bernie leaned over and picked up her coffee and took a sip. "I've talked to myself so long that I'll have to be careful when we get settled in. I might tell secrets that need to be buried with me."

Pepper snored, and she giggled.

"What's so funny?" Clara asked as she came out the back door with a cup of steaming-hot coffee in her hands. "Do you want a heat up? I'll go back in and get the pot if you do."

"No, I'm fine, but I've made a definite decision about selling the bar. You and I just need to visit about your plans before I put it on stone," she said. "Sit down and tell me if you really want to stay here or if you are having doubts and want to go to the Paradise with me. If you and Nash are getting as serious as it looks like to me, remember that it's only an hour to Spanish Fort, and that's close enough that you won't even have to call it long-distance dating."

"Aunt Bernie," Clara answered without even a second's hesitation, "I love you and my Aunt Mary Jane, and I'm glad she and Mama are taking baby steps toward mending things between you. But I don't want to go with you. I want to stay here with Nash."

"How serious are things between y'all?" Bernie asked.

"Let's just say that I'm glad the walls of the bar can't talk." Clara gave her a broad wink. "I'm going to church with him and his grandparents tomorrow morning and the hay barn might be *the place*. If you are selling to him, we'll be living in the same apartment, but quite possibly not the same bedroom. Does that answer your question?"

"Yes, it does, and Madam Fate is telling me to call the lawyer. I'll discuss it with you kids tonight at the cigar therapy session," she answered.

*I've done it,* Bernie thought. *My first mission has been a success.*

"Okay, who wants to go first tonight?" Bernie lit up the remains of the last half of her cigar, crooked her finger around it, and took a long puff.

"I believe it's your turn," Clara told her. "We kind of hit on our stories after you went inside last week."

"All right, then, you pretty well know all that I'm willing to tell you about my life, so I'll just get right to it," Bernie said. "It hasn't been the full six weeks, Nash, but I can see that you love this place as much as I do, so I'm ready to sell it to you. The lawyer has the papers drawn up, and if all parties are willing for the conditions, we will sign them Monday morning at ten o'clock right here at the Chicken Coop. Everything will be transferred at the signing. Insurance on the place is paid up until January first of next year, and that will be included in the sale."

"Fantastic," Nash said. "I'll be here with my checkbook."

"Not so quick!" Bernie said sternly. "I said we would make the transfer if all parties were willing for the conditions, and you didn't even ask me how much I wanted for the building, land, and business."

"I don't care about the cost. If I don't have enough in my savings account, Grandpa said he would come in as a silent partner," Nash told her.

"I don't think he'll have to do that, because I'm only going to sell you half the place," Bernie said.

Clara's eyes lit up. "Does that mean you are going to stick around and still own the other half?"

"Sorry to disappoint, darlin' girl," Bernie said with a smile. "No, I'm retiring and leaving Monday afternoon if this works for you kids, right after we make a trip to the tag agency and put my old truck in your name. I'm giving you the other half, Clara. You and Nash are going to be full partners in this business. You have proven your worth these past weeks, and I can see that you are happy."

"I love that idea," Nash said.

"But…you've done so much… Why…" Clara stammered and then started weeping. "It's too much, Aunt Bernie."

"Dry up those tears and just say thank you," Bernie said and blew out a whole string of smoke rings. "My favorite nieces would inherit what I leave behind anyway. This way you just get it before I'm dead instead of having to wait. I don't want you to ever feel like you are less than anyone on the face of this earth again."

Clara swiped the tears away with the back of her hand. "Then thank you. You were right when you said that the toughest pathway often leads us to the place that will be our biggest joy. Maybe not in those exact words, but that's what I got from it."

"Good enough," Bernie said. "Now that is decided, we can get on with our whiskey and cigars."

"You could stick around until the full six weeks is up," Nash suggested.

"Y'all have proven that you can run this place, and now that I've made up my mind, I'm ready to go. I'll always remember the Chicken Coop, but I've only got so many years left and a lot to get accomplished in whatever days the good Lord sees fit to leave me here," Bernie told them. "Before that signing process, Clara and I will be at the tag agency when it opens so that we can get my old truck signed over to her. After we make the transfer, I'm going to wave goodbye and head to Texas. Seems only fitting that I was born and raised up in Spanish Fort, and I'll be going back there to finish out my life. But what was in the middle, that part from womb to tomb, is where all my good memories are stored. I'm hoping that y'all are always as happy as you are now, and as I have been while I've been here."

Nash reached across the distance and took Clara's hand in his. "Down deep in my heart, I feel like we will be, and thank you for doing this."

"You are both welcome. I'm going inside now, and I will be ready for church services in the morning when you come by for Clara. Seems only fitting that I tell the friends I have there a proper goodbye."

"Will you go to dinner with us?" Nash asked.

"I'd be glad to, but I do not want any special treatment. No happy retirement parties or tears when I leave. Let's all just put on our best smiles and wave as I drive away. You'll open up the bar, and I'll be at the Paradise when evening comes. Unless"—she chuckled—"you have plans to move into the apartment all afternoon and enjoy a little time alone behind closed doors?"

"Aunt Bernie!" Clara's eyes widened out the size of saucers.

"Don't tell me you both didn't already think of that," she scolded. "On that note, I bid you both a good night. I need my beauty sleep if I'm going to be ready for church."

"Good night." Clara let go of Nash's hand, stood up, and wrapped her arms around Bernie in a fierce hug. "You are an angel," she whispered softly.

"Not yet, darlin', but I hope that when I draw my last breath, the good Lord sees fit to give me wings to fly," Bernie said around the lump in her throat.

# Chapter 17

PAPERS WERE ALL SIGNED, and all that was left for Bernie to do at noon was get into her new truck and start driving toward Spanish Fort. The kids stayed true to her wishes and stood at the door of the Chicken Coop and waved until she made the corner and couldn't see them anymore. That's when the waterworks let go and she began to weep so hard that she pulled over on the side of the road a few miles out of town and let it all loose. Pepper hopped up on the console, put his little paws on her shoulder, and licked the tears from her face. Half a box of tissues later, she took a deep breath, put the truck in drive, and set her face like flint.

"You are a good friend, Pepper, but now I've had my fifteen minutes of whining, and it's over. I had many good years in the Chicken Coop, and I know it's time to pass the bar on to those kids who already love it as much as I do." She hiccupped a couple of times, took a sip of her lukewarm coffee, and inhaled deeply. "If we ain't movin', we're standing still, and old age grows on those folks who come to a screeching halt."

Pepper yipped once, lay back down on the passenger's seat, and closed his eyes.

"I'll take that as a yes, you are in agreement with me." She put the truck in gear and pulled back out onto the highway. When she crossed the Highway 70 junction, she was berating herself for not letting Nash and Clara give her a going-away party.

"I love parties, and I could have dressed up," she muttered. "I could have worn different pieces from all my costumes. The pants from Labor Day, the top from Easter, and maybe the hat from Veterans Day to celebrate all the years I owned the Chicken Coop, but oh no! I had to be all brave and tell them not to make a fuss."

She thought of what Joe Clay told her the first time she drove down to Spanish Fort. "Don't blink or you'll miss it."

"That's pretty much the story of Cornish except that I just blinked, and it's already gone." To keep her mind off what she had left behind, she switched on the radio.

Blake Shelton singing "Goodbye Time" filled the truck. Pepper put a paw over his ears, but Bernie didn't turn down the volume. The song was about a woman who left a man, but it seemed fitting that afternoon as she saw the sign on the Oklahoma side of the Taovayas Bridge over the Red River. She stopped the truck. When she crossed over to the other side, she would be in Texas.

"A lifetime behind me that accounts for more years than the one in front of me. This is it, Pepper. When I moved into the apartment at the Chicken Coop, I swore I would never go back to Texas." She took the last two sips of her coffee. "There, I just swallowed my words. It's better than getting old and going to a nursing home. I've always heard that life is what you make it. So, good-bye, Oklahoma, and look out, Texas! Mary Bernadette is about to enter the state, and it will never be the same."

She drove across the bridge without a single glance in her rearview mirror.

Pepper hopped back onto the console and was focused on the road ahead the rest of the way. Bernie reached over and scratched his ears, and said, "I don't know if you can read English, old boy, but if you can, that sign back there said, 'Welcome to Texas,' and the little one under it said, 'Don't Mess with Texas.' That doesn't mean something ugly, but it's a warning not to throw litter out on the car window or you will get fined. This ain't *The Wizard of Oz*, and you ain't Dorothy or even Toto, but I can truthfully tell you that you are not in Oklahoma anymore. You are a Texan now, so get ready for a different world."

He wagged his tail and kept his eyes straight ahead.

"Yes, there are squirrels and even rabbits where we are going. You are going to love it there." Bernie wasn't sure if she was trying to convince the dog or herself.

In a few minutes she flicked on the turn signal to turn up the lane lined with pecan trees. No one was on the front porch, so she figured she and Pepper could sneak back to her trailer and unload her things before she even went up to the Paradise to see Mary Jane.

When she rounded the end of big house, she braked so fast that poor old Pepper flew off the console and landed in the passenger seat. A huge banner hung across the front porch posts that Joe Clay had built onto her trailer. She hadn't expected both a porch in the front and a deck on the back overlooking a wooded area, but there they were with a big WELCOME HOME, AUNT BERNIE written in sparkling red letters.

People were everywhere and the aroma of barbecue came right into the truck through the air conditioner vents. She rubbed her eyes, unsure if they were working right, but nothing changed. Finally, Joe Clay carried over a long length of red carpet and stretched it out from the truck to a table where Mary Jane waited behind a chair that resembled a throne. He opened the door and offered her his hand.

"My job is to lead you to the place of honor," he told her. "So, get a leash on your companion over there, and let's go."

"If I'd known there was going to be a party, I would have dressed up," she whispered as she snapped the leash onto Pepper's collar and put her hand in Joe Clay's.

"This is just a gathering," he said out the corner of his mouth. "We didn't know until Saturday that you would be coming today, so this is the best we could do on short notice."

Mary Jane rounded the end of the table with Endora and Luna right behind her. "We are so glad you are finally here," she said as she hugged Bernie and then stepped to the side. "Come on around and have a seat. This is the chair we use at Christmas for Santa Claus, but today it is Queen Bernie's throne."

Endora wrapped Bernie up in another hug. "I'll make you a plate."

"And I will sit beside you and get your dessert when you are ready," Luna told her after a third hug. "We plan to take lots of pictures, and it won't be easy not to show them to the other five sisters, but we will keep your secret. Can you at least tell us why you don't want Ursula or the others to know?"

"I want to surprise them all," she said around the big lump in her throat. "Did Clara tell you…"

"Yep, she did," Mary Jane answered. "But don't you fuss at her. We want you to meet the folks who have hung on here in Spanish Fort with the hopes that some-day it will be back to its former glory, only without the gunfights and brothels."

"Bless that sweet child's heart," Bernie said.

# Chapter 18

THE TWINS, ENDORA AND Luna, assured Bernie just before Thanksgiving that, even though it was the toughest secret they had ever had to keep, none of the other five sisters knew that she had moved to Spanish Fort. Ursula had finished her teaching job and should be there before lunch. Bo was flying in from Nashville. Rae, Ophelia, and Tertia were all driving and planned to be home by suppertime.

More than an hour ago, Bernie had snuck a little Jameson in her sweet tea and had claimed a rocking chair on the front porch to wait for the oldest Simmons girl to get home. She wanted to be one of the first to welcome Ursula home for the holidays. Little, other than this secret, had gone the way she planned since she left Ratliff City. She had thought she would get a phone call a few weeks after moving to the Paradise and Clara would tell her that Nash had proposed.

She had hoped that Clara would ask her to be the maid of honor, but oh no, that's not the way things went at all. One of the first weekly calls that Clara made was to tell Bernie that Hoot's brother, who never married or had children, had passed away and left his small farm up near Shattuck, Oklahoma, to Hoot and Darlene. They had been talking about downsizing for a while, and they would like to move up there, but they didn't want to live more than two hundred miles from the kids.

Then, as if Fate made the decision for them, the Chicken Coop caught on fire a couple of weeks later and burned to the ground.

Clara was inconsolable when she called to tell Bernie the news. "The fire department folks said a squirrel must have gotten into the attic and chewed through some electrical wires," she said between sobs. "When the blaze reached the storage room and the bar, the liquor fueled the fire even more, and it went in a hurry. Oh, Aunt Bernie, I am so, so sorry."

"Nothing to be sorry about, darlin'. Move to northern Oklahoma and start a new bar," Bernie told her. "The Universe has spoken, and we could argue with it until we turn blue, but once its mind is made up, nothing can change it, not even a block of C4."

"Aren't you sad?" Clara asked.

"I am, but we both have our memories. Did you save any of your personal things?"

"Not even what was left of the old cigar," Clara said between sobs.

"Dry your eyes. Kiss Nash and tell him everything is going to be all right. You have both started over before, more than once, so take the insurance money, buy a new bar, take a trip before you settle in to working, and never look back. Think about the happiness you have with Nash, and move on," Bernie told her.

Then, as luck would have it, a small bar not three miles from Hoot's new farm came up for sale. Pepper's Place, named for the man who built it twenty years before and made a drink with jalapeño peppers floating on the top, was located just over the border from a dry county in Texas, and that made the decision for the whole family. Hoot sold his ranch in Ratliff City, and on Bernie's okay, the kids donated the land where the Chicken Coop had been all those years to the city for a brand-new volunteer fire department building. Hoot chipped in a chunk of money to buy them a new shiny red truck.

"The Universe spoke and Fate agreed. Yes, I wept a little at the idea of the bar being gone, but the Good Book says, 'ashes to ashes and dust to dust.' I just mourned and grieved like I would at any good friend's funeral, but when I thought about it, everything seemed fitting," Bernie told Pepper, who growled at the cat who thought she owned the Paradise porch. "They each owned half of the Chicken Coop. Now they own Pepper's Place together. It's like two halves now make a whole, and even though I didn't get to be in the wedding, I'm glad that they got married in Vegas just before they took over the new bar. The name of the place seemed like an omen to me and Clara both, especially when they found that it had an antique jukebox in it with a whole collection of records so they can change them out."

Pepper growled at the cat again, and she flopped down under another rocking chair.

"You'll get her trained, but it will take a while," Bernie assured him and lowered her voice to barely a whisper. "Maybe you'll get that job done by the time I get Ursula and Remy together. It took some doing for me to get him over here today, but I finagled it just right. If I can get a bawling great-niece of mine and a sexy, silver-haired feller together, then this should be a piece of cake. And besides, Pepper, my boy, Remy lives right next door. That's as good as it gets. Mary Jane will have another of her girls close by, and maybe even have her first grandbaby by the time another Thanksgiving rolls around.

"I hear a vehicle coming down the lane. I'm so excited that I could dance a jig right here on the porch." She shaded her eyes with the back of her hand. "Yep, I believe it's Ursula, and here come Joe Clay and Remy around the end of the house. The Universe is with us today and life is good, Pepper. Even though I grieved when the Chicken Coop burned, I've moved on. Now it's time to work my magic on Ursula and Remy."

# THE
# MATCHMAKERS

# Chapter 1

"THIS ONE IS GOING to be successful," Minnie said as she and her two friends, Sookie and Dotty, got in line to go through customs so they could board the cruise ship. "I can feel it in my bones."

Minnie was just under six feet tall and had gray hair that she kept cut short and blue eyes set in a bed of wrinkles in her slim face. Built on the slender side, she hated anything that made her sweat and loved good food. Her motto was that she would eat what she wanted and die when the good Lord saw fit to take her, and bless her heart, she never gained a pound.

"You said that last time, and it was our first failure in six months, but then it could be your arthritis talking to you, not your intuition," Sookie told her as the three of them moved forward a few feet. Today's group moved along at a pretty good clip, but it still seemed to take forever to get to the customs desk. Boarding and then deboarding was the only bad thing they'd found about living on one cruise ship after another since they had sold their homes and refused to go to an assisted-living center.

"Oh, hush that kind of talk." Minnie shook a finger at her friend. "You'll jinx our next mission, and we depend on you to make the plan once I spot a target."

"I already see my target," Dotty whispered and nodded toward a tall, dark-haired man in the line next to them. "He looks absolutely miserable, doesn't he?"

Dotty's green eyes sparkled with orneriness. Her honey-blond hair did not have a single gray in it because she was as careful to keep them plucked out as she was to keep her light-brown eyebrows. She claimed that good genes and DNA kept her round face from being wrinkled, but if the truth were told, it was the fact that she loved food as much as Minnie did and carried around twenty extra pounds. Her theory was that if she ever got sick, she could depend on the extra weight to keep her from dying.

"So does that cowboy over there…" Minnie started and then shook her head when a tall blond joined him and planted a kiss on his lips.

"I'd say that he's taken," Dotty said with a giggle. "I'll bet you ten bucks they're on their honeymoon."

"I see a sparkling new ring on her left hand and a wide gold band on his." Minnie sighed. "I guess it'll have to be Mr. Tall, Dark, and Lonesome. I don't see a wedding ring on his hand, so you're off to a good start, Dotty. Maybe we'll have good success on this trip."

"I see a white ring around his left ring finger. He could possibly be ready for a rebound," Dotty whispered as they moved forward in the line.

Sookie eyed him closely. "I'm not sure about him, my friend. We like to see more than rebounds. We want the cake, the dress, and the whole thing when we put a couple together. It's like half the job is done if it's nothing but a booty call."

"And you'd know a lot about those booty calls," Minnie teased.

"Of course, I would. Being middle-aged doesn't mean I've already got one foot in the casket." Sookie tucked a strand of brown hair—compliments of the hair stylist on whatever ship they had been on when she needed her roots touched up—back behind an ear. Cut chin length, her hair matched her milk-chocolate-colored eyes. She had jogged since she was a teenager and had a firm body to prove it, and nowadays, she always spent an hour every morning in the ship's fitness room and then jogged up and down the staircases several times.

"Middle-aged?" Dotty snorted. "Seventy-five is a little past that."

"Not if I plan to live to be a hundred and fifty," Sookie eyed Mr. Tall, Dark, and Lonesome out of the corner of her eye.

"Well, we've got eight days. If we can't make a match in that time, we should give up our snowbirds-in-residence status and check into an assisted-living place," Minnie said. "Looks like we're next in line. Are we ready for another cruise?"

"Hell, yeah!" Sookie and Dotty high-fived each other.

"Are we ready for another challenge?" Sookie asked.

"Damn straight!" Dotty and Minnie gave her the thumbs-up sign.

"Who's ready for a drink at the launch party?" Dotty asked.

All three hands went up.

"Next." The lady at the front of the line motioned for Sookie to go to the left.

While she handed her passport to the woman behind the computer, Dotty was sent to the right and Minnie to the left. The three of them were veterans at this business, so in just a few minutes they were on their way up the ramp and onto the ship. This time Minnie and Dotty were bunking together, and Sookie had a room all to herself. Minnie and Dotty had a balcony, and Sookie got an inside room, but for the most part, she would only be sleeping and changing clothing in the smaller cabin anyway. That's the way they had been handling things from the beginning when the three of them had decided that living on a cruise ship wasn't as expensive as an assisted-living care center.

All cabins were double occupancy, but having a stranger for a roommate wouldn't be much better than living in assisted living. To save money, one of them took the inside room on each cruise, and the other two got a balcony room. That way, no two of them would get tired of living together, and to make it fair, they added up the cost of the whole trip and split the price between them.

"We'll get our luggage in the room and meet you for the safety event, and then we'll head on up to the lido deck for the launch party." Dotty hit the button on the elevator to take them up to their deck. "And no letting Henry talk you into sharing your room with him on this cruise."

"Not a snowball's chance in hell, but Mr. Tall and Dark might be a different story altogether," Sookie said with a broad wink toward both other women. "I bet I could teach that hunky young man a few things that he would never forget, and all the women he'd spend time with after that would drop down on their knees and thank me."

"Good God!" Minnie gasped. "He's young enough to be your grandson, if you had one."

"Yep, and I bet he wouldn't break a hip if he fell out of a bed," Sookie winked again and stepped out of the elevator when the doors slid open. "And I'm the one with a big bed. Y'all have to sleep on twin beds this go around."

"Remember you're seventy-five years old, so you might be the one breaking a hip while you're trying to keep up with a thirty-year-old man," Dotty said as she and Minnie got out of the elevator.

"Like I told you before, old don't mean dead," Sookie teased.

"No, but it means we're supposed to show good common sense." Minnie sighed.

"I'll pay him when the cruise is over." Sookie's deep southern voice sounded like she had been a long-time smoker, even though she'd never smoked either cigarettes or weed. Her friends didn't know that she did occasionally eat a gummy bear—for medicinal purposes only—when her knees hurt from exercise. "That's good common sense, isn't it?"

The three of them rounded a corner, and only a few doors down, they found their rooms were right across the narrow hall from each other and just a little way from the laundry.

"We decided we were done with men," Minnie said as she rolled her luggage out of the hall and into the cabin.

"Done with them forever, amen, or just done with marrying one?" Sookie asked.

"Forever, amen," Minnie and Dotty chorused together.

"Well, then I guess I'll have to just dream about that pretty boy." Sookie opened the door to her cabin and flipped on the light.

"Go on and get your stuff put away," Dotty said. "They'll be calling our floor for the safety thing soon, and we'd better not find a scarf tied to the door when we come back."

"I'll use the Do Not Disturb sign if I snag a little young thing who needs some training." Sookie tried to get in the last word.

"A young guy could kill you, woman," Minnie said.

"But what a way to die." Sookie closed the door before either of them could smart off again.

———

"You'd think as many cruises as we've been on that we could just show them our green card and skip this part. I could put a life jacket on with my eyes closed," Sookie muttered as she rolled her suitcase into the tiny closet area.

She enjoyed every third cruise when she got a room to herself. She had always been a night owl, and she treasured those couple of hours in the evening when she had complete peace and quiet. By the end of the cruise, she'd be ready for a roommate for a couple of cruises, but for this weeklong trip to the Caribbean, she was grateful for time alone.

After this one they'd fly to Seattle, spend a day seeing the sights for the third time, and then board a ship headed for Alaska. She would have ten days to plot out a matchmaking plan then, but this time she would have to get the job done in only seven, or else they'd have two failures in a row—and they had never had that much bad luck.

She opened her suitcase, hung up her clothing, and put her underwear and nightshirts in a drawer. Then she took her toiletries into the small bathroom. She didn't mind living out of a suitcase—it was really kind of exciting—but she did miss her huge, oversized bathroom in the house that she had sold six months ago. That's when she, Dotty, and Minnie hatched this plan to be snowbirds in residence on cruise ships instead of going to a senior independent living place. Just because they had all turned seventy-five didn't mean they were ready for a rocking chair.

Sookie remembered the conversation that they'd had when Minnie and Dotty asked her to join them. She'd already been trying to think of ways to have more fun than moving into one of those assisted-living homes, and their idea seemed to be perfect.

"It's cheaper than those places that senior citizens go," Minnie had done her research before she presented the plan to the other two, "and we don't have to cook, clean, or even make our own beds."

"I've heard that the food is excellent," Dotty had said.

Minnie had whipped out a fistful of brochures and laid them on the table. "And if we watch the sales and book in advance, we get a free drink ticket, too. There's always entertainment, and God knows, it'll beat having the same people around us all the time."

"Pushing walkers and watching reruns on the television in the nursing home lobby." Dotty nodded.

"I'm in," Sookie said. "Where do I sign? I want to slide up to the Pearly Gates with every ounce of me used completely up. I'll be hollerin' for someone to open the gates and let me tell them all about the wonderful life I had the last few years."

"You're the planner among us," Minnie had said. "We want you to do the logistics. That means figuring out how to go from one ship to another for at least three months. We need you to plan where we'll be staying in a hotel for a night or two between our cruises, and the flights or transportation to and from ships."

"I can do that." Sookie had nodded.

The captain's voice came over the intercom system, telling everyone on their deck to go to the auditorium for the thirty-minute safety class and jerking Sookie back to the present. The loud knock on the door caused her to grab her sparkly lanyard with her room key on it, slip it over her neck, and cross the floor.

"I'm ready," she said. "Let's go get this over with so we can have a drink."

"I'm spitting dust," Minnie said, just like she always did before they were finished with the class and could head to the lido deck for the launch.

"I love the launch," Dotty said. "It's as exciting as a first date."

"You *remember* first dates?" Sookie asked. "I thought we were *old*."

"We are old, but our minds are as good as they were when we were teenagers," Dotty threw back at her. "If you hadn't had so many first dates, you might be excited."

"Oh, honey." Sookie's brown eyes twinkled. "Blanche on *Golden Girls* has been my role model for years. I don't let an opportunity to have a little fun pass me by."

"You look more like Rose with brown hair, or maybe that tall actress on *Hot in Cleveland*." Dotty led the way to where the safety course was being given.

"Add in that I'm smart like Dorothy, and I've got them all covered." Sookie flipped back her hair with a flourish.

Dotty nodded and frowned at the same time. "She's right, Minnie. She's managed to outrun Henry for the last four cruises, so she has to be pretty smart."

"Or maybe she hasn't," Minnie disagreed. "Maybe she's telling him exactly what ship we're boarding next, and she's just leading him on."

"Nope, I'm trying to get you fixed up with him, Minnie," Sookie teased.

Minnie laid a hand over her heart. "Sweet Lord! I had a good marriage and planned a good retirement with my sweet Walter! I most certainly do not want another husband!"

Sookie opened the door into the big auditorium and stood to the side. "You don't have to marry 'em, just because you sleep with 'em."

"I'd have to get a *Sex for Dummies* book to even know how to do that anymore," Minnie said, giggling.

"It's just like riding a bicycle. Once you get the wheels to rollin', you remember all about it," Sookie teased.

Dotty headed in first and took a seat. "I'll look around for a good candidate for the guy in our matchmaking game. I just know in my soul that the guy I pointed out is the one for this trip, but I want to be certain before I make a declaration."

"Well, honey," Sookie said in her Texas drawl, "I hope your soul hasn't been keeping company with the devil and is lying to you." She sat down beside Dotty and only listened to the demonstration with half an ear.

"You're the one who talks to the devil, not me," Dotty told her.

"I do not talk to the devil!" Sookie said. "I love Jesus, even though I drink a little and still enjoy a romp between the sheets."

Their matchmaking scheme had started on their fourth cruise when they'd befriended a single woman and introduced her to a guy that had been seated at their table one evening. They'd had so much fun putting the two of them together that they'd decided to try their hand at it again. Now it was a game that they had only lost twice in the past six months.

———

Dotty claimed a table for four on the lido deck while her two friends went to the bar. The band up on the next level played "It's Five O'Clock Somewhere," by Alan Jackson and Jimmy Buffet. Dotty checked the time on her phone and smiled. It really was after five, and the launch would be happening anytime now. Drinks were flowing and folks were having a good time. In a week, they'd be ready to go home, but today, everyone was excited to get underway.

Minnie and Sookie returned with drinks, and Minnie handed a dirty banana off to Dotty. "Here you go, girl. I don't know why you always order one of these for the launch party."

"It's my good luck charm. I didn't have one on the last cruise because y'all talked me into a strawberry daiquiri—and look where it got us. We failed in our mission to put a couple together. You didn't listen to me on the guy I picked out, either, so I went with a different one. My mojo was off, and it was all because I didn't have my dirty banana. I'm considering having another one to start off this launch to be sure we'll have good luck."

"Excuse me," a young woman said. "Is this chair taken, or would I be intruding? Seems like all the tables are full."

"Have a seat, darlin', and tell us your name." Dotty smiled at the cute little red-haired woman.

She raised a beer. "Ava Cargill."

"I'm Dotty, and this is Minnie, and that one over there eyeing every single man on the ship is Sookie. Glad to meet you, Ava."

Ava smiled, but it didn't reach her emerald-green eyes. "I won't challenge Sookie for any of the guys on this ship—or in the world for that matter. I'm done with all of them."

"That's good," Sookie said, "because with your looks, I wouldn't stand a chance if you set your sights on one of them."

Ava raised her can of beer. "Thank you for that. You've made my day. Is this your first cruise?"

"Oh no, honey, we're snowbirds with green cards," Dotty answered.

"What's that?" Ava asked.

"It means we live on cruise ships, and after so many trips, we got a green card saying we are residents," Minnie told her.

"That's the short form of it anyway," Sookie said. "Is this your first cruise?"

Ava nodded. "I'm supposed to be here celebrating my fifth anniversary with my husband, but we're taking some time apart. I decided to come on the cruise anyway."

"Getting away from the forest so you can see the trees?" Minnie asked.

"Yep, and I shouldn't be unloading on y'all," Ava said.

"Darlin'," Minnie said with a broad smile, "it's easier to unload on three old women than anyone else..."

"Oh! My! Goodness!" Ava had to swallow fast to keep from choking on a swallow of beer.

"Are you okay?" Dotty asked.

"I'm not sure," Ava shook her head and continued to stare across the deck. "That's my husband over there in the white shorts and blue shirt. I arranged this cruise to celebrate our fifth anniversary. I spent the night of our anniversary alone until about midnight because he had an important business event. He sent roses, but I'm sure he had his secretary call the florist. When I gave him my gift of this cruise, he said that he couldn't take a week off work. The next day I moved out of our house into a hotel." She shook her head. "And yet, here he is. I wonder why he's even here."

Dotty, Minnie, and Sookie followed Ava's gaze. She was nodding toward Mr. Tall, Dark, and Lonesome.

"I still love him even if he has broken my heart," Ava said with a sigh.

Dotty caught Minnie and Sookie's eyes. They had helped get lots and lots of relationships started, but not one time had they ever put one that was on the rocks back together. They smiled at one another, without a word, and accepted the challenge. With slight nods, they began to plan their next matchmaking job on this cruise.

# Chapter 2

ACCORDING TO THE BROCHURES Ava had almost memorized back when she was planning the trip as an anniversary present, there were about three thousand people on the ship. That meant it shouldn't be all that difficult to avoid Vince for a week. She had managed to avoid him for days on end in their two-story brick home in the suburbs of Dallas, and that house was a whole lot smaller than the big cruise ship. Of course, he had probably been avoiding her, too.

If he would just wake up and think about the dreams and hopes they'd shared in the beginning of their relationship, she'd walk—no, she would run—right back into his arms.

She picked up the phone and started to order breakfast brought to her room but put it down before anyone answered. She would not hide in her cabin or even pass the whole week sitting on the balcony. With a workaholic husband, she was used to eating alone, but she didn't intend to do so on this cruise. No, sir! She was going to the dining room, loading up her plate with all kinds of wonderful breakfast foods, and sitting among people. Maybe those sweet little old ladies she'd met at the launch party the evening before would be in the dining room, and she could visit with them a little more.

She dressed in white capris and a cute little hot-pink halter top, slipped her feet into a pair of pink-and-white polka-dotted flip-flops, and pulled her red hair up into a messy bun on top of her head. She didn't bother with makeup because when she finished eating, she planned to claim a chaise on the top deck and get some sun. Within thirty minutes, she would sweat off any makeup and every one of her dozens of freckles would shine forth like stars in a dark sky anyway.

She took the stairs rather than the elevator, since passing Vince going up to the lido deck would be easier than getting stuck with him in a tiny cubicle. Walking into the dining hall, she smiled when she noticed all three ladies waving at her and pointing to the fourth chair at their table. Her mood lifted, and she forgot about the problems she and Vince had for a few seconds as she made her way around other tables full of people and sat down in the empty chair. She loved him too much to put him completely out of her mind. That was just a fact.

"Y'all are so sweet to invite me to join you," Ava said.

"Anytime, honey," Sookie answered and then lowered her voice. "You're doing me a big favor by sitting with us. There's an elderly gentleman who's been flirting with me—God love his soul—and although I appreciate the fact that he finds me beautiful, I'm just not interested in a relationship with some old guy who I'd have to take care of later in life."

"And besides all that, if she got all tangled up with Henry, she would be thinking about putting down roots instead of using her wings to fly," Dotty said. "We made a pact when we left our homes behind that we wouldn't let a man come between us."

"Like that old song says about 'Lord help the mister who comes between me and my sister,'" Sookie said. "We are closer than any blood sisters could ever be. We've helped each other through tears, fears, marriages, PMS, menopause, joys, and sorrows."

Ava thought of her blood sister. They hadn't done anything but argue and bicker their whole lives. "I see," she said with a nod. "But what's all that got to do with me sitting at the table?"

Dotty patted her on the shoulder. "It's like this on a ship, darlin'. If there's an empty chair at a table, it's impolite to tell someone they can't sit in it, so when you join us, you are really helping us old ladies out."

"Please don't wait for us to invite you. Just consider the fourth chair yours anytime you see us," Minnie said.

"Thank you so much." Ava picked up the menu and had already made her choice when the waiter reached their table.

When they had all ordered, Ava picked up her glass

of water and took a long drink. "So, what's on your agenda for this first day we're at sea?"

"The same as all our first days," Sookie said. "We go out on the deck, watch the people, and make up stories about them until midmorning, when we have an order of fries and a milkshake for a snack."

"After that, we go back to our lounges and plan whether or not we'll do any excursions on this cruise," Minnie chimed in.

The waiter returned with four cups and a full carafe of coffee that he left on the table.

Dotty poured for all of them, and said, "After lunch, we go to our cabins for our afternoon nap or to sit on the balcony and read. Then we meet up on the lido deck to watch the pool people and have an afternoon drink."

"And you, darlin', are welcome to join us anytime that you want," Dotty told her.

"Or while these two *old* ladies nap and read, you can join me in the exercise room," Sookie offered. "I run up and down the stairs from the first floor to the ninth a total of three times. It's kind of like running bleachers at the football field. That way, I can eat like I want to and not have to worry about the calories or buying bigger clothes."

"Thank you. I just might have a run with you, Sookie. Now, what's this about stories?" Ava put a package of artificial sweetener and a little container of skim milk in her coffee.

"I'll show you rather than explain," Sookie said in a low voice. "See that couple over there by the window? The woman is wearing a yellow sundress."

Ava nodded, and remembered a little green sundress a lot like that one that she'd worn the first time she met Vince.

"Notice that they're both wearing wedding rings," Sookie said, "but he keeps looking around at other women coming and going. If I'm reading his lips right, he's telling her about how beautiful each one is."

Dotty added a package of sugar to her coffee and then poured in half-and-half from a tiny pitcher. "His wife has gone to the trouble to curl her hair, put on a pretty sundress, and…" She leaned over to better see the couple. "Yep, and even shave her legs. The expression on her face is screaming, 'Look at me,' but her husband is stone-cold blind to her."

"From the looks of them, they've been married maybe twenty-five years"—Dotty picked up on the story—"and their marriage has gone flat. Their kids are off to college and she's wanting to rekindle the love they used to have, but it ain't goin' to happen on this ship unless he wakes up and sees her."

Ava bit back tears and took a couple of drinks of her coffee to swallow the lump in her throat. She wished Vince would think about something other than making money. She pointed to another couple across the room. "What about them?"

"Oh, darlin'." Dotty grinned. "They aren't married—yet—but he's going to propose on this cruise. She comes from money, and he's a poor boy. Kind of like she's a princess who lives on a big horse-training estate, and he's the stable boy. He's saved his money for two years to bring her on this cruise so he can give her a romantic proposal."

"Y'all should be writing romance novels." Ava visualized the night that Vince proposed to her. He'd taken her to a fancy resort in the Bahamas for the weekend. The same one where they'd met at her college roommate's wedding. Back then, she had been the poor elementary school teacher, and he had been the prince—so to speak. After a dinner that probably cost as much as half her monthly salary, they'd taken a walk in the gardens and he'd proposed under a full moon with stars dancing around it. She would never forget the feeling in her heart that night as he'd slipped the diamond ring on her finger and they'd talked about their plans to move away from Texas—maybe to another country. Their future was bright. Vince had just passed the bar exam and he loved her. She loved him. Nothing could change that.

*Yeah, right,* the voice in her head said. *Five years later, the future is dim. His family's acceptance of you and his obsession with his job have changed everything you had in the beginning.*

Ava looked down at her naked ring finger. "Is she going to accept the young man's proposal?"

"Of course," Sookie answered. "This is the love ship where miracles happen, and there's always a happy-ever-after."

"What about that couple that's been married twenty-five years, and the husband is ignoring his wife?" she asked.

They all glanced over that way in time to see the woman stand up, lean across the table, and say something to the guy. He shook his head in denial, and she removed her rings and laid them beside his plate. Then she walked away.

"That doesn't look like a happy-ever-after," Ava said.

"Yes, darlin'," Dotty said with a smile, "it is. You just got to look at it in the right way. If he comes to his senses, it's a happy-ever-after for them both. If he doesn't, it's a happy-ever-after for her, because she can move on with her life and find someone who will treat her the way a woman should be treated and appreciated."

"Someone who will have eyes for her and see *her* instead of looking at every other pretty woman on this ship," Sookie added.

That's exactly where she was with Vince these days in their relationship—on a fence and trying to figure out which way to fall. Only it wasn't a woman that Ava was battling; it was the two M's, as she'd begun to think of them—money and mother.

Ava had three choices really. Number one was to go on living in a world where she was just a fixture in a big, fancy house. Number two was to make Vince understand that time with her wasn't time wasted, and money wasn't the most important thing in the world. Number three was to start divorce proceedings. She couldn't bear to open door number one. What was behind door number two was what she wanted most, but Vince had proven that his job at his dad's big firm came first in his life. Door number three beckoned to her like a shot of whiskey to an alcoholic. Just end the misery and move on with her life in hopes that there was someone out there who would treat her as an equal and not see her as a poor little kitten he had picked up on the side of the road and was now ready to take to the animal shelter because she wasn't cute and cuddly anymore.

"You look like you're about to cry," Minnie said.

"I thought I'd cried out all my tears, but it seems like my body keeps producing more," Ava declared.

"Do you want to talk about it?" Sookie asked. "We're just three old women, but we're good at listening."

"I wouldn't know where to begin," Ava said.

The waiter brought their food and set it in front of them. "If you need anything else, just signal me," he said with a smile.

"Thanks," Dotty said. "This all looks great."

Ava smeared cream cheese on her bagel and bit into it. She would only be on the ship a week with these spicy old gals. What would it hurt to confide in them? She didn't have a grandmother or even a mother to talk to, and her older sister would tell her to suck it up and live with whatever Vince did or didn't do so she wouldn't lose all those lovely dollars she had at her disposal.

"I met Vince at a wedding a little over five years ago. We had a whirlwind romance, and he flew me down to the Bahamas to the very place where we'd met and proposed to me. He comes from a long line of oil money and works in a huge firm as the in-house lawyer for his father, who owns the business now. I *was* an elementary school teacher."

"Kind of a Cinderella story, right?" Sookie asked.

"I thought so at the time, but then Vince's mother decided that I shouldn't teach school anymore," Ava said.

"Why?" Dotty's eyes narrowed into slits. "I was a teacher for ten years. There's no more honorable position in the whole world as far as I'm concerned."

"Cargill women have educations, but they do not work," Ava mimicked her mother-in-law's British tone and then went back to her own southern accent, "I wanted to fit into the family, and I tried so hard. After watching my mother die with cancer when I was a teenager, I wanted to be a part of Vince's family. I agreed to do a little charity work with her, learn to throw a good dinner party, and all those things that Cargill women do, but nothing I did pleased his mother."

"Maybe you tried too hard," Sookie said.

"Probably, but Vince is an only child, and I just chalked it up to her wanting the best for her son." Ava picked up the wrong cup and took a sip of Dotty's coffee. "Oh. My. Goodness! That tastes so good, but I'm so sorry that I drank out of your cup."

"No problem, darlin'," Dotty said with a grin. "You got to have a few things to make life worth living. Real cream and sugar are a couple of those that I indulge in."

"Hmmph," Sookie almost snorted. "A couple?"

"Hey, I love food, and my fat cells love me," Dotty told her and turned back to Ava. "Now where was your evil mother-in-law brought up?"

"Wales, where she rubbed shoulders with royalty from the time she was born. My father-in-law met her on a business trip. When Vince and I were first married, things weren't so bad, but it's slowly gotten worse through the years. He spends more time with his job and his folks than he does with me. They have job-related dinners that his mother tells him I wouldn't be 'interested in'…" She air quoted the last few words. "So he goes without me. I wouldn't say we've grown apart, but more that we've been split apart. Other than marrying me in a wedding that she told me was shabby and a disgrace to her son because we had it out on my grandparents' old farm, I'm sure he's never done anything against her will."

"Does he still love you?" Sookie asked.

"At this point, I don't know," Ava admitted. "I still love him, or at least I love the man I married. I'm not so sure about the man I'm living with at this point."

"What can we do to help?" Minnie finished off her eggs, bacon, and biscuits.

"You've already done a lot, just by listening to me. My only living relative is a sister who is ten years older than me and thinks I fell into a honeypot when I married Vince. She tells me that I should just live with whatever it takes to keep him and the money."

"Money doesn't mean everything," Minnie said with a sigh.

Ava raised an eyebrow. "Do I hear a note of regret there?"

"Yes, you do," Minnie answered. "My husband made Midas look poor, but all that money didn't save him when he had an acute heart attack and dropped dead on the bathroom floor at the age of fifty-five."

"And my late husband's fortune wasn't worth much when he got terminal cancer," Sookie said.

"Or mine when he worked hard on a huge Texas ranch his whole life, and didn't live to see sixty-five," Dotty told her.

"I'm so sorry for all of you," Ava said.

"And we're sorry you are in this place in your marriage, but we're here to help if you need us," Sookie said. "Looks like we're finished here. Let's go out to the deck and watch the world go by. Everything always looks better out there where all we can see is sky and water."

"Puts things in perspective." Dotty placed her napkin over her plate and pushed back her chair.

Ava followed her lead and stood up. "I hope so," she muttered.

———————

Vince sat on his balcony, watched the sun rise beyond where water touched sky, and felt miserable and empty. Stupid didn't begin to describe his actions. He was man enough to admit that this separation from Ava was all his fault. She'd done her best, only to be shot down at every turn by his folks.

In the beginning of their relationship, he and Ava had talked for hours and hours about their dreams and hopes, and how that they wanted to travel to another country. Then his folks offered him a fortune to go into the family business—and he couldn't say no to his mother. Ava had begged for time with him, but he'd kept telling her that they would have time to spend together later. His excuse was that he had to learn all he could about running a multibillion-dollar oil company.

He finished off the breakfast he'd ordered from room service, poured himself one more mimosa, and then stood up, opened the sliding glass doors into his private cabin, and went inside. He should have enjoyed the view of nothing but ocean and sky as the ship glided across the water, but all he could think about was that Ava could have been sitting across the little round table from him. What was she doing that morning back in Texas? Had she begun packing to leave him for good?

He dressed in khaki shorts and a red polo shirt and slipped his feet into a pair of sandals. He ran an electric razor over his face. Mother said a gentleman didn't go out in public looking like a beggar, but since Ava moved out, he'd been rethinking listening to everything his mother told him.

*Can you even see what kind of situation listening to Delores Cargill has caused?* the pesky voice in his head asked.

"It's not all on her," he muttered. "I'm the cause of most of this trouble because I haven't stood up to her but three times in my life. Once over my career, and she won that time in a sense. Two when I married Ava, and just this week when I decided to take a week off for this cruise to try to come up with a plan to talk Ava into giving me another chance."

*Sometimes it's too late to do what you should've been doing all along.* This time his grandfather's voice was in his head.

"I hear you, Granddad." He shoved his room key into his pocket and looked back at the bed that he and Ava should be sharing.

He snagged a cup of coffee in the dining room and carried it out to a deck where chaise lounges were lined up. He chose one at the very end of the row and leaned back to enjoy the view. In a few minutes, an elderly gentleman who reminded him of a skinny version of Sean Connery sat down beside him. He sported a gray mustache like the actor had when he played in roles later in his life. His gray hair was feathered back perfectly. His size, posture, hair, and everything about him, other than that little mustache, reminded Vince of his own grandfather.

"Are you saving this for someone?" the guy asked.

"No, sir, and I'll be glad to sit beside James Bond. Can I go get you a cup of coffee?"

"Just plain old Henry O'Dell, who recently sold his ranch in West Texas and decided to take a year's vacation on cruise ships, and I've had enough coffee this morning," the guy said. "And you are?"

"Vince Cargill. Pleased to meet you, Henry."

"Likewise," he nodded. "I see by that white mark on your ring finger that you aren't attached, but you have been."

"Yes, sir, that's right," Vince said with a nod. "I made a huge mistake."

"Can you fix it?" Henry held up his hand. "My white line has gone. My sweet wife died ten years ago, but we had a good long and very happy marriage. Kids were grown and gone on their own paths of life when I lost her. I wanted one of my boys to take over the ranch, but neither of them wanted it, and my daughter couldn't wait to get away from Texas. I gave them all a healthy little chunk of inheritance and decided to treat myself to an extended vacation."

"That's nice." Vince sipped his coffee.

"First cruise I was on, I saw a lady by the name of Sookie Green, and boy, I'd just love to…" Henry chuckled. "I guess what I'm trying to say is that I'd love to spend time with her. I'm seventy-five years old and had prostate cancer a couple of years ago. The surgery to get rid of it ended the sex stuff, but it doesn't end the want to have someone to cuddle with at night. And I wouldn't feel like I was cheatin' on my sweet wife if there wasn't any real sex." He lowered his voice. "I tell myself that she wouldn't want me to be lonely, but truth is I figure she would scratch Sookie's eyes out if I got serious about her."

Vince drank the last of his coffee and started to get up, but then Henry pointed to his left. "There's Sookie now. Looks like the old gals have taken a pretty little red-haired woman in with them. They do that on every cruise. Kind of reach out to help some lady who's here all alone so she won't be lonely."

Vince recognized his wife and slumped back down into his chair. His heart skipped a beat and then raced ahead with a full head of steam. His hands were so clammy that he almost dropped the coffee mug. He figured she would have returned the tickets she had bought for a refund, but evidently not.

They hadn't talked in two weeks, not since the night he had come home and found the note saying she was moving into a cheap hotel to have some space to think about their marriage. She had only sent him one short text since then saying that they needed to talk, but she wasn't ready to do so yet. When and why had she decided to come on the cruise that was supposed to be her anniversary present to him—for *them*? Seeing her across the distance made his heart ache and his chest tighten like it did the first time he laid eyes on her at a friend's wedding reception.

"So, what happened that made you take off your wedding ring?" Henry asked.

"A lot of things, and nearly all of them have been my fault." Vince looked down at his finger and remembered the night he'd taken it off in a fit of anger. Now he wished he had it back. He kept stealing glances at Ava. He hadn't forgotten how beautiful she was—inside and out—but seeing her close enough to drink in her whole essence and yet not being able to even talk to her was painful. Only a complete idiot would have put anything ahead of her happiness, and he had the crown for being that fool.

"You wantin' to get a second chance with her?" Henry asked.

"I'd love one, but I might have blown any hope of that." Vince shifted his gaze toward the horizon where the water and sky met.

"Well, I'd guess that you ownin' up to that would be a good start. You should call her when we have cell service here on the ship, or else figure out what stateroom she's in and just call that room and pour your heart and soul out to her," Henry said.

"It's complicated," Vince whispered.

"Love always is." Henry chuckled. "Did your mother like your wife?"

Vince wondered if Henry was a mind reader. "Why would you ask that?"

"Because what problems me and my wife had was centered around my mother not liking her." Henry chuckled. "There weren't many women on earth that Mama thought was good enough for me. After all, I was born on one of the biggest ranches in West Texas, and I would be inheriting it from my daddy, who got it from his father, and so on and so forth, all the way back to the time before Texas became a state. According to my mother, I deserved a woman better than my Nellie, but the heart wants what the heart wants, and mine wanted Nellie."

"How did you handle it?" Vince stole still another look at Ava.

"My daddy was a smart man. He gave me two sections of land and a hundred head of cattle as a wedding present. He told me that when I learned to run that much of a ranch, he'd deed over some more to me. By the time he passed on, all he had left was one section left to give to me. Mama never did like my Nellie, but that was her loss," Henry said.

"Now how about you, Mr. Vince Cargill? What's your story? We're on this ship for a week, and then we'll never see each other again, so tell me, why are you looking so sad? And why did your eyes come near to popping out of your head when you saw that red-haired woman that Sookie and her posse have taken up with?"

"My mother has rubbed shoulders with royalty in Scotland. My father is an oil baron who inherited a huge company that's been in our family since the first oil was struck in Texas over a hundred years ago." Vince spilled his story to a man he barely knew—and it felt so good. "I'm an only child, so the company will fall to me. My folks are trying to groom me to take care of it when the time comes. Right now, I'm the company lawyer for the Texas office."

"Ranchin' or oil. The story stays the same when it comes to mamas and their baby boys. The way that Nellie was treated is the reason why she didn't say a word when our kids left the ranch, and she made damn sure she was good to her son-in-law and both daughters-in-law. Those three loved her as much as our kids did," Henry said. "You got to do what makes you happy. Money ain't the most important thing in the world, son."

Vince took a deep breath, let it out slowly and said, "That woman that Sookie is sitting beside is my wife, Ava. I didn't even know until right now that she was on this ship. We're separated right now. We were supposed to do this vacation together, and I figured she wouldn't come since I refused to go. My grandfather told me to go alone, sort out my priorities, and come home ready to get back to work. Now there she is and I've got to figure out how to deal with it."

"What's your heart tellin' you, son?" Henry asked.

"It's confused right now, but I know I don't want to lose her," Vince admitted.

"Then you'd better do something about that or you'll be plumb miserable for the rest of your life," Henry told him.

"You are so right," Vince whispered.

# Chapter 3

Ava thought she was in good shape until she ran the stairs three times with Sookie. By the time they finished the last set, she was so winded she could hardly breathe. Her red hair stuck to her sweaty forehead, and she bent forward and sucked air into her lungs.

"That was one more workout," she panted.

"I didn't know how I was going to keep in shape when we decided to live on cruise ships." Sookie wiped her face with a bandanna she pulled out of the pocket of her athletic shorts. "I was used to walking around the football field in our small town several times in the morning and then running the bleachers. I was just fine when I found an exercise room with a treadmill and figured out these stairs are as good as bleachers. And this is in air-conditioned comfort."

"I'm sweating like a hooker on the front row of a tent revival in July," Ava said.

Sookie laughed out loud. "I haven't heard that saying in years and years."

"My granny used to say that when she was all sweaty," Ava said with a smile.

"Were you close to your granny?"

"Oh, yeah," Ava said as she straightened up. "She kept me when I was a little girl while my mama and daddy worked, so we kind of had a special bond. Minnie reminds me of her."

"Not me?"

"Oh, no!" Ava found enough air for a giggle. "Granny hated to get all sticky sweaty, and cooking in an air-conditioned kitchen was enough exercise for her." She heard a noise behind her and looked over her shoulder just in time to see Vince and Henry step out of the elevator.

"Well, hello, Sookie." Henry smiled. "You are beautiful even after you run the stairs."

"That's silly," Sookie told him. "I'm drenched with sweat and look like a wet dishrag."

"Then a wet dishrag must be beautiful." Henry wiggled his gray eyebrows. "Want to go…"

Sookie held up a palm and shook her head. "Don't even go there."

"I meant maybe go sit in a steam room, or maybe do some laps in the pool," Henry said with a big grin. "Where's your mind? In the gutter?"

"Henry O'Dell, I know what you were thinking," Sookie fussed at him.

"No, you don't, but I will explain what I am thinking in detail if you'll go to dinner with me tonight. You can even bring your posse with you."

"No, thank you," Sookie told him with another shake of her head.

The whole time they were bantering, Ava looked at the wallpaper, the carpet, and even the ceiling in the elevator lobby. The few times that she caught Vince's eye, the moment was more awkward than she imagined that it ever would be. How did two people who'd been so in love ever get to this point? she wondered. There didn't seem to be much of anything between them, and yet just standing this close to him sent sparks dancing around the whole area.

"I'd like to introduce you to my new cruise buddy, Vince Cargill," Henry said. "Vince this is Sookie. She's out here alone, but most of the time she runs with Minnie and Dotty, and the three of them are like me. They go from one cruise ship to another. It sure beats living in an old folks' home."

"Pleased to meet you, Vince," Sookie said. "This is Ava Cargill. Y'all have the same last names. Reckon you are kinfolks?"

"Nice to meet you, Sookie," Vince answered, "and yes, ma'am, Ava and I are married."

"Are we?" Ava asked.

"Until you say we're not, we are." Vince gave them a brief nod and hurried down the hall. Ava heard a door open and close. Her heart thumped harder than it had after she'd run up and down the stairs, and her mouth went as dry as if she'd been sucking on a green persimmon. What did he mean when he said that their marriage would be over when she said it was? She didn't have that kind of power in the almighty Cargill family.

*If you've got a second chance, don't blow it!* The voice in her head belonged to her sister, Carlene.

"I'm not the one that needs a second chance," Ava muttered.

"What was that?" Sookie asked.

Ava whipped around to find Sookie sitting on the bottom step of the staircase. Henry was nowhere in sight.

"Where's Henry?" she whispered. "Did I just imagine that he and Vince were right here?"

"He went on up the stairs. Said he was headed to the buffet for a piece of pie and asked me to join him after I turned him down for a dinner date. I'm beginning to think that he's just lonely, and he's wanting to join me and my friends for the company. It's kind of a letdown. I thought I still had it."

"Then I wasn't hallucinating?" Ava asked.

"Of course not. What made you think that?"

Ava sat down on the step beside Sookie. "Vince was there and then gone so quick, I thought maybe my brain was oxygen-deprived from all the exercise."

"They were here, but your ex sure made a hasty retreat. He looked confused and maybe even a little shocked to see you. What do you think he meant by that last statement? I thought he was the one who had the ball in his court."

"I have no idea, but he's never seen me looking like warmed-over sin on Sunday morning, so maybe he's wishing that I will end our marriage." Ava inhaled deeply again and got another whiff of his cologne. That expensive scent always sent sweet shivers down her spine. "Sookie, don't ever doubt that you've still got what it takes to turn a man's head. I want to grow up and be like you."

"Well, thank you, darlin'." Sookie patted her on the shoulder. "Don't worry about how you look. Letting your husband see you at your worst is a good place to start."

"What does that mean?" Ava asked.

"Anything worth having is worth fighting for," Sookie said. "If you want him back, this right here is a wonderful place to start, like I said. To win the battle against his mommy dearest, you've got to strategize. He saw you at your worst. Now it's time to show him your best and to flirt a little."

"I could never take him away from…" Ava started.

"All is fair in love and war with mothers-in-law, and I'm speaking from experience," Sookie said. "The next step is to let him see you at your best, but we'll build up to that."

"What does that mean?" Ava asked.

"Tonight, we'll go to the musical in the auditorium, and you'll get all dressed up. But you'll save your formal gown for the last night onboard when we have black tie. Because we've taken trips on this cruise line so many times, we have a captain's pass that lets us go to the front of the line for the dance and party. You can be my guest. That way, Vince can see you looking like a movie star."

"He won't have a pass," Ava said. "We've never been on a cruise before."

"I'm pretty sure Henry will invite him as a guest since he said they were cruise buddies." Sookie's grin got even bigger. "And if Henry doesn't think of it himself, I'll make sure he does. We may even invite him to sit at our table that night so that Vince can see you looking like the Cinderella you are. Now, it's time to go take a shower, stretch out on your bed and relax, and then get ready for the musical."

"Are we cruise buddies like Henry and Vince?" Ava asked.

Sookie patted her on the knee and then stood up. "Of course, we are."

"But I don't know where y'all call home when you're not on a ship, or…" Ava started.

"That's the joy of being buddies on a ship, darlin'," Sookie said. "You don't have to worry about sending us Christmas cards or coming to visit or even texting us once a week. We're just sweet memories that you can keep in your heart for a while."

"But what if I want to text you?" Ava got to her feet and followed Sookie down the hall.

"Then we'll be three happy old ladies." Sookie opened the door into her cabin.

The ship had already docked in Mexico the next morning when Ava met the ladies in the buffet area for breakfast. She went through the line, picking up a bagel, an individual package of cream cheese and some thinly sliced salmon, hash browns, and scrambled eggs. The ladies had invited her to go with them on an excursion of the Mayan ruins that day, but she wasn't sure she wanted to leave the ship.

"I see that you listened to our words of wisdom." Minnie nodded toward Ava's plate.

"Yep, and I'll probably gain fifteen pounds this week if I don't stop eating so much. I understand y'all are going to see the Mayan ruins today? I'm not sure I'm going. Vince and I were supposed to do that together. It'll be sad to see the ruins alone."

"We'll be with you," Minnie said.

"Y'all have already seen the ruins, right? Why would you want to see them again?"

"Yep, we've seen them twice, or is it three times?" Dotty answered.

"But we want to see them through your eyes," Minnie said.

"It's always fun to go with someone who's never been there," Sookie added as she drank the last of her coffee.

"That's so sweet," Ava said. "I thought this would be a lonely cruise where I would do a lot of crying and trying to figure out what to do about my life and marriage, but you all are making it an adventure."

"I don't have children, and that means I never got to have grandchildren." Sookie nodded when the waiter brought over the coffee pot to refill her cup. "I always wondered what it would be like to go on a vacation with either one. This is a little like having that experience."

"My grandmother would have loved to go on a trip, but that was way out of her financial reach," Ava said. "She passed away when I was in high school. My dad died with a heart attack at fifty, and cancer got my mama when I was in college. I was hoping that Delores and I could…" She shrugged. "She's got more of my sister's traits—all judgmental, bossy, and money-hungry. So, being with y'all is kind of like having a family vacation. Thank you all for taking me in. Crazy thing is that I feel we were neighbors or at least friends my whole life."

"That's the way it is when you live on these big floating hotels," Dotty said. "You sure you don't want to live on ships with us?"

"This is lovely, and I'm enjoying it so much, but I have to have roots," she answered.

"Roots are good at your age, but every now and then you should sprout wings. Maybe once or twice a year you could come cruise with us," Sookie said.

"I would love that."

"Or if we decide to take a month off from cruises this winter and rent a cabin in the Colorado mountains so we can see snow. Maybe you could come see us then?" Minnie asked.

"I'm probably going to go back to teaching in the fall, so that might be doable over my Christmas break," Ava said with a nod.

"But for now, eat your breakfast and we'll go get on the bus that will take us out to the ruins. They are breathtaking," Sookie told her. "We'll probably sit at the bottom of the terrace since these two are too lazy to climb the steps, but I want you to go up there and see them. It's amazing how when you are up on that cliff and looking around, your troubles don't look nearly as huge."

"They really are awesome. The only other thing I've seen to compare to the feeling I got when I saw them was when I visited Niagara Falls," Minnie declared, "and the climb up all those stairs is worth the effort. But Dotty and I are going to wait at the bottom for you. Sookie could take the steps two at a time if she wanted to go. At our age, we should be slowing down, not trying to run a marathon with twenty-year-olds."

Sookie patted Minnie's thigh. "I stay fit so I can outrun Henry."

Ava wondered if she could outrun Vince—or if she even wanted to.

———

Vince didn't know if he wanted to corner Ava and have a talk with her, or if he wanted to avoid her as much as possible until he got things straightened out with himself and his family. Henry had told him that there was no way Sookie and her posse would even consider going to the ruins again since he was sure they had already been at least three times already.

"How can you know that?" Vince asked. "Are you stalking Sookie?"

"No, sir! I'm not that kind of fellow, but I know because each time was an experience. I first noticed Sookie at the ruins. I was so winded that I couldn't even speak to her. The second time, I just sat down in the pavilion at the bottom of the stairs, and she and her friends passed right by me. The third time, Minnie and Dotty sat across the pavilion from me, and Sookie went on up the steps to the ruins. I overheard Minnie and Dotty saying that they wouldn't ever climb up there again, and I had to agree with them. So, I don't reckon they'll be going to the ruins today. They'll probably just stay in this area and do some shopping. Women of all ages like to get a piece of jewelry or a nice purse at the prices they charge around these parts."

"Why would anyone keep going back to the same old places? If you've been there three times, and you know Sookie won't be there, why are you going back?" Vince figured if he got off the ship and paid for an excursion that it would give him time to figure out how to approach Ava for a talk. Would she ever give him another chance if he promised to start over with their original dreams? He wished that they had gone to England, or maybe Australia, or even France when they were first married.

That they would have been a team and come home every night to watch the sunset and talk about their day.

"We go because we like it," Henry was saying when Vince tuned back into the conversation. "That's the same reason folks go to the beach or to the mountains for vacation every single year. Are you going with me or not?"

"Yes, I will. Getting off the ship will give me some thinking time. Do we need tickets or does the excursion come with the price of the cruise?"

"We need tickets, and we'll go on a bus. I just love the bus trips," Henry answered. "I've met some mighty fine folks on the trip that takes us out there, and yes, we need tickets. I'll meet you on the dock in thirty minutes. I got to go back to my room and get my hat, and I'll stop by the booth and get us two tickets. And, Vince, the way to get a second chance is not to run away when you come face-to-face with your pretty wife. You should have said something nice to her the last time, even if she was all sweaty from exercising. You kind of left things hanging in the air."

"I was completely caught off guard," Vince said, "but I won't be again. You are right, and, Henry, I'll repay you for the tickets."

Henry waved him off with a flick of the wrist. "You can get the ones when we get to Belize. You're going to love the howler monkeys and the zoo."

"It's a deal. I'll see you at the dock then." Vince

headed back to his room to get a floppy hat he'd packed. If Henry needed one with that mop of gray hair he had, then Vince figured he should wear one, too.

Henry was already on the dock when Vince arrived, and he pointed toward the bus driver on the other end. The man was motioning toward a vehicle that folks were loading onto.

"That's our tour bus," Henry said. "Windows are up so maybe we got one with air-conditioning."

"You mean that…" Vince started.

Henry butted in before he could finish. "Yep, some of them don't have AC and even with the windows down, it gets pretty warm, but we're lucky today."

When they reached the bus, the guide smiled and said, "Now we are all full. You guys go find a seat."

Vince stepped up into a jam-packed bus. There was only one seat left and that was right behind the driver, so he slid across to the far side to make room for Henry. The hair on the back of his neck prickled, giving him the signal that someone was staring at him. He turned slightly just as Henry was sitting down and locked gazes with Ava. She was right across the aisle from him, sitting with Sookie. Minnie and Dotty were in the seat behind them, and all three older women were staring at him, too.

"Oops!" Henry chuckled. "I should never have said never when it comes to a woman, but remember that what don't kill us makes us stronger. I'm living proof of that."

"I sure hope you are right." Vince smiled and waved at Ava, but she turned and looked out the window. Baby steps, he told himself. Maybe before the cruise was over, she would be sitting next to him on an excursion.

A young lady with dark hair and nearly black eyes came from the back of the bus and stood beside the driver as he started the engine and pulled out on the narrow street. "Hello, my name is Mia. I'm your tour guide today," the woman said. "As we drive, I'll tell you about the places we're going through. First rule of business is don't pet the lions." No one laughed, but a few people leaned over to peek out the windows. "Man, you guys are a tough crowd today. I was joking with you. We don't have lions, but we do have iguanas. If you stop at a place to eat, ask for chicken with bones. That way you get a cluck-cluck and not an iguana."

That brought on a few giggles, but not from Vince, who was trying to think of ways to flirt with his wife. He'd been so busy the past five years that he couldn't even remember the last time he complimented her for anything—from her cooking skills to the way she looked all dressed up.

*Your mama is a good woman, but she likes to have her way.* His grandfather's voice was back in his head.

"Much better," Mia said.

That brought Vince out of la-la land, as Ava called it when his mind wasn't on what she was trying to tell him. He glanced over to find Ava looking right at him.

Their eyes locked like they did the first time he met her, and there was that familiar chemistry that he had been too busy to feel for a long time. Finally, a faint smile twitched at the corners of her mouth—not a brilliant one like she'd flashed toward him that first time he laid eyes on her across the room, but it was a start.

Mia kept up a running story about each place they passed until they reached their destination. "Now, you have two hours to check out the souvenir shop and go up to the ruins. This bus leaves at exactly…" She looked at her watch and gave them a time. "If you aren't here, then you can walk back. If you see a giant lizard, don't try to hitch a ride with him. They charge too much."

That garnered a few more giggles as everyone began to move out of the bus. Henry waited until most of the people had cleared out and said, "I figured we would give them women time to get to the souvenir shop before we leave. Sorry that I didn't do my research a little bit better and you got stuck with your ex again but, son, this is a perfect time for you to talk to her. You might be amazed at what results you'll get from an apology and a promise to do better if she'll give you a chance."

"She's not my ex yet," Vince said.

"That's right?" Henry said. "The way you've been staring at her, it's plain as the snout on a piglet that you want her to never be your ex, unless you've got another woman already picked out. Are you on this cruise to tell her you want a divorce?"

"No, I do not!" Vince declared as he stood up and bumped his head on the bus ceiling. "I'm not sure how I feel. I just came home one night, and she wasn't there. She hasn't answered my texts or calls, and now we're on this same trip, and…" he stammered.

"Did you have an affair?" Henry asked.

"No, I did not!" Vince repeated his previous answer, and his tone went up an octave as he stepped down off the bus and onto the ground. "And I don't think she did."

"Then what's the problem? And remember, you can have an affair with your job just as much as you can with another woman." Henry started walking toward the pavilion which was close to the steps leading up to the ruins.

"Then I guess I did." Vince kept in step with Henry. "I work long hours, and there always seems to be a business dinner that doesn't include her."

"Why don't those dinners include your wife?" Henry kept pace with him.

"Mother usually sets them up, makes the reservations, and does all the work, and she…" Vince stammered.

"Doesn't want to spend that much time with your wife, does she?" Henry chuckled. "Sounds to me like you got a decision to make, son. It's either your marriage or your job, and your wife or your mama. You can't have both in either instance. Is your wife hard to live with? Do you love her?"

"No, she is not, and yes, I love her, but I'm not so

sure that she loves me anymore. I would never abuse her, but the way I've put her at the end of the line when it comes to time with her would tax any woman's love."

"Well, I'd say that you have recognized the problem. What are you going to do about it?"

"I have no idea. Got any suggestions?" Vince couldn't believe he was asking a person he'd only met a couple of days ago for advice.

"Yep, talk to her," Henry answered. "Until you do that, you'll be even more miserable than you are right now."

"Is it that obvious?"

"Oh, yeah," Henry said with a nod. "I'm going to get one of those big, old slushy drinks and sit under the pavilion while you go up and look at the ruins. There's Sookie. Maybe I can get a little visit with her."

———————

"Fate has blessed us today," Sookie said. "I had hoped that Vince would come on this trip. I'm glad I opted to sit with y'all and send her up alone. She needs time to think, and there's no better place to realize that your problems aren't as big as they seem than up there on that cliff."

"Or for her to talk to Vince, either," Minnie said.

"Maybe this will be the beginning of a beautiful love affair." Dotty sighed.

Henry came over to their side of the pavilion and sat

down beside Sookie. "Is your new matchmaking project already up at the ruins?"

"Yes, she is," Sookie said, "and don't you go spilling the beans about what we're doing!"

"Hey, don't be all sassy with me." Henry took a long drink of his frozen cherry drink. "I've been helping you all I can up to now, but I can stop if you're going to bite at me every time we get close together."

"What do you mean helping us?" Minnie glared at him through narrowed eyes.

"I help you with every one of your little games. When you pick out a guy, I get close to him and get him to talking to me about what he wants out of life, what kind of woman and all that, and then I make sure he's wherever y'all are with your lady," Henry said. "We sure enough failed last time, but this time, I want things to work out. Those two kids belong together, and he's so in love with her that it makes my heart hurt. He knows he's made mistakes, and I believe he's willing to try to fix them, if it isn't too late."

"And we thought all this time that you were just flirting with Sookie," Dotty said.

"I have been, but not for a romantic relationship. I want to be in on the matchmaking scheme y'all got going. It sounds exciting and fun. I'm not wanting a serious relationship at my age, but I would like some friends," Henry admitted. "Maybe for a game of tennis, or to have dinner with, or even just to talk about the good old days. These young whippersnappers today don't know what life was all about back before there was technology like cell phones and computers."

"Amen to that," Sookie agreed and thought maybe it wouldn't be so bad to let Henry into their little circle part of the time—as long as he wasn't looking for something serious.

———————

Vince exercised regularly in the gym at the office, but he was still out of breath when he reached the top of the crude stairway. He leaned against the rough, rocky wall of one of the buildings and stared out over the cliff toward the horizon. Waves lapped up on the sandy beach below him, and out there in the distance, birds dotted the sky. Everything seemed so vast and his troubles suddenly took on a new perspective. Henry had been right. He had choices to make, and right now he would give up everything he owned to have a life with Ava.

His mother would probably disown him, and he might even be looking for a job elsewhere. She'd been so excited when Ava moved out. Staying with his wife would mean he could lose his job and possibly even his inheritance. He could very well see his mother influencing his father to cut him out of the will. His grandfather had set up a healthy trust fund for him. He loved his job at the firm, and the people he worked with were great, but he loved Ava more.

"Hello, Vince." Ava appeared out of nowhere and sat down on the stairs leading up to a massive building not far from where he was standing. "This place kind of says the same thing that our marriage did, doesn't it? It was a beautiful thing at one time. Something to be revered and treasured, and now it's just a bunch of ruins on top of a cliff."

"I was thinking about how hard it must have been for all those people to even get the stones up from the bottom of the cliff to this place to build these massive houses," he said without looking at her, knowing that she would be able to tell that he was lying if he did.

"It took teamwork," she said. "When we were first married, we worked together to make our home a place that was filled with peace and love. We had a future and talked about how in a year we would go somewhere other than Texas, and then it all just faded away."

"Had?" He held his breath so long that his chest ached.

"We had something special, but…" She shrugged.

"Do we still have a few pebbles left of what was there?" He sat down beside her.

"I don't know," she said after a long sigh. "You tell me. I love you, Vince, and probably always will, but I can't go on living like we are. You've become a stranger to me."

"What would it take for you to move back home?" he asked.

"You know the answer to that, so why even discuss it? Do you want a divorce?"

"No, but…"

She shook her head. "It's just yes or no. There are no buts. I know what you'll be giving up if you say yes. I'm not sure I even want to be the one to blame for causing that decision. You'd resent me in a few months or years for asking you to walk away from what you have. You like what you do or you wouldn't be doing it."

"I wish I'd had sisters and brothers," he said. "The responsibility that comes with being the only child in a family like mine is overwhelming."

"I understand that, and like I said, I don't want to ever have you hate me for forcing you to make this decision," she told him, "but something has to change."

"I still love you," he whispered.

She laid a hand on his arm. "And I will always love you."

Sparks danced all around them, like a million stars falling from the sky.

He picked up her hand and brought it to his lips. He kissed every knuckle and then laced his fingers in hers. "Ava, why can't that love carry us until I get a hold on everything I'll have to know to run the company?"

"Because we only get one day at a time." She pulled her hand free. "We can't depend on tomorrow, because it might never come. I want to be a part of your life every day. That's what marriage is. It's not money or power or owning big companies. It's sharing life. You decide what you want, and then we can talk about whether we feel like hauling big rocks up from wherever they have fallen to repair our marriage, or if what we had is in ruins like this place. I'm not asking you to give up your job or family. I just want to be a part of your life, to share time with you instead of sitting at home alone, night after night. I'd also like to go back to teaching or at least have a job."

She paused for a moment and then went on. "After the first few months of our marriage, we became nothing more than two ships passing in the night. Your mother managed to schedule something every evening that did not include me. Do you want to be married to your job or to me? That's the question. You have to figure out the answer before we can talk about our future as a married couple," she said as she stood up and walked away, leaving nothing but a hint of her perfume in her wake.

"I can fix that," Vince said with a smile.

# Chapter 4

"What did you find out?" Sookie asked Henry when he joined her at the steps by the elevator.

Henry sat down beside Sookie and whispered, "Vince is miserable. Ava told him they were just two ships passing in the night, and she wanted a relationship that involved more than that. He's got a lot to think about."

"This is a real challenge." Sookie sighed. "We might fail. Seems like he's married to his job and his family more than he is to Ava. She was strong, but it cost her a lot of tears this afternoon. She loves him, but she can't continue to live like she has been."

"I believe in miracles," Henry said. "After all, y'all decided to let me help, and you're sitting here talking to me. I haven't felt this alive since before my Nellie passed away."

"Helping folks get together does kind of spice up our lives, doesn't it?" Sookie said with half a smile.

"Yep, kind of…" Henry frowned. "The word is right on the tip of my tongue, but I can't grab ahold of it."

"The word or your tongue?" Sookie teased.

"The word, smarty-pants," he shot back at her. "It's kind of like putting a good barbecue sauce on ribs."

"Or that we're living vicariously through our match-making?" Sookie heard the elevator doors open and held her breath for a few seconds. An older couple stepped out and waved to Sookie and Henry as they headed back down the hallway.

"Both," Henry said with a nod. "We can help others find the thrill of a new romance, even if we're too damn old for such things, and it adds a little sauce to our dull lives."

"Speak for yourself," Sookie declared. "There's nothing dull about my life."

"You mean you…" Henry sputtered.

Sookie patted him on the knee. "Honey, a woman never gets too old."

"Well, in that case…" Henry grinned.

"No!" Sookie threw up both palms. "You win. I'm not interested in a relationship like that at my age. I tease about it, but I'm happy right where I am in life. No commitments. No snoring man beside me at night. No having to wait on a man to…"

"I get what you're saying, sister, and I agree with you," Henry said with an even wider grin.

"Okay then, the plan is that we send them to the Belize excursion without us tomorrow. We buy the tickets for them, so they'll feel like they have to use them, right?" Sookie asked.

Henry covered a yawn with his hand and stood up. "I've already bought one for Vince, and he thinks I'm going with him, but I'm worn out from the excursion today. And speaking of that, it's way past my bedtime, so I'm going to my cabin. And darlin', I am right glad I don't have to share my bathroom with you or anyone else."

"Right back at you," Sookie said but made no effort to get up. "We'll meet right here tomorrow night after we've got them tucked into their rooms and figure out the next step."

"I'll be here," Henry said with a nod.

Sookie gave him plenty of time to get to his cabin, and then she hurried down to Minnie and Dotty's room. She'd rapped on the door, and Minnie opened it immediately and pulled her inside.

"What did you find out?" Dotty asked. "And before you answer, I'm not trusting Henry to pick out the guy for our matchmaking business. That's my job. Minnie chooses the lady, and you do the planning."

"Having Henry on the team is an asset for the planning part," Sookie said. "I found out he just wants us all to be friends. He teases and jokes around, but I got the feeling that he could never be unfaithful to his wife's memory."

"Not any more than we can to our husband's memories." Minnie nodded. "That said, I don't intend to share a stateroom with him."

"Me neither," Sookie and Dotty agreed at the same time.

———

The next morning, Ava was the last person to step onto the bus that was headed to the forest to see the howler monkeys, and as luck would have it, there was only one seat left—back row to the left, and right beside Vince. At that point she still had choices. She could get off the bus, go shop for a while, and then spend the rest of the day in her stateroom. Or she could suck it up and sit beside her husband. Besides, her new friends would be disappointed if she didn't use the ticket they had given her for the excursion.

"Are you on or off, ma'am?" The driver asked.

"I'm on. I was just trying to decide where to sit," she answered.

"Just one seat left, all the way to the back," he pointed. "I'm leaving in two minutes, so please sit down."

"Yes, sir," she said as she took the first step down the narrow aisle.

"Hello," Vince nodded. "My name is Vince Cargill."

"Ava." She wondered what game he was playing.

"You ever been to Belize before?" he asked.

She shook her head. "Have you?"

"No, I'm a bit of a workaholic. This is my first vacation since my honeymoon. I wish I had taken my wife on a cruise back then. I didn't realize how romantic they could be," he said with a smile.

"Where is your wife?" Ava asked.

"I'm not real sure, but I know that I'm somewhere between a rock and a hard place," he answered.

A young guy who had been sitting right behind the driver stood up. He introduced himself as Rovelle and said he would be their tour guide for that day. "Belize is a small country, but a very beautiful one," he said and pointed out spots of interest as they left. The bus was not air-conditioned, and what few bursts of breeze flowing through the open windows didn't last long. By the time they made the stop at the edge of a forest, rivers of sweat rolled down between Ava's breasts, soaking her bra.

"Little warm, isn't it?" Vince handed her a snow-white handkerchief with his initials monogrammed in gold thread on the edge.

Even though he was her husband, she didn't feel like she should cram the hanky down inside the front of her tank top and sop up the moisture. She dabbed her forehead a few times and handed it back to him.

"Thanks," she said. "I will never take air-conditioning for granted again."

"Me either." Vince took the hanky from her and shoved it back into his pocket.

In the process of the transfer, his hand brushed against hers and there was that familiar old flash of electricity between them. Ava had never felt that sensation before she met Vince and couldn't imagine having those kinds of tingly vibes with another man. She had never believed in soulmates, but after the whirlwind romance with Vince, she had changed her mind. Now, she was afraid she could be on the verge of losing that feeling.

*You've already lost most of it. His job and his mother stole it one tiny piece at a time*, the voice in her head reminded her.

*He could have stopped it,* she argued. *If our marriage meant as much to him as it does to me, he could have protected it with everything he had. You don't fritter away something precious.*

The tour guide told them that they would be walking through the forest for about a quarter of a mile. He warned them to be careful about tree roots and rough patches, and when they got off the bus, he led the way down a narrow path that was barely wide enough for two people to navigate.

The pungent scent of what could only be described as forest reminded Ava of the old pond on her grandparents' farm. The smell wasn't the same, but it brought back memories of times when she was a child and would stay with them—and of her wedding that had been held there just before her grandmother sold the place and moved into a retirement home.

She had felt pretty as she walked down the aisle on her father's arm. Not even the expression of disgust on Delores's face at having an outside wedding not far from a pasture full of cows had ruined her day. She had tried so hard to be what Delores wanted in a daughter-in-law, as a wife for her son, but slowly, chip by chip, the woman had managed to push her out of Vince's life.

A few years later, the farm was gone. Her grandmother

had died in the retirement home. Both of her parents had passed away. Now, it could very well be possible that her marriage was dying, too. Or maybe it already had, and she was just beating a dead horse.

She could hear the haunting sound of the monkeys before they ever stepped out of the dense forest and into a small clearing. It reminded her of the soundtrack on a horror film just before something horrible was about to happen. Was this an omen? Were their screams just a prelude to the death of her marriage?

"The howling can be heard up to three miles away," Rovelle told them as the tourists started whipping out their phones and cameras to take pictures.

"The big guy up there who is making the most noise is the only alpha male in this family." He pointed toward the largest monkey in the tree ahead of them. "That means this is a new family. Later, the male might accept one of the babies you see up there next to the females into the group or possibly even a male looking for a place after he's gone out on his own from another family."

*Family.*

That word stuck in Ava's mind. A family like what her grandparents and her parents had had before they were taken away from her. She wanted to be a mother who made cookies for an after-school snack and helped her child build a science project. She wanted to grow old with a man and someday sit on a porch and watch her grandchild—or grandchildren, if she was blessed—chase fireflies.

Thirty years of age was the new twenty, and she still had lots of time to make those dreams come true. She glanced over at Vince, who was taking a picture of the monkeys with his phone. What kind of father would he make? Would he be one who helped his child build a volcano for a school project, or would he want to send the son or daughter off to boarding school the way his mother had done with him?

The male of the species threw back his head and howled so loudly that a couple of people dropped their phones and covered their ears. To Ava, it seemed as if the family's head honcho was simply telling the people staring at his wives and children that they should keep their distance, or he would get aggressive with them.

"Loud, isn't he?" Vince asked.

"He's protecting his own. Some males howl and threaten. Others…" She shrugged.

"Others do what?" He locked eyes with her.

"Others seem to not care enough to protect what they have," she told him.

"If you are talking about me, and I think you probably are, I deserve every bit of it." Vince locked eyes with hers. "I'm working on something that was sparked by something Henry said. Will you go out to dinner with me tomorrow evening so we can talk, and I mean seriously?"

"We dock tomorrow in Honduras," she said.

"That's not an answer," Vince said. "I won't be getting

off the ship in Honduras. I'll be working on something I need to talk to you about, but the plans are still not set in stone, and I want to wait until they are."

"Yes, I will have dinner with you." For the first time, she felt a bit of hope that things just might work out.

"Pick you up at seven?" he asked.

"I'll be waiting for you at the elevator doors," she answered, and wondered what Sookie and the ladies would say when they heard the news. Would they break out a bottle of champagne?

# Chapter 5

Sookie and the ladies had been on pins and needles all day, hoping that their plan to throw Ava and Vince together had worked. Sookie was on her second beer when Ava appeared in the doorway. Minnie pushed back her chair and stood up so that Ava could see where they were sitting in the buffet area of the ship's dining room. Dotty threw up a hand and waved.

Ava made her way around several tables and sat down in the empty chair. Her expression didn't tell Sookie much of anything at all.

"Did you enjoy that little excursion?" Minnie asked.

"How about the luncheon they serve under the pavilion? Did you make any new friends?" Dotty asked.

"Vince was there, and as luck would have it, I had to sit beside him on the bus which, by the way, was not air-conditioned."

At the mention of his name, Ava's eyes seemed to sparkle just a little, and that gave Sookie a little hope. "Did he talk to you?"

"He did. We're having dinner tomorrow night. He

says he's working on something, but he didn't want to tell me about it until it was definite."

"I'm not real sure that's a good idea," Minnie said as she picked up her whiskey sour and took a sip.

"Why are you saying that? Of course, it's a good idea," Sookie fussed.

Minnie giggled. "I just want her to think about it."

"It's just dinner, and we have lots of things to discuss, so why not get it over with?" Ava's eyes darted around the lido deck as if she was looking for Vince.

"I think it's a wonderful idea," Dotty said and laid a hand on her arm. "He's not here, darlin'. He and Henry are at that fancy Italian restaurant."

"I'm a little nervous about whatever he's cooking up," Ava admitted.

"You were alone with him all day. Were you nervous then?" Dotty asked.

"Not really, but there were folks all around us all day."

Minnie patted her arm. "You won't have a meddling mother-in-law or a sister tugging at you from each side, no matter how many people are in the Italian restaurant tomorrow night."

"But…" Sookie started.

Dotty threw up a palm. "Don't you be the devil's advocate, either. We've got to know what he's cooking up, as Ava said. If she doesn't go with him, then we'll never know."

Sookie giggled. "All right! All right! We all agree that Ava should go to dinner with him."

"Could I come talk to y'all after we finish our dinner?"

"Of course, you can. We'll be out on the deck in chairs waiting for you. Shall I have a bottle of champagne ready?" Sookie polished off her beer. "I'm going through the buffet line now. I'm starving. How about y'all?"

"I am hungry, too," Ava said. "Lead the way, Sookie, and I sure hope we need that bottle of bubbly. I want this marriage to work."

"So do I, and it seems like fate that we wound up on this cruise together," Ava said.

Sookie wanted to dance across the room or maybe hug herself. They had a couple more days to work their magic, but it was beginning to look like the matchmakers would be successful on this cruise.

Ava pointed to the dessert buffet. "And after we eat, I'm having two desserts. That cheesecake over there and the key lime pie are both calling my name."

"That's my girl," Dotty said with a big grin as she picked up a tray and started down the line. "And I feel in my bones that we just might get to pop the cork on Sookie's champagne."

"I hope so!" Ava whispered.

# Chapter 6

"Granddad, I've done some thinking," Vince said the next morning when he finally had cell service to make a call.

"Well, it's about time you stopped being a pushover like your dad when it comes to Delores," his grandfather said. "When you fall off that fence your mama has you on, which way are you going?"

"With Ava, I hope," Vince said.

His grandfather chuckled. "I'm glad to see you finally cut the apron strings. I've got a deal worked out for you if you still want it."

"I sure do, and I've got the scissors sharpened for those apron strings," Vince said.

"Then I will put all this in motion," his grandfather said. "And I'm proud of you, son."

"Thank you," Vince said. "Could you say a little prayer that Ava will like the plan?"

"You got it." His granddad chuckled again.

When he finished the call, he went out to the balcony and looked out over the lovely Honduras beach. If

Ava agreed to his proposal, he would bring her back here for a second honeymoon.

The afternoon dragged on and on, and as each minute clicked off the clock beside his bed, he felt more and more antsy. His grandfather had given him an amazing opportunity, but what if Ava didn't agree with it? He could hear her saying that if they did this, they would just be running from the problems that had brought them to this point, rather than standing up and facing them. If Ava said yes, his mother was going to pitch a pure old hissy fit. She was dignified most of the time, but when she didn't get her way, it was Katy bar the door—as Grandfather often said.

"Too bad, Mother," Vince said as he ran a comb through his hair and picked up his room key on the way out.

He was halfway to the elevator area when Henry stepped out of his room and raised both eyebrows. "How did things go today?"

"I took a page from your playbook," Vince said.

"Which one?"

"Remember telling me about how your dad gave you some land and cattle, and told you to learn to run that much?" Vince asked.

"I do remember that very well," Henry said with a smile.

"My grandfather kind of said the same thing, only in different words. He asked me if I thought I could eat an elephant. Walk with me to the elevator," Vince said. "If I'm late, Ava might not wait on me."

"Can you eat an elephant?" Henry fell into step with him.

"I told him I didn't think so, and he explained to me that trying to learn to run the company was like trying to eat an elephant. He said anyone can eat one, but it's one bite at a time, not grabbing a fork and knife and trying to take care of the whole thing in one setting." Vince chuckled.

"I see where you're going with this and, son, it's good to hear you laugh. So, you're going to start out with a little land and a few cattle to see if you can take care of that much, right?"

"More like a small oil company and a really small house compared to what Ava and I've been living in, and it's not even air-conditioned," Vince answered.

"Sounds like a smart move to this old man. You go on to the place where you're supposed to meet Ava, and I'm going on down the hall a little way. You don't need me to hold your hand for this."

"I might," Vince told him. "It was your story about the ranching business that got me to thinking about my idea. Grandfather thought it was great and said he'd like to meet you someday."

"Tell him to book a cruise." Henry winked. "Tell him to bring a friend, and then tell him that I know three ladies who can be a lot of fun."

Vince stopped long enough to extend his hand. "I will do that, and thanks, Henry."

Henry shook with him and then patted him on the back. "Good luck. A man can't do no better than havin' a woman who loves him and who will stand beside him."

"Amen!" Vince agreed and turned the corner to find Ava sitting on the steps in front of the elevator.

The lights above her created a halo effect above her head where her hair had been pulled up into a bunch of sexy curls. Vince had the sudden impulse to kiss her shoulders, which were left bare by her pale-green sundress, but he just smiled and held out a hand.

"You look amazing," he said.

"So do you. This feels like one of our dates back at the beginning of our relationship."

"Yes, it does, and I hope in the future we have a lot more date nights with just me and you." He kept her hand in his and led her across the hall and pushed the button for the elevator going up. They were the only ones inside it, and he had never wanted to steal a quick kiss as much in his life as he did right then. "I think you were wearing either that dress or one like it the night we met."

"It was one very similar to this." There was hope after all, and her heart was lighter than it had been in weeks. "I'm surprised that you remembered. We were at the wedding reception dinner, and you came over to me and shot me a stupid line."

"Not my best moment." He liked the feeling of her hand in his, maybe even more so than he had the first time he'd laced her fingers into his.

"No, it was not, but it wasn't your worst one either."

The elevator stopped and they stepped off. The restaurant was only a short walk away, and there was not a long wait, so they were seated in a matter of minutes.

"You're right," Vince said when the waiter had seated him across from her at a private table for two in a corner. "I've had far worse ones in the past five years. Don't bother disagreeing with me."

"I wasn't going to." Ava picked up the menu, scanned it, and then laid it to the side.

"I talked to Grandfather today." Vince reached across the table and took her hands in his. "Remember that I told you I was thinking about asking him for a favor? Well, I did last night and it's set in stone now. I'm miserable without you, Ava, and I want a second chance for a do-over for our marriage. Being an only child, I really felt like I had a family obligation, but I have a greater one to you and our marriage, one that's based on love and respect and finding happiness, instead of just responsibility. I'm making a mess of this, but I didn't realize where my priorities had been until you weren't there anymore."

Nothing.

No facial expression.

No nod or shake of her head.

Vince gently squeezed her hands. "Are you even listening to me?"

"I've heard every word. I'm miserable without you, too, but I haven't heard anything yet but more of the same words I've heard for five years when I begged for just a couple of nights a week of your time."

"Fair enough." Vince removed his hands. "Henry actually gave me an idea, and I went to my grandfather with it."

"And that is?" Ava asked.

Vince said. "Mother always wanted me to get a degree in business and geology so I could go into the business, but I wanted to be a lawyer. After I graduated and passed the bar exam, no other firm could offer me the kind of money that she and Dad did, so I took it. You know all this already."

Ava nodded. "Yes, I do, and understanding the problem doesn't solve anything. We're growing farther and farther apart every day."

"The very idea of the responsibility of running that company, even with all the help I would have, has intimidated the hell out of me." Vince looked her right in the eye and didn't blink. "Then Henry told me what his father did to get him ready to run a huge ranch."

"What was that?" Ava cocked her head over to one side in that cute little way that he loved.

Vince told her the story of Henry's father giving him a small ranch so he could learn to run it, and then went on. "We have a new little oil company opening up in Morisset, Australia, or maybe I should say near there. It's actually a few miles out from a small town that has a population of less than four thousand. There's a hospital there, and a school, and a nice beach…"

Ava stared right into his eyes, all the way to his soul and beyond eternity. "Isn't that running from the big problem? You can learn to run a business right where you are."

"No, it is not," he declared.

"Are you thinking of moving there?" Ava asked. "Does your mother know?"

"Not yet. I wanted to talk to you about this first. My folks *will* know as soon as I get back home. I'm going, Ava, whether you come with me or not. I understand if you don't want to join me because it will be an enormous culture change. We'd be living in a rather remote village of maybe three hundred people. We'd go to town for supplies about twice a month. I would be overseeing the operation from the ground up." He stopped and took a breath before he added, "And I would need someone to help me in the office that we'd be running out of the house at first."

"Are you offering me a job?" she asked.

"Yes, ma'am, I am, and a brand-new start for our marriage." He pulled out his phone and handed it to her. "Scroll through the pictures. That's Morisset, and the house at the end is where we would live. It's just a stone two-story, with a couple of bedrooms upstairs, and a living room and kitchen on the first floor"—he paused—"and no air-conditioning, but it's got a really nice porch across the front. We can both learn the business this way—one bite a time."

"What does that mean?" She flipped through the pictures he'd collected, taking time to study each one.

He told her the story of eating the elephant.

"One bite at a time," he repeated.

"That's marriage." She finally smiled. "One bite, or one day, at a time."

She stared at the last image on the phone for a long time. "How long has it been since this house has been lived in? Is that a barn and a shed that I see in the background?"

"A year since the house has been lived in, but the people my grandfather talked to said that there's some furniture still in it. We would have to chase out some spiders," Vince answered, feeling better by the minute. She hadn't thrown the phone at him and stormed out, so that was a positive sign. "So, what do you think of the place?"

She looked at the picture again. "It's charming. It looks like it could hold a lot of love. If it had siding instead of stones, it would look a lot like my grandparents' home out on the farm. I loved that place."

"I remember. There were several properties I could have chosen, but this one also reminded me of your grandparents' place where we got married. It seemed perfect to me."

"I could grow vegetables like my granny did," she whispered.

"Yes, you could," Vince answered. "Does this mean you will think about going with me?"

"You're really going to do this with or without me? You're not doing it for just a second chance?" she asked.

"I need to learn how to run the company and to rekindle our dreams." He reached across the table and slipped the phone from her hands. "What about you, Ava? Yes. No. Maybe. I guess we could build a bigger house after a year or two. You said money wasn't everything."

"I did, didn't I?" she said. "Vince, I love that house. I love the idea of living on a place with a barn and a shed. I can have a dog or cats, but most of all, I love the idea of helping you build something with our future in mind. I want to be a part of your life, so the answer is yes, I will go with you to Australia. When are we moving?"

"Next week, but first we have to tell Mother and Dad," he said, "and I want you to be there with me, right beside me, when I do. Grandfather is setting up a dinner the night we get back, and he's already put the wheels in motion. He's got more pull at the company than I thought he still had, and he loves this idea."

"Will you shove me out of the way when the bullets start flying? I'm sure that Delores and William will both be ready to shoot me." She flashed a smile, one that lit up her eyes.

That's when Vince knew they were going to be all right.

"No, I won't push you out of the way, but I'll shield you with my own body," he answered. "Ava, I feel like I should propose to you again."

"No, darlin', you just need to carry me over the threshold of our new home when we get to Australia," she told him. "I don't care where we live, how big the house is, or if we have a lot of money. I just want the man I married back in my life."

"You've got him, darlin', but I could carry you over the threshold in either of our staterooms. This is our last night onboard," he said.

Ava slowly shook her head. "I think we should wait to begin that new step in our marriage until we get to our new home. How do you feel about starting a family in Australia?"

"I think it would be a perfect place to raise a couple of kids." Vince grinned.

"A couple?" Her eyes twinkled. "I was thinking more like half a dozen."

"I'm game if you are," he said, "and I like the idea of a bunch of children so one won't have to bear the load alone like I've had to do. So…" He sucked in a lungful of air and let it out in a whoosh. "You are really, for sure, going with me?"

"Yes, I am. I love you and I want this marriage to work."

He stood up, rounded the table, and bent to give her a long, steamy kiss. "A kiss like that is what you can look forward to every morning before we leave for work, every evening when we get home, and every night before we go to sleep."

"Then our marriage will be amazing," she whispered.

# Chapter 7

Minnie was first through the customs line that morning and headed over to the orange section to claim her luggage. Sookie was right behind her, and Dotty brought up the rear. Their baggage was all in the same spot, and it didn't take them long to retrieve it.

"Hey, I was hoping I would see you this morning for one last hug and thank you for all you've done for me," Ava called out from the red zone right beside them. She wrapped Sookie up in her arms first; then the other two made it a group hug.

"So, what happened last night?" Minnie asked.

"I was going to come to your room, but it was after midnight when we finished talking," Ava said. "We're going to move to Australia. Can you believe it? He's going to start off learning the oil business from the ground up, and his office will be in our little house that's on company property."

"I guess we'll be planning a cruise to Australia pretty soon," Sookie said as she took a step back.

"I would just love that," Ava said. "You don't even have to call, but we'll be in touch before that happens."

Dotty swiped a tear from the corner of her eye. "I'm glad that things worked out for you, darlin' girl. I see Vince coming over this way. Just one more question before he gets here. Did you spend the night in his room or yours?"

"Neither," Ava answered. "We are waiting for that until we are in our house in Australia. A new start, somewhat like a brand-new marriage."

"That is the most romantic thing I've ever heard," Sookie said with a sigh.

"And he's promised to carry me over the threshold," Ava whispered.

"We'll give you time to get past your honeymoon before we show up on your doorstep," Dotty said. "Now, go on and give Mr. Tall, Dark, and Handsome a good-morning kiss. We've got to get on the shuttle bus to take us to the airport. We're flying to Seattle and boarding another ship for an Alaskan cruise."

They all three grabbed their suitcases and headed out of the terminal, but Minnie turned around at the door in time to see Vince wrap Ava up in a hug and give her a long kiss.

"That was our best job yet," she said.

"Yes, it was," Henry said as he joined them. "Now, let's go see if we can beat it on the cruise to Alaska. I'll buy supper tonight to celebrate our victory. Is McDonald's good with everyone?"

Minnie shot a dirty look his way. "I was thinking about that restaurant at the top of the Needle."

"You got it!" Henry chuckled.

———

Ava was antsy that evening when she and Vince walked hand in hand into the fancy restaurant where Grandfather Bill had booked a reservation. Vince's mother and father and grandfather were already there and seated when they arrived, and Delores looked up at Vince with a shocked look on her face.

"What's going on here?" she asked.

Vince's dad, William, glanced over at his father. "Dad?"

"Vince and I have made a deal," his grandfather, Bill, said. "We've shook on it. The wheels are in motion, and it will be happening very fast. We wanted to be the first ones to tell you about it."

Vince let go of Ava's hand and pulled out a chair for her. Ava missed the feel of his hand and the security of his touch, but she was determined that her mother-in-law would not intimidate her ever again. "We've decided to give our marriage a second chance," she said with a bright smile.

Delores's eyes flashed anger. Her lips set in a firm line, and she jerked her head around to stare at Vince. "You want to explain what is going on? I thought you were going on a cruise to get your mind settled and come back ready to work."

"I was, and I did. Ava wound up on the same ship, and we managed to work things out this past week, and…" He reached under the table and took his wife's hand in his. "We are moving to Australia." He went on to tell them the story that Henry had told him and the plan that he and his grandfather had worked out.

When he finished, Delores glared at her father-in-law. "You can't do this. You turned the business over to William, and that would be his decision to make, not yours."

Ava's heart took a nose dive all the way to the bright, shiny hardwood floor.

Bill stared her down without blinking, "I don't think that would be a smart idea. I'm not dead yet, and most of what I signed over to William won't officially be his until I'm six feet under. All it takes is a call to a lawyer, or hell, for that matter, we've got a good one right here at the table with us. Vince can redo my will, and I'll step back in as CEO of our oil business. Vince needs to understand all the aspects of the job he'll be taking on someday, and there's no better way to do it than to start from the ground up with a small company. And it will put him and Ava out there on their own to work on their marriage."

"I think this is a wonderful idea," William said. "I wish you would have thought to do something like this for me when I was his age."

"It can still be arranged," Bill said with a chuckle. "There's a little company out in Arizona, way back in the desert, that I've been looking at. You want to move there? The nearest town is about twenty miles from the site and has maybe a thousand people in it."

"No!" Delores gasped.

"Then let's celebrate Vince's and Ava's new start tonight with a bottle of champagne," Bill said.

"I'd rather have a beer, right out of the bottle," Ava said.

"Then beer it is." Bill motioned for the waiter. "I think that's what I'll have, too."

Vince leaned over and kissed Ava on the cheek. "Welcome home, my love."

"I'm glad to be here, but I can't wait to get to our place in Australia," she whispered.

"Me, either," Vince told her.

"Are you sure about this?" Delores asked.

"More than anything in my life, including getting my degree and asking Ava to marry me. I don't deserve this second chance, but I intend to make the best of it," Vince answered.

"And so do I," Ava seconded.

"What if you fail? Do you expect to walk right back into this cushy job?" Delores's tone dripped icicles.

"I can always go back into teaching to support us," Ava told her, "but we aren't going to fail. Don't you know that love conquers all?"

"Yes, it does, and we will prove it." Vince brought

Ava's hand to his lips and kissed the knuckles.

"The kids are leaving day after tomorrow," Bill said. "That will give them time to get settled in their new place before the actual business starts next month."

Ava whipped her head around to stare at Vince.

"That's my surprise for you. Grandfather has agreed to take care of the sale of the house for us. The little house in Australia has a few pieces of furniture in it, and we can shop locally for anything else we need," he said, and then leaned over to whisper in her ear. "I'm in a hurry to carry you over that threshold."

Suddenly, everyone else disappeared, and no one else mattered. She smiled up at him. "Yes, I definitely can be ready in two days. I hope part of the furniture in the house is a bed, but if not, we can always sleep on the floor."

# CHASING
# DREAMS

# Chapter 1

"You have got to be kidding me." Ford Holt removed his baseball cap with his old Army Ranger insignia and ran his fingers through his thick black hair.

"What?" His grandfather, Billy Joe, chuckled. "Don't you like my bucket-list look?" He turned around slowly to give Ford a better look at his bell-bottom jeans with a butterfly embroidered on one leg and his neon-green T-shirt with *Chasing Dreams* printed on the front. "Sharlene and Nita have matching shirts."

"Your look was fine for the sixties," Ford said.

"And yours is good for a retired Army Ranger," Billy Joe told him. "Now, let's get these bags in the truck. Henry will take care of the place while we're gone, and then when we get back, he'll be retiring. I'm glad you're here to take over."

Ford picked up the two suitcases and headed toward the pickup truck. "Grandpa, you know I haven't made up my mind about that."

"You've got until the end of summer to get it done, and if you don't want this ranch, I'm putting it on the market to sell." His grandfather's tone had a definite edge to it.

"Yes, sir." Ford fought the urge to come to attention and salute, but it seemed rude and kind of military sacrilege to salute someone who looked like his grandfather did at the moment. Was the old guy going to grow his gray hair out and braid it like the hippies did in the sixties?

The two of them got into Ford's pickup truck, and he drove down the lane to the road and made a left-hand turn. The reflection of the sun in the rearview mirror had him reaching for his sunglasses before they'd gone the three miles to the next ranch, owned by Sharlene, who was one of his grandfather's best friends and was going on the trip with them. Ford was sure glad he had them on when he pulled into the driveway and saw what was evidently the van that his grandfather said they would be traveling in for the next two weeks.

"Holy crap!" he gasped.

"Guess I forgot to mention what Sharlene's van looks like." Billy Joe chuckled as he opened the pickup door and slid out of the passenger seat. "Just keep your sunglasses on and don't take off your cap when we take pictures. No one will recognize you."

"Yeah, right," Ford grumbled. With him at four inches over six feet, and wearing a cap that screamed former military, there was very little doubt that someone on social media would recognize him standing in front of or even beside a VW bus with a trailer behind it. Both of them were painted up like a hippie wagon with *Chasing Dreams* written on the front of the bus in neon-green letters. "So that's where you got the idea for your T-shirt?"

"Yep, and because that's what the three of us are doing. We'll all be eighty this summer, and we've been best friends since before we could even talk, so we've decided to start crossing off items on our bucket lists," Billy Joe said as he got out of the truck. "Hello! Are we ready to get this show on the road?"

Sharlene Griffith, one of his grandfather's two best friends, came out of her house with a six-pack of beer in her hands. "Yep, me and Nita done got our stuff in the trailer. Get yours squared away, and we'll take our first picture. Joelle has taught me and Nita how to use Facebook and how to put our pictures on it right from these newfangled phones we all have. We intend to post pictures every day so the folks at our church and our neighbors can see what a great time we're having. Everyone needs to stand in front of the bus so we can see the Chasing Dreams on the front."

She slid open the bus's panel door, set the beer on the floor, and handed her phone off to her great-niece, who was going along with them as a relief driver. "Joelle, you can take the first picture of us three. Then I'll take one of you and Ford."

Nita Woods came out of the house, took her place at the front of the bus with them, and struck a pose. She was a short little lady with gray hair that had been braided and wrapped around her head in a style that reminded Ford of pictures he'd seen from the sixties when the hippie era really was in full swing. She and Sharlene had either kept the jeans they were wearing more than sixty years ago, or else they'd found a vintage clothing store somewhere in the area.

Ford had been stunned by the hippie wagon, but not as much as he was when his grandfather stretched out on the ground in front of the vehicle.

The whole thing looked like a six-year-old girl had painted it, starting with the base coat that was hot pink. Then there were big daisies, peace signs, and hearts everywhere—all in bright colors. And now three almost-octogenarians were acting like they were on the way to a revival of Woodstock.

Sharlene held up two fingers in the peace sign. "Seems fitting that I take her out of the garage for this trip. I even had the name put on the back doors of the little trailer that carries our supplies and had it all painted up to match the VW." She flipped her long red braid over her shoulder for the picture.

Billy Joe flashed a peace sign like both of his friends were doing. "If I was old, I couldn't do this, now could I?"

"Okay, is everyone ready?" Joelle asked. "Smile for the photo. You are all about to fulfill the first item on each of your bucket lists."

Billy Joe gave her a nod, and she snapped half a dozen pictures. Then he hopped up with the agility of a man half his age. "Are we ready to close the doors to the trailer?" he asked as he dusted off the seat of his jeans with his hand. "Do we have plenty of beer and snacks inside the bus?"

"Yes, and yes." Sharlene answered. "You can close the doors and get in the bus while I take a picture of Joelle and Ford." Sharlene reached out for her phone and Joelle put it in her hands.

"You stand here," Sharlene said and pointed to one side of the vehicle and then looked up at Ford, "and you go on the other side of the sign. It's not just us that are chasing our dreams. Y'all are, too."

"What makes you think that?" Joelle asked. "How do you know what my dreams are?"

"Mine sure don't include anything like driving around in something that looks like this," Ford added.

"We all have dreams, whether we admit that we do or not. Smile or say 'cheese' or maybe say 'sex,'" Nita said with a giggle.

"Nita!" Joelle gasped. "I can't believe you said that."

Ford could believe it. Not one thing would or could surprise him after the last half hour. He took a close look at Joelle, and memories from the past flashed through his mind. That she had a crush on him was no secret, but she was five years younger than he was. He had finished his first stint in the army when she was just graduating from high school. He crossed his arms over his chest and realized now that he was thirty-eight and she was thirty-three, the age difference didn't seem to be such a big deal.

*But the two of you chose different paths, and it's probably too late for them to cross*, the pesky voice in his head reminded him. *And besides you need to get your problems resolved before you even think of a relationship.*

He shook the thoughts from his head in time to hear Sharlene and Nita giggling and see Joelle with her hands over her ears.

"Honey, we all three lived through the free love era," Sharlene said. "We know what sex is and that just saying the word made you smile. Nita, you and Billy Joe lean over here and look what a great picture we got!"

"We got us some good pictures here," Billy Joe said and then led the way around the VW bus. "Now, let's get this show on the road. We've got miles to cover and good times to be had,"

"Holy crap!" Ford muttered.

"Why is it holy? Did you bless it?" Joelle looked nothing like her aunt. She was a tall blond, with clear blue eyes and, as Billy Joe would say with one of his sly winks, built like an hourglass—tiny waist, rounded hips that filled out her denim shorts just fine, and a top that stretched the knit of her T-shirt. "Are you ready to get this trip started, or do you want to take a minute and tell me about 'holy crap'?"

"Are we really going to drive this thing?" Ford asked.

"It's their party, and they are in the bus ready to go," Joelle said with half a giggle. "They're not only doing the top thing on each of their bucket lists, but they're chasing their teenage dreams. They were all born right here in Whitewright, Texas, and were groomed to be ranchers, and all they've ever done is work. They never moved or even got to go on vacations. Now if you and I don't step up and take their places, they are going to put their land on the market and move into a fancy retirement village in the city."

"Three places?" Ford followed her around to the bus. He'd thought he might be running his grandfather's ranch and there was a possibility that Joelle would take over Sharlene. But Nita's ranch?

"If we decide to be ranchers, then Nita's place separates Billy Joe's and Aunt Sharlene's." She paused at the door and looked up at Ford's. "She's going to deed half of it to you and half to me since she doesn't have any family left, with the stipulation that she and Sharlene can live in her house together until they have both passed away."

"Holy crap!" Ford said again.

"Is that your favorite saying?" Joelle asked. "Didn't Billy Joe tell you the whole story?"

"I guess he was so excited over getting to make this trip that he forgot," Ford answered. "It's going to be a long two weeks."

"Y'all going to stand out there all day, or are we going to get on the road?" Sharlene called out.

"Guess we've got some decisions to make on this trip, but I wouldn't call it chasing dreams," Ford said as he opened the door for Joelle.

"We're lucky," Joelle said as slid into the passenger's seat and fastened her seatbelt. "At least pot is legal now, and we're not headed for another Woodstock."

"Woodstock!" Nita squealed. "Are they having another one? Can we squeeze it into the schedule?"

"No," Joelle answered, "but if they were, we'd do our best to get y'all there."

Ford settled in behind the wheel and started up the engine. The nightmares caused by what he'd endured in his Army Ranger days could very easily be replaced by the mental image of giant flowers painted on the VW bus that just might overpower him in his sleep.

"Okay, Joelle, start up the playlist," Sharlene said and handed her niece her phone. "Sorry you kids can't have good cold beers, but you're on the clock as of right now, and you can't drink on the job."

"Playlist?" Ford asked as he drove down the lane lined with pecan trees, turned onto the highway, and headed through town. "And it's only eight o'clock in the morning. Isn't that early for beers?"

"It's five o'clock somewhere." Billy Joe laughed as he twisted the cap off his bottle.

―――――

"Hope you like music from the early sixties and seventies,"

Joelle said as she started the playlist that she and her aunt had set up the night before.

When the first song began, Billy Joe said, "That's The Association singing 'Cherish.' It came out the year we were all full of piss and vinegar, weren't we?"

"Back then?" Nita asked. "Billy Joe, darlin', we *still* are full of it."

Joelle glanced up in the rearview mirror to see him flash a crooked smile toward his two best friends who were sitting across from him. "And we're out to prove it." He raised his bottle of beer. "A toast to getting to do what we always wanted to and making memories that we can talk about the rest of our lives. I just wish that Mae Ruth would have lived long enough to join us."

Nita touched her bottle to Billy Joe's. "To chasing our dreams. Mary Nell is watching from above, and I know that she's real happy that you finally get to go to the dude ranch."

"And you get to play and sing on the streets of Nashville, Nita, and Sharlene gets to lay on the beach in Florida," Billy Joe said.

Sharlene took a drink, then clinked her bottle with the other two. "To the trip of a lifetime, and to making memories that will last forever."

"I'm wondering if they've packed bikinis and if your grandpa has a Speedo in his duffel bag," Joelle turned back toward the front and whispered.

"Now, why did you have to say that?" Ford groaned

softly. "I won't be able to get that picture out of my head for the rest of the day."

Joelle laughed softly. "It'll be gone by the time we reach the first campground tonight."

She had known Ford her whole life. After all, he had grown up on his grandfather's farm down the road from her aunt Sharlene's place—sometimes she called it a farm, and other times she referred to it as her ranch—where Joelle spent the most part of every single summer. Her mama and daddy were both military people, and she'd been a military brat until she graduated from high school. But every summer she had spent several weeks on the old family farm that Sharlene still ran with a firm hand. Nowadays Joelle taught fifth grade in Prosper, Texas, which was less than an hour from Whitewright, so she still spent most weekends at the farm.

She glanced over at Ford and remembered having a terrible crush on him when she was a teenager. Trouble was that back then, with five years between them, she was just a child to him. Then when she was old enough to really fall in love, she had already vowed that she would never get involved with a serviceman. Relationships could become permanent, and early in her life she had vowed that if she ever did get married, it would be to someone who was already grounded and had roots.

Creedence Clearwater Revival's song "Proud Mary" blasted from the phone, and all three of the passengers sang along at the top of their lungs. Joelle turned around to see them doing a chair dance, wiggling their shoulders and bodies down to the waist, and holding their beers high as they kept time with their feet—all three in colorful flip-flops.

She smiled at their happiness and turned back around to find Ford staring at her with his brown eyes that were so dark they were almost black.

"What?" she asked.

"I was just doing the math. How are we going to spend time in each of these places and be home in two weeks?" he asked.

Sharlene shook her head slowly and raised both eyebrows. "Is that what Billy Joe told you? Two weeks?"

"I figured you wouldn't go with us if I told you we would be out longer"—Billy Joe chuckled—"and you need a vacation to unwind before you take over Henry's job as foreman of the ranch. We'll be home when we get home, but I promised Sharlene we'd be there by the middle of August so Joelle can get back to her teaching job."

"You can't be serious!" Ford grumbled.

"Serious as one of them cardiac arrests my doctor keeps fussing about if I don't stop eating bacon," Billy Joe said. "By the time we get back home, you'll be tired of traveling and be ready to put down some roots."

Joelle jerked her head around to look at her aunt Sharlene. Her aunt just smiled and closed her eyes to listen to the next song on the playlist. Did her aunt feel the same way? Was that what she meant about the trip being what Joelle needed to realize that she should be on the ranch and not in the classroom?

"It takes a lot of greenback dollars to live at that fancy place y'all have been looking at," Ford said. "You need to sell the land to pay for the next twenty years."

"You think I'm going to live to be a hundred, do you?" Billy Joe laughed out loud. "Boy, I'll do good to make it another ten years, and for your information, I've got enough of the greenbacks buried in quart jars out in the backyard to keep me in a fancy place until I'm a hundred and twenty."

Joelle shivered at the thought of her aunt having money in the ground, but she wouldn't put it past her. All these folks had lived through tough times, and not a one of them was very trusting when it came to banking and finances.

"Why would I want to tie myself down to raising cattle and cutting hay?" Ford asked.

"To help you get rid of those bad dreams," Billy Joe answered. "Until you put down some roots and find a good woman to keep you warm at night, those things are going to follow you around. Onliest way you're going to outrun them is stand your ground and fight, just like you did in the army. But enough about that. We're on our way to the first campground. We'll be getting our instruments out and playing around a campfire tonight. Got to get all polished up to do some sidewalk singin' when we get to Nashville. We're a bit rusty right now."

"From the pictures Aunt Sharlene showed me, it's more like a firepit than an open campfire," Joelle whispered.

"That *would* be safer," Ford said out the side of his mouth. "We don't want to have to dig up the backyard for enough money to bail them out of jail for setting the west part of the state on fire."

"Amen!" Joelle agreed.

———————

In the middle of the afternoon Ford pulled into the Ole Towne Cotton Gin RV Park where Nita had made reservations. Ford parked in front of the office building, and Nita got out of the back of the bus and went inside to collect their permit.

In a few minutes Nita returned waving a brochure. She got back in the bus and closed the door, opened up a map and started giving directions. "Drive straight ahead, and then…" She pointed. "Our spot is just around the next bend over there. These old oak trees will give us good shade, and we can get the barbecue grill going. Pull up right there, and we'll help unload the tents and everything."

"I'm ready to cook us up some hot dogs, some beans, and fried potatoes as soon as we get the tents set up," Billy Joe said.

"Where's the food?" Ford asked.

"In coolers in the trailer," Sharlene answered. "We brought enough stuff for the trip. We just have to get fresh ice every day before we start out."

"They had ice and some supplies at the office back there," Nita told them. "It's just two more days to the dude ranch. I still don't know why in the world you want to go to a ranch when you've lived on a ranch all your life, Billy Joe."

"Why are we going to Nashville?" Billy Joe countered. "You've been singing country music all your life. Why would you want to go to Nashville?"

"Okay! Okay!" Nita snapped. "I get your point, but I think what really got your attention was the shooting contest, the mechanical bull, and the two-stepping at the honky-tonk."

"You got it!" Billy Joe said. "I'm going to dance some leather off the bottoms of my old boots with any pretty woman who will dance with me. And I'm going to beat you and Sharlene both in the shootin' contest."

"Hey, now," Sharlene scolded. "I could outshoot and outride you any day of the week."

"We'll see about that," Billy Joe shot back at her.

"Day one of an eternity," Joelle muttered. She had been dreading sleeping in a tent, but even that sounded good after listening to their music for the past three hundred miles and now their bickering. What she would give for some Blake Shelton, Chris Stapleton, Jason

Aldean, or Luke Combs couldn't be measured in dollars and cents.

*Are you talking about the distance you have to travel or having to sit beside your old crush for two weeks?* the voice in her head asked.

*Both,* she answered without hesitation.

"Think we'll live through it?" Ford asked as he parked the bus.

"You know what they say: That which don't kill us makes us stronger," she answered.

"Then we should each be able to bench press an Angus bull when this is over," he said, chuckling.

"We got to get these tents up before we can cook," Sharlene said as she crawled out of the van. "And Nita gets downright bitchy when she's hungry."

"All I've had today was a beer and a little snack from the gas station back down the road, and the kids today call it 'hangry,'" Nita told her.

"I guess that's our cue to help with the tents," Ford said as he got out of the bus. "I'm starving. Did someone mention fried potatoes back there?"

"Yep, we'll cook soon as we get the two tents…" Sharlene said.

*Two tents* was all Joelle heard. Did that mean she would be wedged in between Nita and Sharlene?

"Me and Nita will be taking one tent." Sharlene was removing stuff from the trailer and setting it on the picnic tables.

"Me and Ford will get the other one," Billy Joe said as he carried one of the tents to a place under a shade tree. "Man, it feels good to stretch my legs. I'm glad we're getting to our ranch on Saturday so I can go to the honky-tonk and dance away all my stiff muscles."

"Hmph," Nita snorted. "It'll take more than one night of dancing to work the soreness out of eighty-year-old muscles. I just now heard your knees cracking, and you were trying not to groan when you got up from that position you were in for our first picture."

"I ain't eighty yet," Billy Joe shot back at her as he rounded the bus to get the supplies out of the trailer, "and there's a lot of good left in this old body."

Sharlene patted Joelle on the shoulder as she got out of the bus. "You'll be throwing your sleeping bag on the floor back here at night. When we get to the ranch, we've rented a big cabin with three bedrooms, so you can even have your own room then."

Joelle didn't realize she was holding her breath until it came out in a long whoosh. She'd gladly sleep in the bus rather than crowd into a two-person tent with two old ladies—especially with her aunt who snored like a six-hundred-pound grizzly bear. She had learned years ago to bring earplugs when she visited the farm. She had often wondered if the neighbors—that would be Nita on the next ranch over, and Billy Joe just past that one—could hear her aunt. But then she figured that if she stepped out onto the porch in the middle of the night, she could probably hear them making just as much noise.

"What are you thinking about?" Ford asked as he opened the driver's side door.

"Snoring," she answered honestly.

"I hadn't thought of that," he groaned. "I didn't bring my earplugs. I may be bringing my sleeping bag and joining you on the floor of this thing."

"Would you really sleep in a pink hippie wagon?" she asked. "Won't that ruin your big he-man Army Ranger image?"

"To get some good sleep, I just might," he answered. "And I finished my twenty years in the service as of two weeks ago, so the image, if I ever had one, retired with me."

She gave him a slow once-over, from head to toe. "I don't think the image knows that yet."

"If it doesn't know now, it will by the time this trip is over. Did you really not know how long this trip would last?" he asked.

"Not until this morning," Joelle answered, "but I'd planned to spend the whole summer with Aunt Sharlene anyway."

# Chapter 2

A COOL MORNING BREEZE flowed through the open door of the bus when Joelle awoke the next morning. When she got her bearings and realized that she was in a sleeping bag on the floor, she turned over to find Ford right beside her—eyes wide open and a big smile on his face.

"Good morning," he whispered.

"How…why…" she stammered.

"I told you that I might be joining you," he said. "Grandpa snores. If you listen…"

Joelle quickly pushed back the part of the bag that she'd used for cover, pulled the edge of her sleep shirt down to cover more of her legs, and made her way on her knees to the door. The sun had just begun to light up the sky, and the snoring coming from the two tents was causing a poor old possum that was between them some major issues. The animal would sneak up to one of the tents between the loud noises and then run back to the safety of a tree when the chorus of snores started up again.

"You've got to see this," Joelle said.

Ford came out of his sleeping bag and eased over beside her. "What am I looking at?"

She pointed toward the tents and the tree where the possum had taken refuge. "Watch for it! Watch for it! Here it comes."

"That's a possum," Ford said.

"Yep, watch what happens when the noise starts," Joelle said with a giggle.

The animal eased up to the edge of Billy Joe's tent and sniffed at the edge. Then the snoring started, and it made a hasty retreat to the tree.

Ford chuckled. "And that is why I'm sleeping in the bus. I found one set of earplugs in my duffel bag, and even they didn't block out all the sound. But I am a little worried about you."

"Why would you worry about me?" Joelle asked.

"You didn't even open your eyes or wiggle when I slipped in here and crawled into my sleeping bag. I could have been anyone…"

She stopped him by putting up a palm. "I knew when you arrived, and I sleep with a Smith & Wesson under my pillow. If you'd been someone about to harm me, I would have shot you and kicked your sorry carcass out the door."

"I think I love you," he said with a grin.

"Why? Because I can take care of myself?" she asked.

His grin widened. "Because I slept like a baby last

night for the first time in weeks. I think maybe you have magic powers."

"Sure, I do," she teased. "But, honey, it wasn't me that helped you sleep. It was finally getting some peace and quiet after a long day on the road, a heavy supper, and getting away from that tent out there."

"Don't forget the power of earplugs," he teased—or was he flirting?

———

Sharlene, Nita, and his grandfather hadn't lost a bit of momentum during the next two days on the road, but they perked right up as they got closer to the dude ranch. Ford wondered if this was what it would be like to take a bunch of young kids to an amusement park. That made him think about having a family and all he had given up to make a career of the service.

*You are only thirty-eight years old, boy.* His grandmother's stern voice popped into his head. *That's not too old to start a family, and it's high time you settled down. It would be a shame to let the ranch that's been kept in the family for years go to strangers.*

Ford might have argued with her, but Sharlene yelled and startled him. "Stop! Don't go past it!"

"Past what?" Ford asked.

"The sign that we're coming into Colorado," Nita said. "We want to get our picture made with every welcome sign we pass."

"Yes, ma'am," Ford pulled over close to the WELCOME TO NEW MEXICO sign and a few miles on farther down the road he did the same at the WELCOME TO COLORADO sign and let them all get out of the bus and take pictures. Two pickup loads of folks honked and waved as they went by at the last sign. Another stopped long enough to ask if they'd sell the bus and trailer.

"Not in a million years or for a million dollars," Sharlene told them.

Ford shook his head in disbelief that anyone would really be interested in buying anything as unsightly as the VW bus. If it could talk, he figured the poor thing would ask to hide in a garage with a cover thrown over it.

"We're almost to the dude ranch," Joelle said. "Are y'all ready to sleep in real beds tonight?"

"Yep," Billy Joe answered, "but the camping out has been fun. I could do this all summer."

Ford bit back a groan. "You'd get tired of tents when it gets really hot."

"Are you speaking from experience?" Billy Joe asked.

"Yes, sir, I am," Ford answered. "Next stop…"

"Is the first place to buy gas and use the bathrooms," Nita told him. "My last two bottles of sweet tea have hit bottom, and I noticed the gas needle is below a quarter of a tank."

Ford nodded. "That's exactly what I was about to say, and while we're in the store, I'm going to buy a big cup of coffee."

"You don't like my campfire coffee?" his grandfather asked.

Ford shook his head. "That's not coffee. That's road tar mixed with motor oil."

"I would've thought a he-man soldier like you would like a cup of good strong joe," Billy Joe argued.

"I would," Ford said as turned off on the next exit, "and I'll buy one when we stop for gas."

Joelle covered a yawn with her hand. "And I'm getting one, too."

"Good Lord!" Sharlene groaned. "We've raised a couple of pansies, Billy Joe."

"Hey, now," Joelle argued. "I teach school. That's a tough job."

"And probably as rough as a war zone in some ways." Ford took up for her.

"Point taken," Billy Joe said, "and by the time we've been out on this road trip for a while, y'all might even be able to be tough enough to drink my campfire coffee."

———————

Joelle hadn't been asked to drive a single time since they left Texas. The few times she had mentioned taking over for a while, Ford had told her that six hours a day wasn't a big chore. She wondered just exactly why she was even on the trip if she wasn't needed to help out. They made a quick stop for gas and a bathroom break, and then it was off to the dude ranch. Ford slowed the bus down to a crawl on the winding dirt road that lead to the place, and what should have been a short trip turned into a thirty-minute ride.

The three older folks had unfastened their seatbelts and were sliding open the back door as soon as Ford brought the bus to a stop. With Sharlene right behind her, Nita made a dash for the office door to register and get the keys to their cabin.

"Wait for me," Billy Joe called out as he joined them. "I want to know where the honky-tonk is, and the dining hall where we're having supper."

Nita gave him a thumbs-up and kept walking. Joelle thought about getting out of the bus and going with them but figured that her aunt might take that as a sign that she couldn't take care of her own business.

"You are fighting with yourself," Ford whispered.

"Yes, I am," Joelle told him. "Aunt Sharlene is almost eighty. She has run a ranch on her own, but here I am, wondering if I should go into the office with her to make sure she gets everything she needs."

"I understand," Ford said. "Those three can probably run circles around us. Yet, we are driving them around and thinking we need to help them. They could easily do their own driving, so why did they insist we go with them?"

"They've got high hopes that we will take over the ranches," Joelle answered. "And they're out to prove to us that they're getting so old that they need us."

"Huh!" Ford almost snorted. "They'll be pulling calves and hauling hay every day until they drop."

"Yep, but they want assurance that when that day comes, what they have worked for is going to be in good hands," Joelle told him. "Do you think you'll give in and take over for Billy Joe?"

Ford removed his cap and ran his fingers through his hair. Joelle remembered him doing that same thing when she had the crush on him years ago, and crazy as it seemed, she thought it was downright sexy—both then and now. He put his cap back on and shrugged. "I don't know. It would be the smart thing to do, and I enjoy ranching. I think I'm rebelling against the idea of someone else making decisions for me. I've lived in a world of higher powers for twenty years, and I think maybe that's long enough. What about you?"

Joelle had nodded in agreement with every word he said. "You are preaching to the choir. I was a military kid, and we lived by strict rules. Neither my granddad, nor my dad ever wanted a thing to do with ranching, but now Daddy is telling me that I should leave my teaching job. He says that it would be a shame for the family land to fall into a stranger's hands."

"I've heard the same things," Ford said. "Looks like we've got some tough decisions to make before we get home, but on a different note, are you going to this honky-tonk place with them tonight?"

"Are you?" Joelle asked.

"Grandpa will throw a fit if I don't," Ford answered.

"Maybe I should take my pistol to protect you from all the women who are going to flock around you," she teased.

"Maybe if you'll dance every dance with me all evening, I won't have that kind of problem. The women will think I'm taken, and all those guys whose jaws will drop when they see you will leave you alone at the same time," Ford said.

"Now, that sounds like a win-win situation to me," Joelle agreed and stuck out her hand. "It's a deal."

Hot little sparks danced around the cab of the VW bus when he clasped her hand in his and shook it. Seemed like the infatuation she had had with him back when she was a teenager wasn't as far in the past as she had thought it was.

Sharlene came out of the office with a map of the ranch and handed it to Ford. "It's only about a city block from right here, so I'm going to walk. I need to stretch my legs."

Billy Joe fell in beside Sharlene and pointed to a building across the gravel road. "Me, too, and right there is the honky-tonk, which means that it's close to our cabin."

"And what does that mean?" Nita asked as she joined them.

"That we won't need a designated driver," Billy Joe answered with a chuckle. "We can all three get sloshed if we want to, and so can these kids."

"We're a little old to be called kids," Joelle objected.

"Honey, all three of us are more than twice your age, so you are kids to us," Sharlene told her. "Just drive straight ahead. We're in cabin number three on the left side of the road. We'll meet you there."

As they drove from the office to the cabin, Joelle noticed several older folks milling about. Some were all decked out in western gear complete with chaps, six-guns on their hips, and fancy boots with designs stitched into the uppers. She picked up the brochure with the map on the back and giggled when she read that this week was senior citizens' week.

"What's so funny?" Ford asked.

"You don't have to outrun a bunch of beautiful, young women chasing after you at the honky-tonk tonight, but you might have to worry about the cougars," Joelle answered. "This is senior citizens' week. Except for the folks that are assistants, you have to be at least sixty-five to be here."

Ford eased the vehicle into the parking space beside the cabin. "Then I guess we aren't drivers anymore, but assistants from this point on? I wonder if that job pays more."

"I wouldn't know," Joelle joked. "How much are you getting paid?"

"Same as you," Ford answered. "All the food we can eat, a place to sleep, and the promise of a huge ranch when we get home."

"You got it," she told him as she opened the door and headed across the small yard. The cabin was the same as all the other buildings on the dude ranch—rustic-looking and made of split logs. A breeze had set the rocking chairs on the front porch in motion, and a wreath made of barbed wire and bright silk flowers graced the door.

"I've got the keys to the trailer," Sharlene yelled from the edge of the yard and tossed them across the distance toward Ford.

He caught them in midair and set about getting things unloaded and onto the porch while the three older folks made their way out of the bus and to the cabin.

"We've got about an hour to explore this place, and then it's suppertime, and after that is a meet-and-greet dance at the honky-tonk," Billy Joe said as he stepped up onto the porch and sat down in a rocking chair. "You two young'uns are on your own for a little while. But part of your job is to go eat with us and go dancing with us tonight."

"You don't need to bring the tents inside," Sharlene told them.

"Do assistants get paid more than drivers?" Ford teased.

"Nope, the pay is the same," Sharlene answered for him. "Room and board and a lovely vacation. I'll unlock the door, and we'll go pick out our rooms. Y'all can just put all the luggage in the living room, and we'll sort it out from there."

"A real bed sounds pretty good," Joelle said as she picked up a suitcase in each hand.

Ford stacked three suitcases up and carried them all at once. "Yep, but I might be sleeping on the porch if my grandpa keeps snoring once he's in a bed and not out on the ground in a tent. I've kind of enjoyed sleeping with you. I'm surprised you haven't asked me to make an honest woman of you."

"Hey, now," Joelle scolded. "We were sleeping in the same area, not together, and you haven't asked me to make an honest man of you, either."

"Touché," he said with a grin.

The old folks claimed their luggage as quickly as it was brought inside. In just a few minutes, they had hauled it all into their rooms and had left the cabin to go explore.

"We'll see y'all at supper," Nita had said over her shoulder.

Joelle plopped down on a buttery-soft leather sofa set in front of a stone fireplace. "We might need that later, but right now, the air-conditioning feels pretty dang good. I worked up a sweat bringing all that stuff in."

Ford opened up a cooler and took out two longneck bottles of beer, twisted the caps off both, and handed one to her. "We deserve a cold beer after these past three days."

"They are cute, though, aren't they?" she said and

then took a long drink. "This is so good, but I got to admit, even with all the hippie music and riding in a vehicle that looks like it sprang up in a bougainvillea forest, it's good to see them all having such a good time. I was afraid they'd get bored or homesick."

"Trip ain't over yet." Ford grinned.

"You've got a point," she said and pointed toward an open door. "I would guess that my room is that one over there since the other doors are closed. I see two beds in it, so if the noise levels get too loud, come on over. I won't need them both, and we've slept in closer quarters than that the past two nights."

Ford picked up his duffel bag, crossed the room, and opened one of the doors. "This looks like Grandpa's stuff, so I guess this is where I'm supposed to be for the next week."

"I'm going to unpack"—Joelle stood up—"and then I'm going to sit in one of those rocking chairs out there until suppertime."

"See you out there in a few minutes," Ford said.

Joelle didn't mean to fall asleep when she finished unpacking and stretched out on one of the beds, but she did. An hour later she heard excited voices in the living room, checked her phone, and groaned.

"Took a little nap, did you?" Sharlene asked. "Well, darlin', it's time to get up and go to supper with us. We thought you two kids might already be at the dining hall."

"Do I need to get all dressed up?" Joelle asked.

"Nope, it's casual tonight. The last night we're here we can dress either in vintage clothes or semiformal," Sharlene answered. "If you comb the tangles out of that mane of hair, I reckon you'll be fine in your jeans and shirt. And right after supper, we're going over to the honky-tonk. It closes at ten on senior week so us old biddies can get our beauty rest."

"And tomorrow?" Joelle asked.

"Horseback riding in the morning and a shooting contest at two o'clock. You kids can do whatever you want," Sharlene answered and then clapped her hands. "Chop! Chop! Everyone is waiting on the porch."

———

Ford lay perfectly still in the sand waiting to finish his mission so he could throw off the camouflage and get to his exfil coordinates. The targets were moving toward him, and his finger was on the trigger. Then he heard the whirring of helicopter blades coming over his head and knew in his heart that they were not the calvary coming to help him, but the enemy arriving to rain hellfire down upon him. He began to sweat, hoping that they couldn't spot him in the sand-colored suit he wore. Then the bullets started coming down like a hard rain. The only thing louder than that noise was the beating of his heart.

"Wake up, Grandson!" Billy Joe touched him on the shoulder.

Ford's eyes popped wide open, and he sat straight

up and hoped that hadn't given away his position. For a split second, he wondered how the weather had dropped from downright scorching hot to cool enough to make him shiver, but then he remembered that it was just another bad dream.

"Nightmares again?" Billy Joe asked. "I thought the VA was supposed to have helped with all that."

"They did their best," Ford said as he swung his legs over the side of the bed, "but they said it will take time. Personally, I think it's going to take a miracle. Is it suppertime already?"

"It is, and then we're going right over to do some dancing. I hope your grandma don't mind if I two-step around the floor with some of these women. I ain't held a woman in my arms since she passed on, and she was one jealous lady," Billy Joe answered.

"She would want you to be happy," Ford assured him.

Billy Joe patted him on the shoulder. "She would want the same for you. Maybe a good supper and a few beers will help you sleep better tonight."

"That would be great, but I don't expect miracles," Ford said and headed out of the bedroom. He glanced over at Joelle's room and wondered if she was the miracle that kept him from having the vivid dreams. He hadn't had one in the two nights he'd slept beside her on the floor of the VW bus, and yet when he just lay down for a short nap, the dreams had returned.

"Seems to me like just looking at all those flowers

and symbols would cause more nightmares than being the lone survivor of a mission that took out the rest of my team," he muttered.

"What was that?" his grandfather asked. "You got to speak up. My hearin' ain't what it used to be."

"I was talking to myself," he answered.

"No problem. A man's got to visit with himself at times to straighten things out," Billy Joe said.

Ford and Joelle hung back and walked behind the three older folks on the way up the road to the dining hall. As they walked, his hand brushed against hers several times. He felt a little like a teenager, not knowing whether it was an accident or if maybe she was making the first move.

The place was buzzing with excitement when they arrived, and the smell of fried chicken and fresh-baked bread filled the room. Supper was served buffet style, and the guests sat around tables that seated ten. That left five places for strangers at their table, but by the time the meal was over, they were already friends and talking about what part of the country they came from.

When they had all finished, they went next door to the honky-tonk, where Billy Joe bought the first round of beers for all ten of them, then plugged five dollars' worth of quarters into the jukebox and grabbed Nita by the hand.

"I'll be back soon as this song is over to dance with you, Sharlene, so get ready." Billy Joe winked at her.

"One of us needs to hold down the fort at all times, which means stay at our table, so that the old people who are here don't steal it from us."

"Joelle and I can hold down the table," Ford told him. "And Grandpa, *you* are old."

Billy Joe and Nita both shook their fingers at Ford.

"Who are you calling old?" Nita asked.

"Ain't a one of us going to be eighty until this summer, and old ain't a number anyway," Billy Joe said. "It's a state of mind, and I ain't never going to get old."

"And one more thing," Sharlene added as she shook her head. "You are not going to hold down the table. You are going to get out there and dance—like right now."

Joelle took a long drink of her beer and stood up. "Yes, ma'am. Come on, Ford. You can step on my toes for one dance anyway."

"Hey now, I'm a great dancer," Ford said as he grabbed her hand and pulled her out onto the dance floor to Travis Tritt singing "Can I Trust You with My Heart." He wrapped his arms around her waist and felt the vibes twirl all around him as she put her arms around his neck and fell into perfect step with him. The song ended, but he held on to her while Kenny Chesney sang "You Had Me from Hello," which was one of Ford's favorite songs, but that night the lyrics meant more than they ever had before.

"I wonder why Billy Joe played these songs," Joelle whispered, her breath warm on his neck.

"Because they're slow songs, and a fast one would

take too much energy for him," Ford suggested, but he knew that subtlety wasn't Billy Joe's long suit. His grandfather wanted him to listen to the lyrics and really take a look at Joelle as a woman he could put down roots with. She was a great person, and the issue wasn't with her, but more with the fact that Ford wondered what she would see in a veteran who was dealing with PTSD.

# Chapter 3

"This week has been like that roll of toilet paper folks compare to old age," Sharlene told Joelle as they packed all their belongings into the trailer.

"What?" Joelle asked.

"Haven't you ever heard that old saying?" Nita asked. "'Life is like a roll of toilet paper. The closer you get to the end, the faster it goes.' I got to admit, I wasn't looking forward to a dude ranch, but we all got to pick the first thing on our bucket list, and this was Billy Joe's."

"And we've had such a good time that I wouldn't mind coming back again next summer," Sharlene said with a nod, "but I suppose we'd better not waste another place on each of our lists."

Joelle glanced over at Ford and, without a word, knew that they were thinking the same thing—would they be driving the VW bus again next summer?

"And what other things are on your bucket list, Grandpa?" Ford asked.

"Well, Grandson, the second thing is that I want to eat a Maine lobster, and I want to be sittin' in a little café right by the beach when I do it, so next summer, this"—he patted the back fender of the bus—"old girl is going to take us from Texas to Maine."

"Oh. My. Goodness!" Joelle muttered under her breath.

"Amen," Ford said out the side of his mouth.

"What about you, Aunt Sharlene? What's the second thing on your list?" Joelle asked.

"I want to ride a mule to the bottom of the Grand Canyon," Sharlene told her.

"And before you ask," Nita said as she slid the panel door of the van open, "I want to see Niagara Falls from the Canadian side, so before next year we're all getting our passports ready so we can cross over the border."

Joelle ran down such a trip in her mind. From Texas to Maine to upstate New York to northern Arizona. She wouldn't mind visiting Maine and having lobster on the shore or seeing Niagara Falls, but riding a mule to the bottom of the Grand Canyon was another thing. What-ifs began to flash through her head. All three of the folks would be past eighty by then. What if one of them fell off their mule and broke a hip, or what if they wanted to do something dangerous and drowned at Niagara Falls?

Ford closed the door to the little trailer. "Are you picturing what I am?"

"Oh, yeah," she answered.

"My VA therapist told me not to borrow trouble from tomorrow, so I'm going to lean on that this morning, but if they're all still alive and healthy by next summer, there's no way I'll let them make *that* trip alone," he said.

"Me either, but I'm sure not looking forward to riding a mule," Joelle said with a sigh.

"Or trying to keep them in the boat if they decide to do that tour that takes them under the falls," Ford said and opened the passenger door for her.

"What are you two whispering about?" Billy Joe asked.

"You can answer that one," Ford said with a wink as he closed the door.

"We were thinking about next summer. I'm not sure I'm up for riding a mule to the bottom of the Grand Canyon," Joelle admitted.

"Where's your sense of adventure?" Nita asked.

"It died when she decided to become a teacher," Sharlene answered. "She would be a crackerjack rancher, but she won't give in and accept the family farm that is her inheritance. I'm not so sure I'm ready to sell the place. If I hang on to it a while, she might come to her senses and step up to do what she knows is right."

"I'm sitting right here," Joelle said with another sigh.

"Yes, you are," Nita said. "And you know the conditions I've set forth for my place. You two are all we have, and I've always considered you as much my own kids as you are the grandkids of these two old renegades I've run with my whole life."

"What's going on?" Ford asked as he slid in behind the wheel.

"We're talking about you kids taking over the ranches," Billy Joe answered. "But I know you're going to do what's right. Right now, I'm thinking that we can do two trips a year. One in the summer and one at Christmas, so y'all don't plan anything for December of this year. That one will have to be short since Joelle will only have two weeks."

"But it could be longer if she moves to the ranch," Sharlene piped up from her place in the back.

"Maybe we'll take turns with the next thing on our bucket list for the December trip," Nita suggested, "and just go to one place."

"I'm thinking warmer places that don't have snow," Billy Joe said. "If I can be first in line, since I am the oldest by six weeks, I would suggest that we go to Disneyland in California for the Christmas trip. Sharlene, can we take the bus every time?"

"Of course. She's got lots and lots of miles left on her before I put her out to pasture," Sharlene replied.

Ford started up the engine and pulled out onto the road leading out of the dude ranch. "This keeps getting better and better."

"It sure does," Joelle muttered.

Billy Joe popped the tab off a can of root beer. "I'm glad y'all think so. When we get home, we'll start planning the trip to Disneyland. I figure three days out, five days in the park, and maybe four or five days coming home. We might want to stop and play at a few tourist sites on the way back, or stop in Las Vegas to play the slots and watch a show or two."

"But for now, we're going to talk about Nashville and the next leg of the journey we're on now. I've got us reservations at a sweet little RV park in Salina, Kansas, for tonight," Nita said. "We'll need to stop right before we get there to buy food. Ford, I hear that you are good at grilling, so I'm thinking steaks for supper tonight."

"I can do that," Ford said. "I'll pick up some fresh vegetables to grill to go along with them."

*He can cook and probably sleep through mortar fire, but snoring wakes him?* Joelle wondered about that as they drove down the highway toward the Kansas border.

*Like a worm in hot ashes.* That's what Sharlene used to tell Joelle when she couldn't sit still, and it's what the folks in the back of the VW bus reminded her of that morning.

Joelle was surprised that not a one of them had teased her about Ford spending his nights in her room on the spare bed. Surely, Billy Joe hadn't slept through the entire night all week, but then he had mentioned taking a sleeping pill.

*Think about it,* the pesky voice in her head reminded her, *Ford was the first one up all week. Remember when everyone thanked him for having the coffee already made?*

"You've been awfully quiet this morning," Ford said.

"Just thinking," she answered.

"I did, too, lasso that calf faster than you did." Billy Joe raised his voice slightly.

"The children are getting fussy," Joelle said with a smile.

"Well, if you did it was by seconds," Nita told him.

"And I beat you both at the shootout," Sharlene told them. "I put three right smack in the bull's-eye."

"They'll be talking about all the fun they've had for months, and planning their December trip at the same time," Ford whispered. "What's the top thing on your bucket list?"

"To find Prince Charming and live happily ever after," Joelle admitted. "I'm an only child and the last living survivor of the Cheadle family. I wouldn't want the line to die with me."

"Your folks are both gone?" Ford asked.

Joelle nodded. "They went down in a freak plane crash when I was in college. They had decided to stay in the military for thirty years before they retired, but they didn't make it that far. Aunt Sharlene is all I've got."

"I'm so sorry," Ford said. "I guess we're paddling the same canoe. I'm an only child of an only child. My mother didn't have siblings, and she and my dad died within a year of each other, both of cancer, and neither of them made it to age fifty."

"I'm sorry for your loss," Joelle said. "Were you close to them?"

Ford nodded. "Especially to my mama. Dad was a

long-distance truck driver and gone from home a lot. He couldn't believe that I loved the farm like I did. He often told me that he couldn't wait to get away from a place where you had to watch where you stepped."

Billy Joe leaned up and patted Ford on the shoulder. "My son hated the farm, but I was glad that he settled down close to Whitewright and that your mama let you come stay with us a lot when you were little. He used to tell me that the Travis Tritt song 'Where Corn Don't Grow' was written special for him, even if it didn't come out until long after he'd left the farm."

Joelle glanced over her shoulder at her aunt.

"Same story." Sharlene answered the unasked question. "Your grandpa left as soon as he could, leaving me behind to take care of the ranch and then to be there to help with our parents when they got old. Then one day, I woke up and realized I was too old to have a family of my own, but I don't have regrets. Your folks were good enough to let me keep you, and you've been a good daughter all these years."

"Well, thank you," Joelle said with a big smile. "You've been a *great* aunt, and I mean that as in awesome, not just a title."

"See there, I'm great!" Sharlene told the other two.

"And I'm great at lassoing calves," Billy Joe countered.

"And I'm great at riding a mechanical bull. I stayed on for eight seconds. Both of y'all got bucked off in half that time," Nita added.

Joelle went back to thinking about that first item on her bucket list. She really did not want to reach the age that those three in the back of the bus were and not have a family. She stole a long sideways look over at Ford and remembered the vibes when their hands brushed against each other.

*No!* She fought the urge to stomp her foot on the floorboard. *That old crush has been buried for years, and there's no digging it up even if the chemistry is strong, and that's probably just on my side.*

*But,* her mother's voice popped into her head, *you could start all over and see if there's something still there to build on.*

# Chapter 4

FORD WAS GLAD THAT the sun was bright and there were no threatening clouds in the sky the afternoon that they rolled into Nashville. The bucket-list crowd, as he'd begun to think of them, would be so disappointed if they couldn't have a jam season in a parking lot. The first one that Nita had found wasn't right across the street from the strip. The folks wanted to have supper and listen to some music at one of the bars after their concert, so he really hoped that one would work out. Driving the bus and trailer was no big thing on the open road, but navigating narrow streets was a different story.

"Are we almost there?" Billy Joe's question reminded Ford of the times when his folks were taking him to the ranch to spend some time with his grandfather and he'd asked the same question about a million times.

*And when we got there, you were so happy,* his mother's voice whispered in his ear.

Ford couldn't argue with that, not when the happiest times in his memories were on the ranch with his grandpa. *So why am I kicking against the idea of settling down there?*

"Just another mile. What are we going to play and sing first?" Sharlene asked.

"Hank Williams Sr., all night long," Nita answered. "He would have been over a hundred years old by now, so it seems fitting that we honor him while we're in Nashville. We'll start off with 'My Bucket's Got a Hole in It.'"

"So, your bucket list has a hole in it?" Joelle asked from the front seat.

"It sure does, and the top item has done leaked out, but we'll plug that hole and refill it when we get home," Nita answered. "Are y'all going to play and sing with us?"

"We'll be your groupies and hold up lights when it gets dark," Ford said as he got in line behind a car waiting to get into the parking lot.

"The concert is over when it gets dusky dark, and then we'll go have supper at one of the places on the strip," Nita said. "After that we're going to the Gaylord for a few nights. I've told them that we'll have a late check-in."

"No camping out?" Ford asked.

"Nope," Nita answered. "We need a base camp where we can catch shuttles and the tour buses. We can't drive the bus all over the place. And besides, the bus needs to be in a safe place. We'll have it valet parked, and no one can scratch it. I don't want to live with Sharlene if someone hurts her baby."

"Thank you," Ford said as he pulled forward when it

was his turn. "That way, I can see all the sights and not have to worry about parking this thing."

An older guy who didn't look to be much younger than the bucket-list crew took a step forward with a brochure and handed it to Ford through the window. "You're ridin' in style. I haven't seen something like this in more'n fifty years. That'll be ten dollars for the rest of today. I should charge you double, since you'll be taking up two parking spaces, but this thing is too cute to make you pay more. I loved the hippie age, and I hate that I ever let my VW bus get away from me. It wasn't painted up pretty like this one, but if it was still with me, it could tell some really good stories." He winked at Ford.

Nita unfastened her seat belt and handed a bill over the seat to Ford. "Can we play and sing in the parking lot?"

The man tipped his cowboy hat toward her. "Yes, ma'am, you can. I'm here until we close the gates at two in the morning, so I'd love some live entertainment. You might draw quite a crowd with this vehicle and a bit of music."

"Thank you, and we appreciate the discount," Nita said.

Ford nodded in agreement. "Thanks again."

"I'll be listening for some music in a little bit," the man said with a grin.

"What kind of stories could *this* bus tell us, Aunt Sharlene?" Joelle asked.

"Oh, honey," Nita said with a giggle and twinkling eyes, "not a one of us three kiss and tell."

"Except to each other," Billy Joe said, "But we're all leaning toward memory loss, so we can't be sure if what we remember is what really happened."

"Yeah, right!" Joelle pointed to a parking spot big enough for the bus and trailer.

Nita was already out of the van before Ford could open his door, and long before Joelle could get out of the passenger side. By the time he made it to the back to help take things out of the trailer, Billy Joe had opened the doors and was setting lawn chairs up in a circle.

Billy Joe and Nita went to work tuning their guitars, while Sharlene took her fiddle out of the case. Ford sat down in one of the chairs and got ready for the show just like he had on the nights when they camped out. That evening was different in that Billy Joe left his guitar case open and set it to the side of his chair.

Ford leaned over and whispered for Joelle's ears only. "You think they'll bring in enough money to pay for the parking fee?"

"If they do, they will brag for the rest of the trip and claim that they are now professionals since they had been paid for a gig," Joelle answered.

"I hate to see them disappointed, so I'll be the first one to make them into professionals." Ford pulled a five-dollar bill from the money clip in his pocket and tossed it into the guitar case.

"Thank you," Billy Joe said in an Elvis impression, "thank you very much."

Joelle's giggles at his antics warmed Ford's heart. For the past three nights, he hadn't even gone to his grandfather's tent, but rather rolled his sleeping bag out on the floor of the van right beside hers. Sharlene had teased them about needing to find a courthouse on the way to Nashville, so he could make an honest woman out of her great-niece. But after that one morning, no one had said anything, which was still a mystery. The way they bantered and bickered, Ford had expected more talking about it and teasing than he wanted to hear.

Nita hit the chords for "My Bucket's Got a Hole in It," and before the end of the song, several people had gathered around.

Ford didn't know if they were there for the music or to take selfies and family pictures with the bus, but it didn't matter, because all the attention sure put big smiles on the band's faces.

Billy Joe took the lead on the second Hank Williams song, "Lost Highway." Ford kept time to the music by tapping his thumbs on the arm of the chair and wondered if his grandfather had chosen that song to mess with him. Ford realized he had to choose a path before long, but until he made up his mind about whether he wanted to put down roots or do some serious traveling, he wasn't going to be goaded into saying he would take over the ranch.

The lyrics became more than just words when they talked about the time when he would curse the day that he started rolling down the lost highway. When the song ended, folks around them clapped and whistled, and Billy Joe smiled and started off on another Hank Williams tune. Sharlene and Nita took turns with the verses and then harmonized with him during the chorus.

The crowd grew bigger and bigger, and several of them threw coins or bills into the open guitar case. When they started singing, "I'm So Lonesome I Could Cry," Ford thought of the nights that he had slept close to Joelle and didn't have those horrible nightmares. Then he remembered the nap he'd taken at the dude ranch and how he had awakened in a cold sweat as he relived the day that he had been the only one to survive the ambush.

*Why have you been fighting so hard against what you feel for Joelle?* his grandmother's voice whispered.

Could his grandfather possibly be right about a good woman and roots curing the problems he'd brought home from the last deployment? He glanced over at Joelle to find her staring at him.

"What?" she asked.

"Do you remember these songs?" he asked, but what he really wanted to know was if she was feeling the same thing he was.

"Oh yeah," she said. "Saturday night at Aunt Sharlene's was concert night at least once a month. You've been gone too long, Ford Holt. I could have used some backup on the nights when I was the only one in the crowd to listen to them."

"I'm here now," he said.

"Yes, you are, and I'm glad," she said with a smile.

Could she mean that she was glad—as in just liking him as a driver? Or could it possibly be more?

———————

Dusk was settling, and the crowd had thinned out a little when Sharlene stood up. "We'll be closing out our tribute to the amazing Hank Williams Sr. tonight with one of his hymns. When I was a little girl, it was a good night when my mama could pick up the *Grand Ole Opry* on her radio. It was an awesome night when Hank Williams ended the show with this song. Thank all y'all for coming around and thank you for your contributions."

She put her fiddle to her shoulder and pulled the bow across the strings. The light breeze picked up the haunting whine and carried it across the parking lot and down the strip. Then Nita and Billy Joe started picking their guitars and singing, "I Saw the Light."

"Think they're talking to us when they sing that?" Joelle asked. "Maybe not in the spiritual sense, but in seeing the light of what we should do in the future?"

Ford turned to look at her, and she could see that he was struggling with the same thoughts that she was. Did they take over the ranches? Did they step back and ask for more time? Where was the light, and what was it showing them?

"Good night, folks," Sharlene said when the song was over. "Thanks again for coming around to make us old folks feel like stars."

"Old Hank sure set the bar high for country music, didn't he?" A gray-haired man stopped and put a bill into the guitar case.

"Honey"—his wife looped her arm in his—"Hank didn't set the bar. He was the bar."

"Amen," Nita said with a smile as she put her guitar away.

Joelle glanced over at her aunt, who was loosening the strings on her fiddle. She had set the bar high—no, she was the bar—for the kind of independent woman Joelle wanted to be when she was almost eighty.

She picked up her aunt's fiddle case in one hand and Nita's guitar in the other. The three of them had drawn their chairs up around Billy Joe's case and were sorting and counting money. In that moment, seeing the happiness on their faces, she knew what decision she had to make if she was ever going to be like Sharlene. She was already thinking about the wording when she wrote her resignation while she put the instruments in the trailer. Peace that she hadn't known in many years flooded her heart and soul, telling her that she was on the right path now for sure. No more lost highways for her.

"That was quite an experience," Ford said.

"And just look at how happy they are," Joelle said with a broad smile.

"You look pretty happy yourself," he said.

"Yep, I am," she admitted. Ford would have to come to his own decision about ranching, but if he made the right one, she wondered if maybe they could pursue this attraction that had popped up between them.

# Chapter 5

JOELLE OPENED HER DOOR to her bedroom at the Gaylord and stepped into her room, which was two floors up from the other two rooms that Nita had booked for them. Two queen beds, a chair and a desk, and a gorgeous view of the atrium greeted her from out the window.

"This is pretty fancy compared to the floor of the VW bus," Ford said as he pulled his suitcase into the room. "Are you sure you're comfortable with us sharing the room?"

"We are two adults, and if you haven't noticed, there's about three feet between the beds. We're probably less than six inches apart on the bus," Joelle reminded him. "And we shared a room at the dude ranch, remember?"

"But that seems different. I was up before everyone else, so I'm not sure they even knew that we were sleeping in the same room back there, and camping out is a whole 'nother story, as Grandpa says." Ford crossed the room and looked out the window. "Looks like this is another city that never sleeps."

Joelle left her suitcase and went over to join him.

"The view is beautiful. Maybe tomorrow we'll have time to do a walk-through while the others take a nap."

"Maybe after supper, which Grandpa says we're having here in the hotel. The tour bus picks us up at the front entrance at nine in the morning. We won't be back until evening. It's one of those stop-and-go things. We can get off at the Ryman, spend as much time as we want there, and get back on to go to the next place," Ford said.

"Aunt Sharlene says that we will meet them for breakfast at seven, and she told me to be ready to leave," Joelle said. "Truth is, I'd rather stay right here and read a book or sit down there in the atrium and watch the people as spend a day on a tour bus."

"Me too." Ford covered a yawn with his hand. "But they might get into trouble if we aren't there."

"Amen!" Joelle said. "I'm calling dibs on the bathroom. After sitting out in the open and fighting mosquitoes, I'm ready for a shower."

"Don't use up all the hot water," Ford teased.

Joelle turned and walked away. "Wouldn't dream of it."

She picked up what she needed from her suitcase—glad that she had brought shorts and tank tops for sleeping. She usually slept in the nude, but not knowing if she would be sharing space with her aunt and Nita, she had tucked in sleepwear. She went into the bathroom, adjusted the water in the shower, and then dropped her clothing on the floor.

Ford's statement about not using all the hot water

went through her mind as the pulsating stream pounded her stiff back muscles. "That's easy," she muttered as she washed her hair. "The tank in a hotel this big probably looks like the water tower in Whitewright, Texas."

She had really thought she was over the teenage infatuation with Ford Holt, but the hot water coming out of the shower wasn't nearly as hot as the attraction she had for him, and it was getting stronger every day.

———

Ford slipped under the covers and wondered again if Joelle was the magic that grounded him and made his nightmares disappear. Maybe it was simply the fact that he was on a road trip and was finally moving away from what he had seen in the military—not only physically, but mentally.

He turned over on his side to find her staring right at him. "Having trouble settling down and going to sleep?" he asked.

"Yes," she answered. "I can't get my thoughts to stop running around like a hamster on a wheel. How about you?"

"I've hated closing my eyes for months," he admitted.

"Why?" she asked.

"Nightmares," he answered as he shifted his position to sit up and use the headboard for a backrest.

"Can you talk about them or is it classified?" she asked.

"I have talked to the VA therapists," he answered.

She sat up and shifted both her pillows around to lean against. "Did it help?"

Ford shrugged. "Not so much." Did he dare tell her that it wasn't just his grandfather's snoring that sent him to sleep beside her after that first night?

"Want to get it off your chest now?" she asked.

"You go first. What was keeping you awake?"

"Decisions I've made and ones I need to make." She pushed back the covers and crossed the room to pick up two bottles of water. She handed one to Ford and twisted the cap off hers, then sat down on the edge of his bed.

"Want to elaborate?" he asked.

"I'm going to resign my position at the school where I teach. We'll probably work on moving Aunt Sharlene's things over to Nita's place most of the summer. I can't imagine letting our family land be sold to a stranger, and none of them are getting any younger." She took a long drink of her water. "But I'm wondering if this is really the right path for me, or if I'm doing it to please Aunt Sharlene. I don't like to think about it, but if I put the pencil to the paper so to speak, it's not hard to figure out that if they all three live to be a hundred, I would only be fifty-three when they were gone. That's not old in today's world, and I would have made them happy for twenty years." She took another drink and smiled. "And I'd get two vacations a year."

"Are you willing to give up your hopes and dreams

for twenty years?" Ford asked. "What's the top item on your bucket list?"

"To have a family," she answered.

Ford shifted one of his pillows over to the other side of the bed and propped it up against the headboard. "You might as well get comfortable."

She slung her legs up onto the bed and changed her position. "I can have both. I'm only thirty-three, and Aunt Sharlene is giving me her house. A ranch would be a good place to raise kids, don't you think? But we're talking too much about my insomnia. What's keeping you awake?"

"Of course, a ranch would be a wonderful place to raise a family. I was happy when I got to spend time there and often wished that I could live on the ranch with Grandpa and Granny." Ford could have listened to her read the dictionary or even the Bible for hours, just to hear her voice. "When are you going to tell the folks?"

"Not until we start home. I want to think long and hard about it and be sure. If I told them now and then changed my mind, it would break Aunt Sharlene's and Nita's hearts. I can't do that to them," she answered.

"I understand." Ford could feel the electricity between them and wondered if she was getting the same vibes. "I'm still thinking about the whole idea. Maybe which-ever way we each swing, we could tell them together."

"We'll see, and now enough procrastinating on your

side of this conversation," she said with a smile. "Tell me about the nightmares."

Ford took a deep breath and opened his mouth, but then he didn't know where to begin. He took a drink of water and looked over at Joelle. "The last mission that I went on is what keeps me awake. I don't want to relive it again and again every night and wake up in a cold sweat while I'm frantically trying to figure out what I could have done different."

"In your heart, do you honestly think anything you could have done would have affected the outcome of whatever happened?" Joelle asked.

"It was like this," Ford answered. "My whole team was strung out on high ground in…" he paused, "in a black ops mission. We were in camouflage and thought we were hidden well, just lying there with the wind creating little dust devils in the sand. The target that we were there to take out was coming down a valley, and our fingers were on our rifle triggers. I heard the whir of a helicopter above the loud beating of my heart, and for a split second, I thought it was one of ours. Then I realized it wasn't a chopper coming to take us away once the mission was completed. Bullets began to rain down on us. It was over in seconds, but I was the only one to walk out of there alive. If I hadn't been so focused on my job, I might have warned the others and we might have been able to roll down off that high spot to hide behind the rocks."

"And this is your recurring nightmare?" Joelle reached over and laid her hand on his.

Ford inhaled deeply and thought twice, then three times, about admitting that she was his lucky four-leaf clover. He turned to watch her expression before he spit out, "Except when I'm sleeping close to you. I think maybe you have magic powers."

"The only power I have is that I don't snore. That lets you fall into a deep enough sleep that you don't dream. You've been on alert for so many years that your nerves are strung up like a tight barbed-wire fence," she said and then added, "But, Ford, I'm so sorry you lost your team. Losing my folks was tough, so I understand your pain in a measure. I still have dreams about them, but they are not nightmares. And in my opinion, for what it's worth, you could have done nothing to save them in that split second. Just think of it this way—you were saved for a reason. Find it and move on. Your team members would want you to be happy."

"Have you ever thought of being a therapist?" he asked.

"No, I haven't." She squeezed his hand. "I think maybe we've both had a therapy session tonight, but morning is going to come around in just a few hours, so we should get to sleep."

She scooted down in the bed, turned on her side to face him, and closed her eyes. "Sweet dreams."

"'Sleep tight, and don't let the bed bugs bite.'" He finished the old saying.

He eased down in the bed and wished that he could kiss her good night—even if it was just on the forehead. Before he could do that, he had to get a clear vision of what his future path looked like. There was no use in starting something that couldn't be finished and could end up with broken hearts and hard feelings. He finally closed his eyes and dreamed that he was an old man sitting on the porch at the ranch and watching his grandchildren play with puppies out on the front lawn.

# Chapter 6

"WELL, HOW DO YOU like being able to mark the number one thing off your bucket list, Nita?" Sharlene asked Nita when they had boarded the VW bus and were leaving Nashville.

"I'm not marking it off. I'm adding it to the bottom of the list, so when we start all over again, we can come back. I loved all of it. The Ryman, and getting to sing on the stage, and visiting the Grand Ole Opry House, but what I liked most was wandering up and down the strip and listening to these new and upcoming artists sing," Nita answered. "It gives me hope for the future of country music."

*Hope for the future* stuck in Ford's mind as he followed the GPS and was soon back on the highway headed south toward Montgomery, Alabama. Nita's bucket-list trip also included going to the Hank Williams Museum and to his gravesite.

"Are we camping out tonight, or are we staying in a hotel?" Billy Joe asked.

"I couldn't find a place I liked in that area, so we're staying in a hotel," Nita answered.

"Who made all these arrangements?" Ford asked.

"I made the ones for the dude ranch and picked out the cabin for us. Nita's job has been to take care of the hotels and routes from Colorado to Tennessee and then to Montgomery since this is her part of the trip," Billy Joe replied.

"After tonight, it's my turn for the rest of the trip," Sharlene said. "We'll be at the beach tomorrow and staying in a couple of condos, then we'll take three days to get home. We won't be getting the tents out anymore."

"Thank goodness," Joelle muttered.

"Amen," Ford said out the side of his mouth.

"I loved camping out." Billy Joe's wistful tone sounded pitiful.

"It did remind me of times when we were kids and took a tent to the creek at the back of your ranch," Sharlene said.

"Want to tell us more about that?" Ford asked.

Nita laughed out loud, and the other two joined her.

"We don't kiss and tell," Sharlene said.

Ford glanced up into the rearview mirror to see them all grinning like three Cheshire cats who had just cornered a fat mouse. "Which of you kissed my grandpa?"

"Oh, honey!" Sharlene shook her head. "Neither of us were ever that brave or that stupid. His wife, Mae Ruth, would have done bodily harm to any woman who ever looked sideways at her Billy Joe. She tagged him as her feller when we were in the third grade, and there wasn't a girl in school who dared to even blink toward him."

"That's my granny," Ford said with a smile as the memories flooded through his mind. The one that he remembered most was hearing her say, "What your mama says is right, but what I say is the law, and no means no, and it will never mean maybe or yes."

Billy Joe swiped a tear away from his eye. "Yep, that was my Mae Ruth. I sure do miss her and wish that she could be on this trip with us."

"So do we," Sharlene and Nita said at the same time.

"She would want us to be happy, not sad. Joelle, start us some music. I want to hear something by George Jones and maybe Vince Gill or Travis Tritt. I like those guys a lot," Sharlene said.

Joelle pulled up her own playlist on her phone. The top song on the list was the Travis Tritt song "Where Corn Don't Grow."

The back seat folks started talking about ranching and their own crops, but Ford caught Joelle's eye and gave her a sly wink. "You ever feel like you just wanted to go somewhere where corn didn't grow or maybe, in our instance, where hay don't grow and there are no cows?"

"Not really." Joelle shook her head. "But I *have* wanted both worlds. I wanted a job where I had free time throughout the year, and yet I go back to the ranch and help Aunt Sharlene every weekend and holiday through the year, and in the summer, too. How about you?"

"I guess I'm in the same boat as you are," Ford answered. "My dad hated the ranch and said that long-distance truck driving was a thousand percent better than worrying with cows all day. When I was little, I wanted to be a soldier. I played with those little green plastic army men for hours and hours, but unlike my dad, I loved spending time on the ranch with Grandpa."

"And then you grew up to be a soldier, didn't you?" Joelle said with a smile.

"Yes, I did," Ford answered with a nod, "but now I'm at the crossroads that we've talked about already. I wish my granny was here to give me some advice."

"She is," Joelle told him. "She will always be in your heart. Just listen to it, and you won't have regrets about your decision. If it's got doubts, then give it some more time. If you make up your mind to be a rancher and you feel peace, then you made the right choice."

Ford put on the blinker to make a right-hand turn at the exit. "That sounds just like something Granny would say. We're stopping to fill up the gas tank, folks. Anyone need a bathroom or something to drink?"

"A man of my age never gives up a chance to get out and go to the bathroom," his grandfather answered. "Or to pick up a bottle of sweet tea and one of those packages of chocolate doughnuts, either."

"You've always had a thimble-sized bladder," Nita teased.

Billy Joe shook his finger at her. "Don't you get all

sassy with me, Nita Woods. I know you and Sharlene need to buy chips and pork rinds and a couple of root beers so y'all are just as eager to get out as I am."

"Yep, we are," Sharlene agreed.

"Think we'll ever get them raised?" Joelle whispered to Ford.

He pulled up to a gas pump and set the brake. "Looks like they have got stuck in their late teens on this trip."

Joelle's eyes twinkled. "This hippie wagon has caused most of it. It's like a time machine."

"I believe it," Ford said with a grin as he got out of the VW.

Joelle opened the door, slid out of the passenger seat, and followed the three older folks into the store. Ford watched her walk across the lot. Her eyes reminded him of the sparkle in his grandmother's eyes when she and his grandfather were bantering back and forth.

# Chapter 7

"How could we have already been on the road more than two weeks?" Joelle muttered as Ford parked the vehicle across the street from the hotel in Florida.

"What was that?" Ford asked.

"I was thinking that the past two weeks have gone by so fast," she answered.

"Happiness does that," Sharlene said as she slid the door open and got out of the bus. "Nita, you and Billy Joe stop dilly-daddlin' around. Get on out here and smell this ocean air. Soon as we get checked in and have our stuff in our rooms, I'm going to the beach." She headed toward the hotel office.

Billy Joe climbed out and stopped in his tracks, took a deep breath, and took a step toward the path that led straight to the beach. Nita grabbed his arm and pulled him the other way.

"You can't get there before us. We'll all go together," she said and dragged him toward the office. "You kids get the luggage out of the back. Oh, my goodness! I see a laundry right across the street. Sharlene did good when she chose this one."

Sharlene waved keys in the air as she hurried across the parking lot. "Y'all are going to love this place. We're in the first three rooms over there." She pointed to her right. "Bottom floor. Let's get going. I can't wait to put my toes in the sand." She handed off keys to Billy Joe and to Sharlene.

Ford winked at Joelle, then got out of the bus. "I think that's our cue to get out and take the baggage out for them."

"Wouldn't it be great if we could unload our own mental baggage like that?" She followed him to the back of the trailer.

"I haven't got as much now as I had when we left," he said with a grin.

"Me either," she agreed, "so maybe we've been chasing dreams just like they have."

"Think we'll get rid of the rest of it while we're here?" he asked as he set everything they needed out on the ground.

Billy Joe rolled the ladies' luggage over to them and then popped the handle up on his suitcase. "Get rid of what?"

"Learning not to sweat the small stuff," Ford answered.

"It's all small stuff when you get to be my age," his grandfather said with a chuckle. "Learn that at your age, and you'll be happy every day. Make up your minds what you want out of life and never look back with regrets."

"That's really good advice," Joelle said as she followed the three older folks down the sidewalk to the rooms, "but not so easy to follow."

"Amen!" Ford agreed. "However, I think I'm making progress, thanks to you."

"You. Are. Welcome," Joelle said with a semi-bow. "Glad to be of help, but that goes both ways, Mr. Holt, so thank you for sharing this trip with us."

Ford shook his finger at her. "We have slept together, Miz Cheadle, so I think we can be on a first-name basis."

Joelle laughed out loud. "Lower your voice or your grandpa and my aunt will have us standing before a justice of the peace. Are you taking your suitcase to Billy Joe's room? Or are you going to save trips back and forth and move it into mine?"

"Might as well put it in your room since that's where I'll end up anyway," Ford said and then added, "If that's all right with you."

She opened the door into the room, and left it standing in the entrance as she explored the rest of the place. "Holy smoke! This is an apartment or condo, not a hotel room. Look, Ford, there's a bedroom plus two bunk beds, and a living room and full kitchen."

Ford had already opened the drapes and the sliding glass doors. "And a view of the ocean and swimming pool, our own private patio, and would you look at those waves?"

The excitement in his tone was so contagious that Joelle rushed over to stand beside him. "This is my favorite of all the bucket-list ideas. I'm going to change into my bathing suit, do a couple of laps in that pool, and then see if that gorgeous white sand is as nice as it looks. Want to join me?"

He crossed the room in a few long strides, grabbed the handle of his suitcase, and threw it up onto the bottom bunk bed. "You can have the bedroom. I'll change in the bathroom."

Joelle took her luggage into the bedroom, opened it up, and dug through it until she found her two-piece bathing suit. She didn't think twice about shucking out of her clothing and putting it on—until she stood before the long mirror on the back of the closet door. She turned sideways and then all the way around and peered over her shoulder at her backside.

"What was I thinking?" she groaned. "Ford is going to see me in this and think I look fat."

*Stop it,* the niggling voice in her head scolded. *He's slept right beside you when you were wearing a nightshirt and bikini underwear.*

She flipped her blond hair up into a ponytail, took one last look at herself, and headed out into the living area. The bathroom door was open, and Ford was nowhere in sight, so she wandered on out onto the patio.

"Come on in. The water is so warm," he yelled from the pool.

No one else was in the pool or even sitting in the lounge chairs surrounding it, so there wasn't even strength in numbers to cause her to hesitate. She turned to the left, through a gate, and down a couple of steps and noticed the rest of their traveling party was already walking toward the water. "Looks like our bucket-list folks have beat us to the beach."

"They waved at me as they went by and said they might get in the pool later this evening after supper," Ford said without taking his eyes off her.

Joelle was shocked when she stepped into the warm pool and sat down on the middle step. "This is heated!"

"Yep, and it feels wonderful after driving all day," he told her. "And by the way, you are stunning."

"You look pretty dang good yourself," she said with a smile.

Keeping her hands to herself wasn't easy when the dark hair that covered his chest beckoned for her to reach out and touch it. Even though he'd slept beside her every night for the past two weeks and two days, he'd always worn pajama pants and a loose-fitting T-shirt, so she hadn't realized just how muscled up he was, or how broad his shoulders were.

"Do you work out?" she asked.

"Haven't in a while, and I suppose if I take Grandpa up on his offer, I won't need to lift weights or run several miles a day. I'll be tossing hay bales and chasing cows," he answered. "You're every bit as toned as I am. How often do you hit the gym?"

"Every day after school," she admitted. "But like you say, I won't need to do that anymore since I'll be doing ranch work."

"Have you told Sharlene?" he asked as he swam over and sat down on the step beside her.

"Not yet. I want to wait until we start home. Don't ask me why. I can't even answer that for myself, but it just seems to be the right time," she answered. "Are you going to make up your mind before we go home?"

She wanted to blame the warmth of the pool on the slight heat in her cheeks, but that wouldn't be honest. The electricity between them seemed to heat the water up another twenty degrees. He covered her hand with his and the heat rose even more. "I'm still teetering on the fence, but I feel myself falling over on Grandpa's side. I'm too young to do nothing. I've tried and tried to think of something I want to spend the rest of my life doing, but…"

"Make up your mind and don't ever look back or regret your decision, like Billy Joe said," she reminded him.

He nodded and looked at her without blinking. She felt as if she were drowning in his dark-brown eyes, and yet at the same time, she could have sworn he was seeing into the depths of her soul. Her left hand trembled, but the right one that he had laid his hand on was steady as a rock. A fluttering in her chest made her breath catch, and her pulse raced. For a minute, she thought he was going to kiss her, but then he blinked and turned away.

"What is this between us, Joelle?" he whispered.

"Attraction," she answered honestly.

"Where do we go with it, and what do we do about it?" he asked.

"What do you want us to do with it?" she fired back.

"I want to ask you out on dates, to get to know you even better than I do now, and yet, if I decide not to stay in Whitewright…" He stopped midsentence.

"Why start something that has no future, right?" she asked.

He gave her hand a gentle squeeze. "Exactly."

"I would never want you to make a decision about staying on the ranch or not because of me," she said, even though at that moment she would have given anything to know that he would be that close to her for the rest of their lives. "That kind of choice has to be for yourself so that you won't look back and wish you had done something different."

"How did you get to be so smart?" he asked.

"I'm not that little teenage girl who thought you hung the moon and stars and that the sun just came up every single morning to shine on you," she teased.

"I'm flattered that you ever thought that about me but, honey, you aren't that girl for sure." His gaze started at her ponytail and traveled all the way down to where her toes rested under the clear water.

Her pulse had barely settled from the staring contest, and now it was racing again. "Stop looking at me like that."

"Can't help it," he said with a grin. "You are beautiful, but it goes beyond physical beauty."

"Are you flirting with me?" Joelle asked.

"Tryin' too, but I'm more than a little bit out of practice." He leaned over and kissed her on the cheek.

"I don't believe it for one minute. You are definitely not out of practice," she whispered. She fought the desire to touch the place where his lips had been and see if it was as hot as it felt. Suddenly, she either had to get some space between them, or she was going to drag him back to the room and lock the door. She stood up, pushed off from the step, and did a complete lap with him right beside her the whole way.

"So, I've still got it?" he asked when she started out of the pool.

Joelle turned to face him. "Don't ever doubt your effect on women, Ford."

"I don't care about other women. What about you?"

"You've still got it," she said with a nod. "So much so that we better get down there on the beach with our crew so that we'll have some chaperones."

He stepped up out of the pool with water sluicing off him, and she was reminded of those Greek god statues. Oh, yes, sir, he still had it. No question about that—at least in Joelle's opinion.

# Chapter 8

JOELLE SAT IN THE last of five lounge chairs lined up close to the water on Sunday morning. Ford was in the chair next to her, then Sharlene, Billy Joe, and Nita. It hardly seemed possible that they'd already been there two whole days, and only had three more until they started home.

"I'm glad you thought of watching the sunrise this morning, Aunt Sharlene," she said.

"If you decide to be a rancher, you'll get lots of sunrises in your life," Sharlene told her.

"And you will love every one of them," Nita said.

"Yep, and if you make that decision…" Billy Joe said as he leaned forward and pointed at Ford. "You will thank the good Lord for everything he gives you. Whether it's summer, winter, spring or fall, it's a thing of beauty."

"Right now, I'm just enjoying this one," Ford said.

"'One day at a time, sweet Jesus,'" Nita sang.

The other two harmonized with her through the first verse and chorus of the song. Joelle remembered the song well, but she just listened instead of joining them. Maybe that's what she needed to remember the most—just to take one day at a time and not rush or expect anything from tomorrow, to just enjoy each sunrise and each sunset and be content with what you got done that day.

"Amen," she said when the singing stopped and the first edge of the sun appeared on the eastern horizon.

"It'll be coming up fast," Billy Joe said. "Now we can have our breakfast." He pulled a holder with five large cups of coffee and a box of doughnuts from under his chair. "Thank you, Ford, for driving down to that little shop and getting all this for us."

"You are welcome," Ford said as he handed a cup to Joelle.

All the feels were there when his fingertips brushed hers—the hike in her pulse and that extra little beat in her heart, the desire to have more than a chaste kiss on the cheek—but did she dare pay attention to any of it?

Nita grabbed a doughnut with sprinkles and a chocolate one as soon as Billy Joe opened the box.

"What's your hurry," he snapped.

"I got to get them while I can or you'll steal them," Nita shot back at him.

"Y'all better leave me one with maple icing," Sharlene said.

"The answer is no," Ford said out the side of his mouth so that only Joelle could hear.

"No to what?" Joelle whispered.

"No, we aren't ever going to get them raised, and I

guess we'd both better stick around to see to it that they behave themselves," he answered.

"Are you saying what I think you are?" Joelle's breath caught in her chest. Could there be a future for them?

"I'm saying I'm about to fall off the fence into hay and cows," he said.

Billy Joe whipped around to look at his grandson. "What did I hear about cows and hay?"

"We were wondering if y'all are ready to get back to the ranchin' life of hay and cows?" Joelle said.

"Great cover," Ford mouthed without saying a word out loud.

"I love the peace here in this place, but in another three days, I will be ready to start that way," Sharlene answered. "It's been fun, and I can't wait to start planning our Christmas trip, but I miss home."

"If you miss it that much, then why would you want to live with Nita and let me have your house?" Joelle asked.

"Home isn't a house," Sharlene answered. "It's a feeling in the heart."

"Couldn't have said it better," Nita said with a nod.

"Amen! And amen again," Billy Joe agreed.

————

Billy Joe declared he was tired of eating out, so he made a pot of pinto beans and fried a skillet of what he called a summer mash-up that included potatoes, yellow squash, peppers, and onions for supper that night. Nita brought a no-bake pineapple pie and corn bread from their room, and Sharlene contributed a small ham she'd baked all afternoon.

"Now I'm homesick," Billy Joe said after he'd finished his second round. "Ain't no food we've had anywhere that tasted as good as this did."

"You got that right," Sharlene agreed.

Nita had a mouthful of food and just nodded.

"Well, I for one have eaten way too much," Ford declared, "so I'm going for a long walk on the beach. Anyone want to join me?"

"Lord, no!" Sharlene answered. "I'm going to sit here for a little while and then have another piece of that pie."

"I'll go," Joelle said. "We started off the day by watching the sunrise. Seems only right that we watch the sunset over the water this evening. Just don't expect me to jog."

Ford slid off the barstool and opened the sliding door for her. "Wouldn't dream of it. You'd probably embarrass me." He was glad that she was going with him because he wanted some time alone with her. Sure, they had slept together—as in the same bed, but a foot apart—for more than two weeks. The last couple of nights, falling asleep had been a chore. His mind kept running in circles like a hamster on a wheel. The nightmares hadn't plagued him in weeks, but he wasn't at peace and wouldn't be until he decided what he was going to do about the ranch.

When they stepped out onto the still warm sand, he took her hand in his. "I wanted to hold you last night, to snuggle up with you, and maybe even kiss you good night."

"Ooo…kay." She dragged the word out to three syllables.

He took a deep breath and let it out slowly. "I figured it out over a bowl of beans and a plate full of food tonight. The ranch is where I belong, and I want to be with you."

Joelle stopped in her tracks. "For real?"

"Yes," Ford answered.

"I want to spend more time with Grandpa, not just go on a couple of vacations a year, and thinking about selling the ranch that generations of my family have built makes me sad. I sat there at the supper table tonight and thought about working for a private security firm. I've had several offers that I didn't mention to you until I'd made up my mind. Then I thought about ranching and having time with all of you, and that brought me peace," Ford admitted.

Joelle took a step forward. Her arms went around his neck, and she moistened her lips while she stared right into his eyes. "Does this mean?"

"It means that we could be a couple," he answered as his lips met hers in a fiery kiss that made him even more sure he had made the right decision.

# Chapter 9

"I CAN'T BELIEVE THIS is our last day of the trip," Sharlene said with a sigh the next morning.

The others, who were sitting around the table on the balcony having doughnuts and coffee for breakfast and gazing out at the reflection of the sun on the water, just nodded in agreement.

Billy Joe's sigh was even louder than Sharlene's. "I hope we all live until Christmas so we can go to Disneyland."

"Oh, stop it!" Nita scolded. "This is just the last day at the beach. We've still got three days left after today, and I'm planning places for us to see and eat along the way home. Besides, we need to remember the fun we've had, not be sad that it's over."

Joelle reached over and patted her aunt on the shoulder. "We'll all be talking about this trip for years to come." This would be a perfect time to tell them that she was resigning her job as a teacher and moving to the ranch that summer, but she and Ford had decided to tell them after they'd loaded up the van and started home the next day. She glanced over at him just in time to see him slide a sly wink toward her.

"I've planned something special for today," Ford said. "We're going on a dinner cruise out to see the dolphins."

"Are you serious?" Sharlene's expression went from sad to happy in an instant. "I've been hoping to see them, but they haven't come up close to the shore while we've been here. What time do we need to be ready?"

"Ten o'clock would be great," Ford answered. "By the time we get home from the three-hour cruise, it will be time to get things packed and ready to load up in the morning."

Joelle nudged him with her shoulder and whispered, "Well done!"

"Can't have the children pouting because they have to leave," he said in a voice for her ears only.

"What are you two whispering about?" Billy Joe asked.

"I was saying that we'd better not forget our phones so we can take pictures," Joelle answered and then, like a little child, crossed her fingers under the table.

"Oh, honey, I've taken more than four thousand pictures since we left home and plan to take even more on the way back," Sharlene said. "I'll have to sort them out when we get back and decide which ones to put in the memory album I'm planning to make." She pulled her phone from her shirt pocket and began to show Billy Joe and Nita all the photos she'd taken.

"Now, they're excited again. You did a good thing," Joelle told Ford.

"Can we call this our first real date, then?" he asked.

"Depends on whether you kiss me good night at the door," she teased.

"Then it will definitely be a first date," he said with a grin.

———————

Joelle felt like butterflies were flittering about in her stomach all during the cruise. The older folks had gone to get a better view of the dolphins for their pictures, leaving her and Ford at the dinner table alone.

Joelle hadn't dated in a while, but when she had in the past, she hadn't had this antsy feeling. While they ate the supper on the open-air cruise boat, she tried to figure out if it was because Ford was right there beside her or if it was because they would be heading home the next morning. She had less than twenty-four hours to change her mind about ranching. Once she and Ford let the cat out of the bag and told Sharlene, Nita, and Billy Joe that they were going to move to Whitewright, they couldn't take it back.

Or was she feeling what she was because she'd always been in love with Ford, and now the life she'd only dreamed of could be a reality in a few months? Those pesky what-ifs popped into her mind—the major one being, what if after a few dates, one of them decided they weren't happy?

Ford nudged her on the arm. "Penny for your thoughts. You seem to be fighting with yourself."

"I was," she admitted. "We've only got a few hours to be sure."

"I'm at peace," he said with a frown. "How about you?"

"Yes, but worried about us," she said. "What if…"

He laid a hand on her arm. "No regrets, darlin'. We'll watch sunrises and sunsets together and have no regrets. It takes most people a long time to figure out how they feel about each other. They have to get to know one another and go from there. But we've known each other since we were kids. Other folks go on a date or maybe two a week, talk for a few hours during each one. We've been together twenty-four seven for three weeks. I figure that's maybe a year's worth of conventional dating."

What he said made sense, and the doubts that plagued her disappeared, leaving her with nothing but peace.

"You've given this a lot of thought," she said.

"Yep, I have," he admitted. "Two dates a week for maybe four hours each multiplied by fifty-two weeks in a year is a little over four hundred hours a couple would spend together. We have spent more than five hundred hours together."

"And even slept together without sex," she said.

"Hopefully, we'll remedy that when the time is right," he said with a smile that melted her heart.

"Maybe we'll save that milestone for when we move in together at the ranches?" she suggested.

"So, it's a milestone?" he asked, and his smile widened even more.

"Yes, it is," she answered.

He took both her hands in his and leaned forward. "I've fallen in love with you, Joelle Cheadle. You make me happy and take away all the sadness from my heart."

Her heart thumped so hard in her chest that it sounded like a drum in her ears. "I'm not sure that there was a lot of sadness in my heart, but I can honestly say that you make me happy and bring peace into my life"—she stopped for a breath—"and that I've fallen in love with you all over again on this trip. I loved you when I was a teenager, but now I love you as an adult, and that's even better."

———

Ford slid in behind the steering wheel and started the engine the next morning just after the sun had risen. Joelle fastened her seat belt and shot a brilliant smile toward him. The idea that he could wake up every morning with her beside him for the rest of his life was almost more than he could even imagine.

"Wagons ho!" Billy Joe said from the back seat.

"I'm actually looking forward to going home," Sharlene said.

"Me too, but this has been too wonderful for words," Nita agreed. "Let's build a bonfire and roast hot dogs and make s'mores when we get home to celebrate marking things off our bucket list."

"Sounds good to me," Billy Joe said. "You kids ain't got to be in a rush about leaving, do you?"

"Nope," Ford answered. "Matter of fact, I'm not planning on leaving at all."

"Me either," Joelle said.

Time stood still in the bus for several moments. All that Ford heard was the rustling of paper behind him. No one said a word or even squealed, like he thought they might.

"Did you hear us?" he finally asked.

"We heard," Sharlene answered. "We're marking off the real first thing on all our bucket lists before you can change your minds. Once we cross them out, then we can hold you to what you just said."

"Real first thing?" Joelle asked.

"Everyone of us have wished for, hoped for, and even prayed to God that you would come back to the ranches and take over," Nita answered. "Now it's all taken care of, and…one…two…three…"

They all shouted to the top of their lungs, produced a bottle of champagne from what seemed like the air, and Billy Joe popped the cork. He took a long swig of it right out of the bottle and passed it over to Sharlene, who downed a good bit and gave it to Nita.

"Life is good now," Billy Joe said.

"Yes, it is!" Ford reached over and took Joelle's hand in his.

# *Epilogue*

**Six months later**

JOELLE CHOSE A DRESS made of white eyelet, and a circlet of white baby roses rested in her hair. Ford wore jeans, a white shirt, and his cowboy boots that morning as they stood before the judge at the Grayson County Courthouse in Sherman, Texas. In just a few minutes, he pronounced them man and wife, and Ford gave Joelle a true Hollywood kiss.

Ford scooped Joelle up in his arms and carried her outside into snow flurries while Billy Joe, Sharlene, and Nita tossed red rose petals over them all the way to the VW bus. Ford set his new wife down on the sidewalk and opened the door for her, then drew her into his arms and kissed her once more.

"I can mark something off my bucket list now," he said.

"Me too," Joelle said breathlessly. "Now let's get this honeymoon on the road. Disneyland waits for us, and besides, I'm freezing."

Ford reached into the vehicle, brought out a denim duster, and draped it around Joelle's shoulders. "I'll make sure to warm you up to the steaming-hot point tonight, darlin'."

"I'm looking forward to it," she told him as she slid into the passenger's seat.

"I can't believe you're letting us go on your honeymoon with you," Sharlene said as she settled into one of the chairs in the back seat.

Joelle turned around in her seat and smiled at the three of them. "A trip in the hippie wagon wouldn't be the same without y'all. We're all chasing dreams together."

# About the Author

Carolyn Brown is a *New York Times, USA Today, Wall Street Journal, Publishers Weekly,* and #1 Amazon and #1 *Washington Post* bestselling author. She is the author of more than one hundred novels and several novellas. She's a recipient of the Bookseller's Best Award and the Montlake Romance's prestigious Montlake Diamond Award and a three-time recipient of the National Reader's Choice Award. Brown has been published for more than twenty-five years. Her books have been translated into twenty-one languages and have sold more than fourteen million copies worldwide.

When she's not writing, she likes to take road trips with her family, and she plots out new stories as they travel.

**Website:** carolynbrownbooks.com
**Facebook:** carolynbrownbooks